Arborview

by

Karen Guzman

Arborview

Cover Art by *Kim Mendoza*

The Wild Rose Press, Inc.
PO Box 708
Adams Basin, NY 14410-0708
Visit us at www.thewildrosepress.com

Publishing History
First Edition, 2021
Trade Paperback ISBN 978-1-5092-3649-7
Digital ISBN 978-1-5092-3650-3

Published in the United States of America

The light was dying in Arborview. Ellen had to get going, but she wasn't ready. Descending the ladder meant reentering her life. The time she spent here, suspended among the branches, did not banish the uncertainty that crept back when her feet hit the ground, but it did give her reprieve.

The stillness, the silence, slowed her mind. *Be still and know that I am God.* She used to love that old Psalm. This must have been what it meant. Her thoughts unraveled in Arborview, exposed in a cool, piercing light, a calm glow giving her hope.

It had been a week since she'd heard from Alice, and the memory of her guilty laundry-room face lingered. Perhaps Ellen had been too harsh, too judgmental. That was a big thing today, wasn't it? Judging. Nothing was supposed to be off limits, nothing truly wrong, or shameful. Ellen had broken down and left a voicemail, but Alice had not returned the call.

The warm impression William had left in her bed, the faint whiff of his cologne on the pillows, had stayed with Ellen, too. He was coming to take her to dinner in an hour.

William had struck a chord with his pastry shop idea. It had taken root and grown all week within Ellen, its tendrils reaching into her heart. She could see it: a little storefront place, a jingling bell on the door, cakes and pies in the window, a soft wash of light on the gleaming display cases inside.

Praise for Karen Guzman

Winner
of the 2013 Fiction Attic Press First Novel Contest

~*~

"A pitch perfect debut novel."

~Jacqueline Sheehan,
New York Times bestselling author

~*~

"In the tradition of Ann Patchett and Julia Glass, Guzman weaves a brilliantly layered tale of family, forgiveness, and reinvention."

~Michelle Richmond,
New York Times bestselling author

Dedication

For Ethan, with love now and always

Acknowledgments

This novel would not have been possible without the help of so many people. Chief among them is Cathy Cruise, my co-conspirator in the writing life, for her sterling editing skills, sound advice, and dear friendship. I owe a debt of gratitude also to Nichole Bernier for encouragement during the early drafts; Susan Schoenberger, Rosalind Wiggins, Colleen Kearney Rich, and Teresa Allen for their helpful input; to Rafael Roca Gonzales for his linguistic sensitivity; and to Michelle Richmond for loving my writing even when I didn't. Many thanks also to Judi Mobley and the whole team at The Wild Rose Press for bringing this book into the world.

~

And last—but truly first—
I thank Michael and Ethan
for all their support and love.

There let the way appear,
Steps unto heav'n;
All that Thou sendest me,
In mercy given;
Angels to beckon me
Nearer, my God, to Thee.

~Sarah F. Adams, 1805-1848

Chapter One

Morning came, and with it the play of light that made her yard seem alive. Late summer sun burst through the trees, dazzling the water in the stone birdbath and casting shadows beneath the ancient elm. Ellen stepped barefoot onto the cool gray slate of the patio. It was early to be up, but she'd had another bad night. She drew a deep breath filled with the scent of the lilies and lilac she had spent years cultivating.

At moments like this, Zach became an abstraction, an insect buzzing at the border. Five months since the divorce was settled, twenty years of marriage, two children, and a man who had once sent her heart racing, were now on the periphery. If only she could remain buffered in this yard, mistakes fading in the glow of a new morning. Impossible, of course. Without a job, and soon, she wouldn't be able to hold on to this yard, or this house. That was the way of things, pay up or give it up.

Sunlight crept across the lawn, and a quiet vitality infused the air. Ellen sensed it every morning—this silent assurance that, whatever her problems, things were on track and proceeding. Even the darkness of the night to come was simply a necessary part, not to be feared or resisted. All she had to do was go along.

She walked to the edge of the patio and sat down, her bare feet in the grass. At forty-eight, she was still pretty limber. Exercise paid off. Her best friend, Alice, was right. Alice still had the body of a thirty-year-old. "Hit the gym, Ellie," she'd said. "That's what divorced women do, the smart ones."

Ellen scanned the tree line at the far edge of the lawn. Breezes riffled in from the woods like stealthy, untraceable breath. How familiar these trees were, every branch and gnarled trunk, like old friends. She would miss them. There would be new ones, of course, but they would never be *her* trees. There had to be a way to hold on to this place.

Bzz, bzz—a loud and jarring intrusion made Ellen flinch. Her cell phone, rumbling to life on the patio table. If she had her way, she would silence the thing. But then she could miss a call from one of her children. Maybe in trouble, maybe needing her.

She stood and looked down at the screen. The number was not one of her children's. It was him. Again. Ellen's stomach churned. Now that they were no longer married, Zach had begun calling at odd moments to tell her something or to ask a question, and once, puzzlingly, just to "check in." Early morning seemed to be a favorite time, when he was in his car or leaving the airy apartment where his girlfriend, Lydia, still lay asleep.

Ellen sighed. "Hello?"

"Too early?" he said.

"Nope. I'm wide awake. Is anything wrong?" She knew nothing was wrong.

"Nah, I'm just touching base."

Ellen's jaw clenched. What sort of "base" did he imagine she was now?

"I'm on my way to a training conference in

Stamford," he said. "Remember when Taber was in that spelling bee in Stamford? At the Marriott, wasn't it? She got disqualified in the semi-final round. What was the word? What was the word Taber couldn't spell? For the life of me, I can't remember."

Ellen heard the dinging chime of what must have been his key sliding into the car's ignition. He was in his car, heading to work, and this was a pressing question? A spelling bee eleven years ago? Alice was right. He was coming unglued.

"Synchronicity," Ellen said. "Stopped her cold."

"Synchronicity, yes." Zach laughed. "Taber's coming next week, right?"

"They both are. I'm planning a little dinner for them."

"Ah, good."

A beat of silence. Did he expect an invitation? Ellen's mind raced. "I'm sure they'll be in touch. They'll want to get together with you. Jimmy told me he already left a message?"

"Oh, yes. I meant to call him. I've been a little under the gun, handling a few things right now, and I'm…"

"There's still plenty of time." Her voice rose in false, sing-song levity on the last word. She could have kicked herself, but she was relieved to have dodged him. She didn't want to know what he was "handling." There were still too many potential landmines: He and Lydia were buying a fabulous vacation house or planning a trip around the world. He had met Lydia's family and just loved them. Or worst of all, his sheepish admission, maybe after he'd had a drink or two, that he had never been more content, more at home, in his

3

entire life. It was not beyond him to feel it was somehow okay, somehow permissible, to tell her things like this, to believe he had her blessing, no matter what.

"Have a good trip to Stamford," she said.

"Yeah, thanks. Take care."

That was how he ended every call, *take care*, as if he were signing off for good, wishing her well before disappearing, never to be heard from again. *Take care.* And then he'd call again in a few days.

Did Lydia know about these calls? Ellen felt a nasty satisfaction at the thought of Lydia, slumbering and oblivious, unaware of Zach's calls, of how his voice resonated with sad yearning. Not that it made any real difference. Ellen was beyond vengeful solace. It sometimes seemed she had moved beyond any solace.

She dropped the phone on the table. She shouldn't have answered. Even now, she was still the dupe, playing nice for everyone's sake.

She gazed into the trees, and something caught her eye. At the far edge of the yard, a wink of light, a spark blipping in and out. She squinted. Was it coming from the branches of the massive elm, or from Arborview, the kids' old tree house, perched in its arms? The wink faded.

Probably nothing. Ellen looked away. The tiger lilies at the patio's edge were opening so nicely this year, spreading their brilliant orange petals. Maybe she'd divide a few and replant them at the top of the driveway.

Wink. From the corner of her eye, she saw it again. Definitely coming from Arborview. But what in the world? Taber and Jimmy hadn't been up there since elementary school, except for the time Zach discovered the beer they were stashing there during high school.

The grass was cool and damp beneath her bare feet as she crossed the lawn. Wink, wink. It was stronger now. The rising sun hit whatever was in there, at just the right angle. Did this happen every morning? Why had she never noticed it before?

Arborview was a simple wooden platform, its plywood walls streaked and weathered. It sat at the edge of the woods, where the yard ended and the forest took over. The kids had named it after discovering the term in a travel brochure featuring lush photos of Vermont's canopied forests. The pitched roof onto which Zach had crudely nailed rows of shingles was chipped and moss-covered now. A ladder of wooden steps nailed into the tree trunk led to the small square opening in the floor.

Ellen climbed, holding tightly to the steps, wincing as she wedged her feet against the rough trunk. She emerged through the opening and hoisted herself up onto the floorboards.

A familiar hush greeted her. Sunlight filtered through cracks in the walls. It filled the glassless, rectangular window opening overlooking the dense woods.

Ellen's breathing slowed. The tree house smelled like a dusty, old attic. She scanned the walls and floor. Splotchy water stains dotted the plywood ceiling, where a papery gray wasp nest was tucked in one corner. This place was forgotten, but something still laced the air. A presence, steady and expectant. Ellen sensed it the way you sometimes become aware of your own heart beating, a nudge deep within, a reminder that this vigil is going on all the time.

She turned in a circle. It was amazing, really, the thing was still standing. Had it always been so calm, so *still,* up here? Where else had she felt this—this sudden quiet banishing the outside world? Her childhood church. The old church with the stone steeple and the cool marble interior, cloistered yet stirring with welcome, as if it had been waiting for her to arrive.

Stepping into the Lord's presence, old Mother Margarita had called it. Ellen smiled. All those years of Catholic school had left their mark. She could recall the soft wool of her uniform and the reverent hush of the chapel where the sisters said our words—and even our thoughts—are always heard. The benevolent assurance that it all mattered.

Wink. Another spark, low down, along the scuffed floorboards. Ellen crouched and looked closer. There, a sliver of round glass. She reached through a tangle of cobwebs and grasped a solid object—a magnifying lens, a toy for little hands to hold. She held it up in the light. Yes, Jimmy and Taber had once run around the yard with these things, turning them on hapless insects or plucked blades of grass, delighting in the joy of simple discovery. That's what was flashing up here, catching the sun in a little prism and sending out solitary sparks. She closed her hand around it.

Ellen stepped to the red beanbag chair in Arborview's center and dropped into it. The beans crunched and shifted as she sank in and leaned back, letting go. She hadn't realized how tired she was.

Something—a squirrel—scrambled across the roof and sounded its chattering scold from the branches of a nearby tree. Ellen closed her eyes. No words came to her mind, but a heavy silence gathered around. She felt grounded, protected. Should she pray, maybe? She'd forgotten how. And what would she pray for? A winning lottery ticket?

Mother Margarita was surely long dead now, probably buried in the same cemetery where Ellen's parents lay. Ellen had stopped going to church after she married Zach. He had no capacity for things which couldn't be measured and quantified. His disinterest was so complete, so final, she hadn't seen any point in pressing him.

All those years, she had focused on Zach as he climbed the corporate ladder, believing in him, believing in "them," despite the rough patches and bruises. And in the end, he'd fought her tooth-and-nail in court. He never gave an inch unless he was forced to. He was the one who had filed for the divorce, and he'd tried to push an immediate sale of the house, even though he knew how much she loved it.

Now she probably would lose it. Her alimony—Zach had driven a hard bargain there, too—wasn't enough. What she needed was money, a new way to earn it, and fast.

The wind rustled the leaves outside, bringing the faint sound of dogs barking in the distance. Ellen stood and walked to the window. A black bear had ambled out of these woods on a late spring evening years ago when she was working in the flower garden. It had stood, watching her. Ellen had frozen, spade in hand. She wanted to run, but something stopped her. She felt like she was witnessing a privileged moment, that an entity, powerful and ever-present, had emerged before her eyes.

The bear considered her, bobbing its massive head

up and down. Then it swiped its pink tongue over its nose, turned and trudged back into the trees. The low branches swayed in its wake, as if a ghost had passed.

Everyone she'd told about the bear thought she was crazy to not flee for the house. Ellen couldn't explain why she had stayed. How do you tell people that these moments simply appear sometimes, unbidden, confusing and disconcerting, yet real all the same? That same black bear might be out there still, passing by unseen.

The sun was growing stronger now, leaking through the weathered cracks, casting a bright, disjointed halo everywhere it fell.

Chapter Two

Rosa Escamilla placed the tray of plastic water pitchers on the counter next to the deep steel sink. Cleaning and refilling these flimsy, flip-top, raspberry-pink pitchers was the part of this job she figured she would always remember. She had to do it at least ten times a day. Pull off her latex gloves, dump the pitchers in the sink, squirt the soap that smelled like bleach and roses over them, grab the faucet sprayer with the cord that looked like a black snake, and blast all the germs the old people left on them down the drain.

The patients weren't all old. Some were shockingly young—teenagers like her. They were all dying. Some quickly, others lingering—weeks, a few months—but as her brother Javier warned before she took the job, "Ain't no one getting out alive. It's a hospice, *florecita*, not a hospital."

Rosa squirted soap over the heap of pink plastic. When she applied for the housekeeping job at Mid-State Hospice back in June, she really didn't know what a hospice was. No one she knew had ever gone to one.

Mama had shrugged. "A job's a job, and nobody else banging down your door."

Rosa needed the money. River Bend Community College had hiked its tuition again. It was only a small increase, but Rosa had to make up the difference. Mama helped, but she was at her limit. Rosa only had one more year of River Bend, and then—if things went according to plan—she'd be gone.

She rinsed the pitchers and lined them up on the counter to dry. The hospice wasn't so bad. She had gotten used to it. She never went into patients' rooms when they were "nearing the end." It wasn't her job to be there. The nurses and doctors and care aides did all that. Rosa just cleaned the rooms. She stripped the beds and mopped the floors. She sanitized the bathrooms. She sometimes spent her entire five-hour shift running loads of laundry, an endless tangle of sheets and pillowcases and towels.

But she was used to hard work. And the job had some hidden benefits. The main entrance had a soaring cathedral ceiling with cool ivory walls. A star-shaped window made of layers of glass, high over the front door, bent the sunlight so that multicolored beams spilled into the hall, glinting like gems along the floor and walls. She liked to stand in the middle of the floor and let them spill over her.

There was also the chapel, a big room with rows of chairs and a stained-glass window up front. Not many people used it. Rosa liked to sit there on her breaks and think. Not pray. They weren't a praying family. "God left this town a long time ago," Mama liked to say. But Rosa wondered, had God left Mama, or had Mama left God? It wasn't something she would have said aloud, but it was interesting. In any case, God probably didn't even exist. If He did, how could all these people be dying behind every door in this place?

Rosa dried her hands and glanced at the clock on the wall. Break time. Maybe she'd head to the chapel and sit for a minute or two. It had been a quiet day.

Some days she saw an ambulance pull up and a crush of family and friends fill a patient's room, spilling into the hall, looking stricken and tired and incredulous all at the same time. But today no one had died.

Rosa had noticed a new patient last week, a girl. She couldn't have been much older than Rosa. Passing in the hall, Rosa had smiled at her, this pale girl, pretty in a delicate way. Her sandy blonde hair was pulled back in a ponytail, and her eyes were the softest shade of green, like Easter grass. The girl was skinny, but Rosa had sat next to girls just as skinny in high school. She didn't look sick, much less like she was dying. Doctors weren't always right. Miracles did happen, even if the notion made Mama snort.

Rosa passed through the main foyer on her way to the chapel, glancing at the sky beyond the window. A couple more hours and she could head home and pull some lunch together. Mama would be home. She didn't work Mondays. The best restaurants, the really fancy places, didn't open on Mondays. They needed to recover from the weekend crowds.

The chapel was tucked at the back of the building, out of the way, private. Its door was open when Rosa got there. She stepped inside to see Mr. Janssen walking down the aisle toward her. Bumping into him was another good part of this job. He was the money guy, and she had to stay on his radar.

"Rosa, good to see you." He smiled. He always smiled when he saw her, which Rosa took as a good sign. He was the head of financial aid at River Bend. The hospice was a volunteer job for him, which had stunned Rosa when he first told her. Imagine having so much money you work for free? Mr. Janssen did some sort of accounting work for the hospice.

"I'm good," Rosa said. "I'm, ah, enjoying my job here, and it's, you know, helping me save for…for tuition and everything, after River Bend." Rosa smiled as sweet as she could, because Mama always said to just smile when you don't know what else to do.

"Well, you've got a good head on your shoulders, Rosa. You're a practical soul."

Rosa nodded. "I know it's a busy time, with the new semester starting in a few weeks and everything, but can I come see you soon? I have a plan for next year, for what I want to do."

"Of course, that's what I'm here for. We've pulled it off so far, haven't we? With scholarships and loans and part-time jobs, there's always a way. That's my motto."

"It's mine, too," Rosa said. It wasn't. She didn't believe there was always a way. There were plenty of times when there was no way, when you were stuck good and deep, and pushing ahead could only come at a great cost.

"I've been working with a nineteen-year-old single mother on state assistance whose parents have disowned her," Mr. Janssen said, shaking his head. "This poor girl just enrolled in the nursing program. We patched together a quilt of financing that will get her to May—as long as nothing goes wrong. If she can do it, Rosa, so can you."

"As long as nothing goes wrong." Rosa glanced at the floor. "I feel sorry for that girl."

Mr. Janssen looked at his watch. "Don't. She's got a good head on her shoulders, too. She'll be fine." He smiled again. "And so will you, Rosa. I'll see you on campus."

"See you."

Rosa drifted down the aisle to a seat. She stared at the stained glass—muted patches of blue and red and yellow waiting for the sun to bring them to life.

The problem was things did go wrong. They went wrong all the time. And then what? That's what she should have said to Mr. Janssen. Not that he would have understood what she was dealing with.

Chapter Three

The next morning Ellen made coffee, standing in her kitchen in the tattered pink paisley bathrobe and T-shirt that now passed as pajamas. Alice would trot up the front walk soon, brimming with optimism, her little heels clicking on the slate. She would take Ellen by the hand, insisting that the world was waiting, insisting that anything could happen.

Alice was accompanying her to River Bend Community College, where Ellen was determined to find a paying job in the tutoring center. The Academic Support Lab, they called it online. She'd taught high school, and community college kids were just a little older, so how different could it be? Since so many of the River Bend students spoke English as a second language, she was sure the school could use more English tutors. It would no doubt be a small paycheck, but something to buy time until she found a more permanent solution.

Ellen poured a cup of coffee and slipped through the sliding door to the patio. The temperature was already in the high seventies. A stifling day loomed. She sat down at the wrought iron table, squinting at the paint peeling in a few spots around the kitchen windows. Winter snows would bring more peeling. The maintenance on a house like this never ended. Zach had done a lot of the work himself. She'd need to hire people now.

"It looks like a runny egg yolk," Zach had said of the creamy, sun-kissed yellow house the day, nearly twenty years ago, when they first laid eyes on it. His burgeoning success had emboldened them to leave the drafty loft apartment in Hartford and take on a monstrous mortgage to finance this house of their dreams. Ellen had planted the gardens and placed the bird houses. She'd chosen all the interior colors and painted the living room herself.

She gazed now at Arborview in the corner of the yard. Too bad there wasn't time for a quick visit this morning. Strange, maybe, but she wouldn't have minded stopping by again. Imagine if people found out she was sitting up there? Ellen Cahill: doting mother and smiling wife, PTO bake-sale queen, the woman who had it all under control, newly divorced and praying in a decrepit tree house while her alimony ran out.

"Ellen? Ellen?"

Alice's voice, calling from the front yard.

"On the patio!" Ellen called. "Come around back."

A moment later Alice appeared at the corner of the house. She wrinkled her nose when she saw Ellen. "You're not even dressed? Is that what you sleep in now?"

"I sleep alone these days, remember?" She didn't tell Alice that she had also been sleeping in the guest bedroom since Zach left. Failure haunted the bedroom she had shared with him.

Alice wore a sky-blue summer dress with a dazzling sash of deep peacock teal tied around the waist and strappy sandals of the same color. She looked like she had just stepped out of a catalogue, Nordstrom or Bergdorf, the kind of places that always struck Ellen as extravagant. She raised her hands in a surrender gesture, a stack of colorful bangle bracelets clinking on her arm. "And that is another situation we've got to remedy. Maybe it should be our next objective: a new man to get your juices running."

"Ugh, too early for this. No 'juices' before lunch, okay?"

Alice laughed. "Fine, but remember—today is the first day…"

"Of the rest of my life," Ellen said. "You really are tireless, you know that? A tireless, bawdy old broad."

Alice gave Ellen a swat on the arm. Then she wrapped her in a warm hug. "How are you?"

"Well, I've been worse, as you know. But today we get down to business. It's find a job or face eviction."

Alice arched one of her delicate eyebrows. "Aren't you being a bit melodramatic? Eviction? All you'd face is a fast sale of this place." She glanced around the yard. "Which wouldn't necessarily be a bad thing."

"We're not going *there* this morning either, okay?" Ellen had built her whole life in this house. She couldn't leave now. Alice didn't seem to understand this.

"Whatever you say. Now, what do I have to do to get a cup of coffee around here?"

Ellen steered her into the kitchen and handed her a coffee mug from the cabinet. "I'm going to run up and get dressed," she said. "Be right back."

Upstairs, she slipped on a blouse—a white button-up with three-quarter sleeves—and a pair of khaki Capri pants. From the jewelry box on her bureau, she drew out a golden friendship-knot necklace—a long-ago Mother's Day gift from Taber—and put it on. She pulled her heavy, shoulder-length chestnut hair—the grays strategically whisked away by her stylist every six weeks—back in a ponytail. It would be too hot this afternoon to leave it hanging.

Ellen surveyed herself in the full-length mirror. She looked like every other reasonable, middle-aged mother in this Connecticut town. When had she become so cookie-cutter?

Alice, of course, would have something to say about her ensemble. She had always cut such a buoyant figure, dashing about with her ashy blonde bob and fair, glowing complexion. Even when their children were young and all the mothers in town went about in yoga pants and T-shirts, Alice wore flowery sundresses with cinched waists, or white linen trousers, her toenails pedicured a rosy hue.

They had seen each other through so much over the years: husbands and lovers—that is, Alice's marital lapses— and children and jobs: parsing one's self among them, what is lost, what is gained, love that inspires and love that depletes, the scramble to adapt, to heal and redeploy, and then the face of a stranger emerging in the mirror as the first fine lines appeared, navigating now into a time when so much seemed behind them.

Back downstairs, Ellen saw Alice eyeing a tray of pastries on the counter.

"Trying out a new recipe?" Alice said and sipped her coffee.

"I couldn't sleep last night. The chimney cleaner was here for the annual cleaning yesterday. He told me the flue needs a new steel liner. Three thousand dollars."

Alice shrugged. "Ah, you'll get over the hump."

"This time. But you know how the taxes go up every year in this town, and then there's the maintenance, snow blowing and roof raking, the lawn and the gutters and cracks in the driveway, all of it."

Alice gave her a pleading look. "And you absolutely won't consider selling?"

"No way." Ellen picked up her purse from the counter. "Ready when you are."

"Is that what you're wearing?" Alice asked.

"Yes. Why?"

"Those are mom pants. Not jeans, but mom-type pants."

"Well, I am a mom, so…"

"You're a divorcée now, my dear."

"Thanks for reminding me."

Alice frowned, a quick tension tightening her soft, lovely face, an expression that Ellen knew signaled retreat. Ellen patted her back, then gently nudged her toward the front door and out to Ellen's Audi wagon, parked in the driveway.

"Let's swing by the grocery store?" Ellen said, as she buckled in. "I want to make a cobbler for the kids, and some tarts. Taber loves them."

"I'll run in with you." Alice nodded. "Earle's grilling tonight. He needs marinade. Are you coming? Bringing dessert, maybe?"

"Zach called again this morning," Ellen blurted. She jammed the key into the ignition.

"What? That's twice this week. What did he want?"

"To know what word it was that tripped up Taber in a fourth-grade spelling bee."

"You're joking?"

"Nope." Ellen gazed through the bright windshield and started the car. "It's like he wants something from me."

Alice's lip curled. "*He* wants something from you? He's the one who owes *you*. He owes you the courtesy of leaving you alone."

Ellen looked down at her stubby fingernails on the steering wheel. She'd begun picking at the cuticles again. "We do have two children to…"

"Grown children, hundreds of miles away. Hundreds of miles, and Zach can call them whenever he wants. The kids are a smoke screen. They always are in these situations."

Ellen sank back into the seat. "These situations?"

"Divorces like yours, messy ones with dangling strings and second-guessing."

"I think they're probably all like that." Ellen adjusted the rearview mirror, then started down the long, curving driveway.

"Remember Leanne Kenniston?" Alice's face lit with the memory. "George wouldn't move out of the house? The divorce was final, and he was still there—what? Four, five months later?"

"Oh, yes. I was so glad you didn't have a hand in that one."

"Oh, come on. George Kenniston? Not even at my most confused, okay? Give me some credit. Anyway, Leanne had to change the locks, remember? She had the sheriff haul George's stuff out to the curb. When George came home after work, he put his fist through the window. It was a horrible thing to see."

"You watched?"

"They lived across the street. Police cars came, sirens, the whole thing. How could I not watch that? But, you know, what Zach is doing is just as horrible. Dragging things out, playing in the ashes like this."

Ellen slowed at the end of the drive, then pulled onto the main road, a ping of irritation stirring inside her. "It is starting to get to me."

"Of course it is."

"Maybe he's looking for closure."

"Please," Alice said. "How I hate that term. Everyone throws it around. What does it even mean? I'd say a divorce is closure enough. What did you tell him this morning?"

"I told him the word. Synchronicity."

Alice groaned, a throaty growl humorously at odds with her chic dress and heels. "He's cracking up. And I wonder what little Lydia has to say about it all."

"I doubt she knows."

"Maybe somebody should do her a favor and tell her." Alice chuckled.

"Are you crazy? It's none of my business what Lydia knows or doesn't know. And she's not so 'little.' She's forty-five with thick ankles, thin lips, and grooves around her mouth—traits you pointed out. With glee, if I remember correctly."

"Yes, I had that little tart nailed. Oh, look. That new boutique's about to open."

Ellen gazed at the Opening Soon sign on a lingerie store they were passing by. A "better match" Zach had called Lydia, the night the whole story came out. He had not planned this. It had simply happened: "She fits who I am now. She thinks like me."

What did that mean? Lydia had done things Ellen should have done? She had seen a magical light and arrived in middle-age, intact and deserving of love? Zach did not say he was in love.

Nevertheless, there it was: Lydia, never married and childless. *A better match*. The words had stripped away all the stories Ellen told herself about her life.

"I should pick up a nightgown there," Alice said. "I'll tell you, Earle was a wild man last night."

Ellen laughed.

"It's the Viagra. That stuff is a miracle."

Ellen braked for a stoplight. "And I bet he'd be just thrilled to know you're discussing his sexual performance with me."

"Oh, you know Earlie. He'd be horrified. But that's how I've survived twenty years of marriage. Strategic little secrets. They hold everything together."

Ellen shook her head.

Alice blinked. "Oh, come on. Just the hurtful parts. That's all I keep from Earle—the stuff he's better off not knowing."

Coming from anyone else, Ellen would have called this a pathetic rationalization. But this was Alice, and somehow rationalizations, even on this scale, bounced off her. Underneath it all, Alice had a good heart. Ellen had lived through her affairs and the very real contrition that always followed. There had been two "slip-ups," as Alice called them, short-lived, punctuated with high drama and coinciding with milestones in Alice's life: when her daughter Caroline started kindergarten; when Alice turned forty; times when she had been bubbling over with losses, real and imagined.

Still, Alice was the best listener Ellen had ever known. She was the first one Ellen called after Zach packed his bags and left. Alice called in sick to work and drove right over. She stayed by Ellen's side all day, bringing tea and tissues, listening for hours, nodding her head in the slow way she had when she really understood. Her gaze never left Ellen's face. In the early days of their friendship, Alice's tenderness had been such a surprise. It was like discovering the most popular girl in school was just another girl with problems of her own, and she needed a friend, too.

Ellen didn't tell Alice everything, though. She would not tell Alice how she sometimes woke at night with a hollow ache filling her chest. She would not mention how she would rise and walk the dark hallway to the master bedroom, to the closet she and Zach had shared, where she would snap on the light and stare at the rows of empty hangers, the place where his clothes—the jackets and shirts and slacks she knew so well—had hung.

Chapter Four

Alice pulled down her visor and checked her makeup in the mirror. "Are you sure about this tutoring? I mean, after all these years, dealing with a bunchy of pimply teenagers and putting up with their crap. Yech."

"It's a start, a first step," Ellen said. "And if you have any better ideas, I'm all ears."

"Prison guard?"

"Ha-ha. Seriously, it can't be any worse than high school, right? It's only tutoring."

"You're asking the wrong person. One dose of teenager was plenty for me. One dose of parenthood was plenty, as a matter of fact."

Ellen laughed. But she knew Caroline, Alice's only child, meant the world to her. Caroline was also away at college.

They exited the highway and snaked through the side streets that wound back to the campus. Turning onto the wide, paved drive, Ellen sat up a little straighter. She pulled into a parking space in the lot next to the college's cement, bunker-like administration building. "It hasn't changed since Jimmy took that introductory college chemistry course here, I guess three years ago."

"I hear they're expanding." Alice applied fresh lipstick. "The state just gave them a big pot of money for a technology lab or some such thing. I wish a little more of that funding would come into social services. It's crazy how busy we are, and some of our clients don't have great insurance. We need to hire another therapist. Did I mention that?"

"No," Ellen said. "I should have gone into speech therapy. Tell me, why did you choose it as a career? I mean, did you really want to be a speech therapist?"

Alice opened her door. "My mother was a speech therapist, so I became one. I'm not good at strategy, Ellie. I roll with what comes along. You know that."

As they walked to the building, Alice's cell phone rang. She fumbled in her purse. "Hello…yes, yes." Her voice dropped. "No, I can talk now. Just hang on." She turned to Ellen. "I need to take this. It's a client. Go ahead, Ellie." She motioned to a picnic table in the grassy quadrangle next to the building. "Meet me here?"

"I'll be right out." Inside, Ellen walked the cool, linoleum hallway to the end, stopping at an office with a sign that read: *Academic Services.*

Ellen stepped up to the counter.

A painfully thin, bespectacled woman peered at her.

"Hello," Ellen said. "I'm interested in tutoring."

"You're a teacher?" The woman's voice rose on the last word. Her short, skunky gray hair was tucked behind her ears, and her thin lips looked papery dry, as if it were the dead of winter. A nameplate on the counter read: *Kate Mooney, Assistant Director.*

"I was," Ellen said. "I mean, I am, and I'm wondering if you have any need for…"

"Part-time?"

"Yes, sure. Part-time would be fine. I'm very flexible. I can fill in whenever. I was a high school English teacher a while back, so I thought maybe I could tutor or help with the ESL students?"

The woman frowned.

Ellen rushed on, "I could be available really whenever." She had a sudden flash of herself, here all hours of the night and day, trudging through snow and cold, chasing these kids. She pushed it away.

Kate Mooney eyed her. "You an empty-nester?" The corners of her thin lips ticked up into a skeletal grin.

"I guess so. My kids are both in college."

"An empty-nester just dying to fill up all those hours with something."

This was getting weird, right off the bat. "I'm not sure what you're referring…"

"I've been there myself." The woman pushed her eyeglasses up the bony bridge of her nose and gave a surprisingly warm smile. "It's a strange place. One day you're the center of everyone's universe, making it all happen, and the next day, you're waiting for your phone to ring."

And your husband leaves you for another woman, Ellen thought. But she said, "A very strange place."

This hint of kinship must have reassured Kate Mooney. "We have a tutoring lab across campus. I bet you'd be perfect. Go check in with them, or wait a sec…" Kate took a business card from a rack on her desk and handed it to Ellen. "Email the lab director. I'm not sure if she's in today."

"Thanks." Ellen hesitated. "Should I email, or should I call?" Wasn't a phone call more personal?

Maybe people didn't want personal anymore.

"Email. You have been out of the workforce for a while, haven't you?"

Ellen gave a tight smile. "You could say that."

"You'll get back in the saddle in no time. The important stuff, you know, it doesn't change."

A flash of panic lit Ellen's heart. "The important stuff?"

Kate nodded. "The old battle, you know. For us, it's the *need*. We do what we can, but it's never enough. These kids are need-machines. More money, more teachers, more course offerings. The kids can't afford the four-year schools, so they come here to knock out two years and then they transfer. Others just want a technical skillset to get a job. And a whole bunch have no idea what they're doing here."

Ellen's stomach ached. She wasn't here to save the world. She couldn't save herself.

"I don't know much about English tutoring," the woman said, "but what we do need desperately right now is this." She slid a glossy, stapled booklet across the counter. "Course catalogue." She pulled out a sheet of paper and placed it on the counter. "The list of late cancellations. I haven't entered them into the system yet." She shook her head. "We've got enough disappointed people around here."

Ellen lifted the sheet.

"Our students count on these courses being offered when they need them. A lot of the kids are on very tight timetables."

Ellen nodded. But teach a course? A whole room full of faces? "I'll look them over," she said. "And thanks for your help." She turned for the door.

"You'll let me know?"

Ellen glanced back and caught the pleading gleam in Kate's eye. "Sure, right away. If I see a good match." She was sure she wouldn't.

In the hall, she rolled the catalogue into a tight scroll. She'd swing by the tutoring lab now. She still believed in face-to-face, even if Kate Mooney didn't. And she could get lucky. The director might be there.

Ellen gazed down the hall to the rectangles of sunshine coming through the windows. She walked on, stopping at the doors holding back the bright day. People seemed to expect things of her now that she was divorced. Big things. Get a divorce and become a brain surgeon. Start a business. Found an orphanage. Travel the world. There were books and movies about it.

Ellen's mother would have been the loudest voice. She'd seen every crossroads as fuel for new ambition. Her mother had been a legal secretary. Working alongside fancy, downtown lawyers had planted the seed in her head that her own children should "go places" in life.

The old urge to retreat came over Ellen. Just get back in her car, drive home, and lock the door, or better still, climb up into the tree house. The silence would wrap around and hold her still, and maybe she could forget about all this.

Mousy was the word her mother had used when, as a child, Ellen had one of her jam-on-the-brakes-and-retreat episodes. *Don't be mousy, Ellen. Mice do not change the world.* Whoever said Ellen wanted to change the world?

Outside again, she dropped the catalogue on the picnic table beside Alice, who was no longer on the phone. "Hey, let's go. They told me to contact the tutoring lab director."

"So quick?" Alice said. "Do they need you?"

"The woman I spoke with didn't exactly know. She told me to email the lab, but maybe we can stop by on our way out?"

Alice tapped the cover of the booklet. "What's this?"

"The new course catalogue. The woman was all bent out of shape about the courses they've had to cancel this semester—not enough money or teachers or something."

"Interesting." Alice lifted it and thumbed through the pages. "I didn't think they were hurting over here. Ha! Look at this. A cancelled pastry course. Honestly, Ellie, you could teach this one."

"I probably could."

Neither of them said anything for a minute, and then their eyes met. "Don't even go there," Ellen said.

"Go where? I didn't say anything."

Ellen had taken her first cooking class—Baking Basics—here at River Bend long ago, during one of the dreamy, hot summers before she met Zach, when she was living on her own in a tiny apartment and had time to fill. She had spent many a sticky night in a too-warm kitchen alongside her classmates, young women squinting at recipes in books propped before them, hands dusted in flour, perspiration beading on their upper lips, as a metal ceiling fan turned lazily overhead.

But teach a course now? She tucked her chin. Tutoring was better. It would be less…less public. One-on-one, it would give her a chance to find her teaching feet again.

"Ellen?" Alice's questioning eyes.

And Ellen saw, in a flash, how the course could unfold. They'd meet in a kitchen, so there'd be no room to stand in front of, no expectant eyes trained on her every move. She would mill among the students, correcting a technique here, testing a texture there. Sampling and moving on. "I can bake," she said.

"What an understatement! Remember the cake for your niece's wedding?" Alice closed her eyes as if recalling bliss. "That great frothy towering thing with the creamy sugar roses? People couldn't get enough."

"That cake was like wrangling a monster, but what a pay-off."

"You're a pro. Everyone knows it." Alice's voice grew stronger. "Remember the cookies you'd bring to the PTA meetings? Those yappy hens would scarf them all down before the meetings even started."

Ellen looked at the cancellation list again. *The Power of Pastry.* "You know, all my life I've been baking for other people, trying to make them happy or acknowledge them in some way."

"Spoken like a wife and mother." Alice sniffed.

"Maybe it's time I get something out of it."

"That's the smartest thing you've said in a long time." Alice picked up her purse. "Let's do this."

Ellen led the way back to the Academic Services office.

Kate Mooney's mouth dropped open when Ellen volunteered to teach the pastry course. "That was fast!" she said, scanning an open ledger on the counter before her. "I haven't sent the cancellation emails out to the students yet."

"I'd call that fate," Alice said.

"You'll need to contact the Enrichment Department chair to get approval for your curriculum and to give your credentials, but this isn't an academic course, so you don't need anything fancy." Kate Mooney was talking fast, probably afraid that Ellen would change her mind.

"I've taken baking classes, and cooking classes, on and off for years, at some very good culinary institutes around New England," Ellen said. She was surprised to feel a stab of fear that she *wouldn't* be able to teach the course. "And I've done some catering, just for friends, but some pretty demanding menus."

"Her desserts are outstanding," Alice piped in. "She can whip up anything, absolutely anything."

Ellen shot her a cautionary glare.

"Do you have a recent CV?" Kate Mooney asked.

"A CV?"

"A curriculum vitae," Alice said. "A resume. Of course! That won't be a problem."

Kate leaned over the counter. "Please don't sweat these details. The chair will be thrilled to have you. For most of the kids, this is a transcript booster. An 'easy A' on their way out the door."

An easy A? That's all it was? Ellen found this hard to believe. To her, baking had always been so magical. Why get your hands dirty, if you don't really care?

"Just remind the kids to keep their eyes on the prize—that degree at the end of two years and the chance to move on to something better." Kate opened a drawer, took out a sheaf of paperwork, and handed it to Ellen. "And come see me if you hit a wall."

In the parking lot, Ellen turned to Alice. "What do you think she meant, 'if you hit a wall'?"

"Who knows?" Alice shuddered. "She was a gloomy old bird, wasn't she? I guess there are women who've never heard of lipstick."

Ellen shook her head. "I'm glad you were focusing on the important stuff in there."

"I'm sorry, but I can't pretend I don't notice these things."

Back in town, they stopped for lunch at Green's Café, a small place not far from the village green frequented by almost everyone in town. A single daisy in a bud vase graced the tabletop. Outside, a trickle of lazy cars passed in the sunshine.

"Well, you're back where you started, in the classroom," Alice said.

Ellen's gaze followed the traffic. "And no matter what comes, I'm going to make it work. This is the first step."

"Oh please, don't be so dramatic. You're going to a college campus, not off to war."

Alice raised her glass of iced tea. "Let's celebrate your return to the paid workforce. Once a teacher, always a teacher."

"I don't know," Ellen said. "The truth is, I was never all that passionate about teaching. My mother insisted on it. Said it was the practical path, and in time I could become an administrator, a principal, maybe even a district superintendent." Ellen heard the pained note of wonder in her own voice. "Am I being ridiculous? Maybe I should just sell the house and squirrel away my money. Let's face it. I don't have Zach's golden touch."

"Oh, the all-knowing Zach. He's King Midas now, too, huh? You're better off without him, Ellie. You've got to know that."

Ellen did know she was better off. There was an odiousness about Zach now. Maybe it had always been there, and she'd been too blind to see it.

"Zach was an easy man to lose yourself in," Alice said. "It's his type—good looking, successful, sooo confident. Men like that suck up all the oxygen." She looked out the window. The fine lines at the corners of her eyes and mouth—despite her best efforts to banish them—stood out in the sunlight. She looked tired, but in a different way lately. Alice wasn't stressed or busy. She wasn't on one of her melodramatic benders. She was weary. "The only way for you now is forward," she said. "Don't look back, Ellie."

Ellen wondered if this were even possible. It seemed to her people spent half their lives looking back. "Teaching will be a stop-gap," she said. "To get some cash coming in. I just want to keep my house."

Alice sighed. "Then you will. One way or another, you will. After everything that's happened, hanging onto a house shouldn't be asking too much."

Chapter Five

Mrs. Ellman in Room 117 was talking to herself again. She wasn't actually talking to herself. She was talking to Mr. Ellman, who had been dead for twelve years.

"This happens all the time near the end," said the Reverend Dillane. "Sometimes it's a long-dead parent or sibling, or grandparents. I've always found it incredibly touching. Come on, Will, you have to at least admit it makes you wonder?"

Rosa sat in the kitchen, a freshly laundered heap of sheets on the table before her, trying not to listen. The little office where Mr. Janssen worked was right off the kitchen, and it didn't have a door. She could hear everything.

Mr. Janssen sniffed. "It makes me wonder about oxygen deprivation to the brain and hallucinations, and there's nothing touching about it. Gives me the willies."

The reverend laughed. "You're a tough old, cynical dog."

"So I've been told."

The Reverend Dillane worked at the hospice, too. The sign on his door said, *Chaplain*, but Rosa thought of him as the reverend. Mr. Janssen called him "Rev." The two of them were friends, though Rosa got the feeling their friendship didn't extend beyond the hospice walls. Their conversations were sometimes interesting, and even though she knew it was wrong, Rosa enjoyed listening. She'd told Mama, who saw no problem: *Getting a little distraction in a place where everybody's dying? What's wrong with that?*

"I once knew a woman who talked to bees," Mr. Janssen said. It sounded like he was yawning.

"Bees? Was she dying?"

"No, she was crazy. She'd hang around the dumpster outside my old apartment building—this was twenty years ago—and argue with the bees buzzing around the trash. Yellow jackets, I think they were actually."

The reverend chuckled. "I don't think the yellow jackets were channeling dead relatives."

"No, huh?" Rosa could hear the smile in Mr. Janssen's voice. "Do celestial visitations arrive via the insect world?"

"Why not? We're all God's creatures."

Mr. Janssen grunted. Rude. He could be sort of jerky.

"Where was this apartment building?" the reverend asked.

"In Manchester."

"Oh, right. You lived there with your girlfriend. Maybe they'd say 'partner' today, right? Ah, to be young and uncommitted. Those days are long gone."

"Well, the young part at least."

Mr. Janssen was right. He wasn't young, neither of them were, but they weren't too old either. Rosa figured they were a little younger than Mama, or at least thinner and sort of more energetic looking.

"I turn fifty-two tomorrow," Mr. Janssen said.

Creepy, it was like he was reading her thoughts.

"Hey, happy birthday! And classes are starting up, right? At the college?"

Mr. Janssen's seat creaked. "Yep, a new semester, and the drama begins all over again. I hold on to my hat this time of year. There's never enough money, not to get them all where they want to go."

Rosa's breath caught.

A scraping noise, the reverend rolling his chair back and standing up.

Rosa grabbed a sheet and smoothed it across the table.

"You're fighting the good fight, helping these kids," the reverend said.

"That's what I tell myself. But my old girlfriend from Manchester, she once warned me I'd die alone anyway."

"Yeesh. I can see why she became an ex. Let's hope she was wrong. Got any birthday plans?"

"I'll pick up a cigar and a nice bottle of red on my way home tomorrow. You ever go to Morley's near the highway? He's got a great selection."

The reverend must have stepped near the office entrance. His voice had changed. He sounded closer. "I'll have to swing by. I like reds, myself. So does my wife. I'm going back to check on Mrs. Ellman. See you next week?"

"Same time, same place."

Rosa snatched another sheet, snapped it, and folded it. She gave the reverend a quick smile as he passed through the kitchen. "Have you visited the new girl on the second floor?" she asked.

"Sarah? No, I haven't yet, but I'm planning to. I'll be back on Sunday."

"She's young."

"Yes, a terrible situation. Twenty-two or twenty-three years old."

"But she could beat it," Rosa said. "The cancer. God works miracles, right?" The reverend must know a thing or two about this.

The reverend smiled. "You know, miracles are funny things. It seems to me the ones we get are the ones we never see coming. But rest assured, I am praying." He winked and headed for the door.

What was that supposed to mean? Rest assured of what? She watched the reverend walk away. She should have kept her mouth shut. Talking in riddles—what good was that?

Chapter Six

At home in the afternoon, Ellen prepared a lemon meringue pie for Alice and Earle. It sat in the refrigerator, a sweet promise beneath plastic wrap. She showered and changed, and when the first, smoky tones of evening streaked the sky, she drove to Alice and Earle's house.

They sat together on the screened-in porch, a late summer dinner on the table before them, as evening settled over the tidy, picket-fenced yard. Earle had grilled salmon with a citrus glaze over a bed of jasmine rice, and vegetable shish kabob skewers, sizzling and blackened at the edges. A cold cucumber salad topped with chunks of ruby tomatoes filled a deep wooden bowl.

"What you need is a new love," Earle proclaimed, lifting a glass of the rosy sherry he liked to drink when a meal was over. He had the patient, long-suffering face of a department store Santa Claus, minus the beard and mustache. His dark eyes were warm and bright behind his shiny round spectacles. His salt-and-pepper hair was always cut a little too short, giving him a shorn, vulnerable air. He was the kind of man whose shoulder you could cry on. Ellen suspected it was a big part of the reason Alice had never left him. Alice had said as much.

"Careful, you're starting to sound like your wife,"

Ellen said, "and anyway, you know what they say— once bitten, twice shy. I can barely say the word: boyfriend. It sounds ridiculous at our age."

"Who said anything about a boyfriend?" Earle swirled the sherry in his glass. "I simply said 'love'."

"In all its guises, all its—ahem—forms." Alice tittered. She had already had one too many glasses of chardonnay.

"I'll get a cat." Ellen raised her wine glass. "To feline love."

"So that's the plan—a crazy cat woman, kitty litter in your shoes, fur stuck to your clothes?" Alice shuddered.

"How about dessert?" Ellen had to cut it off. "Let me get the meringue from the…"

"Sit," Alice said. "You're a guest."

"When was I ever a guest in this house?"

"I don't know, but you're a bona fide, pastry-teaching chef guest tonight. So sit down."

Alice and Earle lived in an antique colonial in one of the old neighborhoods tucked behind Main Street. Their house was almost as familiar to Ellen as her own. She could easily have dished out her meringue, or even made it, in Alice's kitchen. This was a secret litmus test Ellen had to measure her friendships with other women—if you know your way around her kitchen, you're probably good friends.

"I'll have to show you my new bird," Earle said after Alice had disappeared into the kitchen.

Ellen brightened. "What is it?"

"Snowy owl, magnificent creature."

"I love them. How long did it take?"

"Two months, start to finish. The folds of the

feathers, the speckling, and the golden eyes—such an arresting shade—are very tricky to capture."

"Oh, I bet you captured them fine. I love the bird you gave me. He's hanging in my kitchen window. We have coffee together every morning."

Earle planned to sell the decorative wooden birds he carved. He had topped out at the local bank where he worked and was now coasting toward an early retirement and a hobby business of his own.

"Maybe you could give me a woodworking lesson," Ellen said.

"You'll be too busy whipping out pastries over at River Bend." Earle raised his glass again. "Anyway, to new love."

"I'll settle for a paycheck at this point."

He watched her a moment, his eyes tender and tired. "I've got a feeling it'll happen when you least expect it."

From another man, there might have been a flirtatious suggestion buried in this, a daring overture to a wife's friend when the wife is out of the room. But not with Earle. He was like a favorite old sweater you wrap yourself in to feel better. He had never found out about Alice's brief dalliances, as far as Ellen knew.

Alice's first marriage, right out of college, had lasted three years. It was followed by a four-year relationship, culminating in a two-year engagement, to a tax attorney with cold feet. She had married Earle at thirty-one.

"You're on the verge of great things," Earle said.

"And you're as dizzy as your half-drunk wife."

Earle nearly spit out his sherry, and they both laughed until he had to remove his glasses to wipe the lenses.

Alice, and then Earle, were Ellen's friends originally. She and Alice had met through a toddler playgroup at the town library. Zach had socialized with them, out of a spirit of goodwill and, Ellen knew, because he had found Alice amusing.

Try as he had, though, Earle had never been able to interest Zach in the basement workshop where he carved and painted his amazingly lifelike wild birds. Ellen marveled over the painstaking detail, the intricacy of the coloring, and the smooth folds of the wooden feathers.

Earle had carved her a brilliant red cardinal for Christmas one year, its little wooden beak ajar with a sprig of holly tucked inside. She'd had an urge lately to move the cardinal from her kitchen out to Arborview. There was an empty nail above the window opening. The cardinal seemed to belong there now.

Chapter Seven

Baking is like building a house. You must begin with a vision, a dream of the finished thing, in order to bring it to life. Ellen chose this as the guiding spirit of her course. At the top of the first page of the syllabus, she typed: "If you don't know where you're going, you'll never get there."

She winced at the irony of the statement, coming from her, but the students would be none the wiser. Her failures were her own, and at least baking had never been among them.

On a cloudy Thursday morning, she sat at Jimmy's old desktop computer, which she had moved into a corner of the family room. Finished with their summer internships, Taber and Jimmy had come home for a week before heading back to school. They were both sleeping in this morning.

Ellen squinted at the screen. Which skills to teach and in what order? What mattered most? Baking is a series of decisions, each dependent on and influencing the others. The quality of the ingredients, how seamlessly they're combined, the heat of the oven, the deftness in the hands holding the implements.

It was like a game of dominoes, a house of cards. Which step is the crucial one, the one that can send the whole thing toppling if you get it wrong? More irony. Still, she typed:

Weeks 1&2: Types of Pastry—What they are, where they come from

Weeks 3&4: Ingredients—Parts of the whole

Weeks 5&6: Technique—Mastering the moves

Weeks 7&8: Flavor Combinations—What works and what doesn't—most of the time

Weeks 9&10: All About Dough—No, not cash

Final Project: A Reach Recipe of your own choosing. Only requirement: Must be beautiful as well as delicious.

Ellen sat back and bit her lip. She needed to fill in the specifics, to nail down the details. The course started in two weeks, so there was no time to waste. She rubbed her forehead. She'd finish tomorrow, when Jimmy and Taber would be back on their respective campuses.

She planned to make a cocoa chiffon cake for their last dinner at home. Few things said, "You are precious," better than a cocoa chiffon cake. She would top each slice with a scattering of fresh raspberries.

In the kitchen, she sifted flour. It fell in a tidy, purposeful blizzard into the stainless-steel bowl on the counter. Ellen's hands warmed, her movements growing fluid. To her, pastry's mere presence had always implied honor. Someone spent time creating it, assembling the ingredients and breathing life into them—a painstaking act that yielded something wholly beautiful and comforting. This was what she wanted her students to grasp: You can bring solace and wholeness into the world through simple acts. There are people who can't, or who refuse, to understand this. But this doesn't make them right. It makes them lacking. This is what Ellen should have said to her own parents, if she'd only known the words back then.

Still, a flutter of panic filled her chest when she imagined her River Bend classroom, a sea of blank, apathetic faces before her as she prattled on. An "easy A," a transcript booster, all they really wanted. *You can save the bull-crap, lady. We've got to pay our bills.* Well, Ellen had to pay hers, too, and they were going to start mounting soon.

The cake was cool and ready to frost by ten o'clock. Taber, finally out of bed and yawning, slipped into the kitchen as Ellen filled a pastry bag with a fluffy light French Buttercream.

"Can I help?" Taber asked from the doorway.

Her long hair, a gleaming brown, darker and more lustrous than Ellen's, emphasized her angular face and large brown eyes, their irises flecked with specks of gold. She wore a pink tank top with NYC stitched in tiny, glittery rhinestones across the front.

"Did my clanging around down here wake you?" Ellen wiped her hands on her apron. "How about French toast?"

Taber yawned. "Nah, I've been awake a while. I think I'll hold off 'til lunch. You're frosting?"

"A 'Good Luck in the New Semester' cake for you guys."

"Mom, how sweet. Can I take a shot?"

Ellen handed her the pastry bag. "Be my guest. I was going to do little swirling peaks, like a tiny mountain range."

"Won't Jimmy love it?" Taber cocked her head to the side. "I may work in a flower or two, if you don't mind. A few alpine roses?"

Taber was a merchandising major at the Empire

Fashion Academy in Manhattan. Ellen watched her work the pastry bag, twisting the stream of frosting into rows of breathy peaks and then into the tiny ivory petals of a single flower sitting amidst them.

"Lovely," Ellen said. "You've been practicing."

"You'd be surprised how handy I've become. One of my classes last semester was totally hands-on. I mean—measuring, draping, cutting, and sewing—all the bases. And I've never been good with my hands."

"What did you make?" Ellen asked.

"Well, it was a summer dress pattern that didn't come together. But, you know since I'm on the merchandising side, it isn't a big deal. The point was to give us an appreciation for the craft, for the role designers play, what goes into taking a design from an idea to a model's back to a rack in, say, Bergdorf. The chain of value."

"You've got the head for business I never had."

"Style and substance." Taber raised her arms and snapped her fingers. "Check it out."

It sometimes seemed Taber had fallen from a star—a satiny, stylish perch in the heavens—directly into Ellen's arms as an infant. She was such a bold, savvy girl. She always had been.

"How did things go yesterday?" Ellen asked. Jimmy and Taber had spent the day with Zach and Lydia. Ellen had dropped them off outside the condominium in West Hartford. She had driven by the building the first time months ago, out of curiosity, with Alice in the passenger seat, clucking and shaking her head. It was one of the turn-of-the-century places that lined the main avenue, a stone edifice, gargoyles perched menacingly on the corners of the roof. No doubt the units featured high ceilings and brick fireplaces.

"We went out for Thai food," Taber said. "Lydia came, too, but it was nice. Yeah, it was okay." She nodded, yet a hint of uncertainty creased her brow. "It would have been better if you were there," she said, her voice rising on the last word.

"Honey, you don't have to say that."

"I know I don't, but it's true. It would have been better with you."

"But it was still a good time, and Daddy wanted to see you both so much."

"Yeah, Dad seemed really happy."

Ellen kept the smile on her face. "Remember how we all said this was for the best?"

"I don't like you being here alone," Taber said. "You must get lonely. I would."

"No time to get lonely, I've got a lot going on."

Taber brightened. "It's great you're teaching at River Bend. You'll be a natural, Mom. Was it your idea or Alice's?"

"Mine, but of course Alice had something to say."

"Alice is so cool. I wish I could have squeezed in a visit with her." Taber flashed the same dimpled grin she had turned on Ellen from her crib. "You wouldn't believe how gross Lydia's feet were in sandals. The nasty toenails. Seriously, I bet the woman's never had a pedicure in her life."

"You sound like Alice," Ellen said, but she had to laugh. "How about cutting flowers from the garden for the table?"

"Black-eyed Susans," Taber said. "They look awesome this year." And she was gone, through the sliding glass door, out onto the deck, and into the blooming sunshine of late morning. How easily Taber moved on—bouncing from broken marriages to nasty toenails to flowers and sunshine. Youth made her impervious.

Ellen would make them both—Taber and Jimmy—a dish to take back to school, something they could open in their dorm rooms and find comfort in. She had a couple of hours free this afternoon. She thumbed through the pastry catalogue in her mind. Berry cobbler, a nice summer dish, the berries quietly sweet and draped over velvety crust. It wouldn't take too much time.

She still thought in these terms—time at a premium. When the children were young, mornings had been a frantic dash: breakfast, packing lunches, catching the bus. Ellen had longed for the days when she would see the hours ahead as something other than a to-do list. Now she had them—endless hours to rattle around in her own head and to move through the rooms of her house. She was a person who pondered, a ruminator, a quality Zach, at first, had appreciated.

"He's someone who is going places," her mother had said, a touch of disbelief in her voice when Ellen told her Zach had proposed. What Ellen should have said was she wanted to go places, too. She just hadn't known where yet.

****

At dinner that night, Jimmy described his escapades in the mountains of New Hampshire. The soft light of evening fell across the dining room table as the three of them feasted on the kids' favorite meal: chicken piccata, all bubbly and succulent over a bed of fluffy rice, and sautéed asparagus. Taber's tiger lily bouquet glowed in its glass vase.

Jimmy's skin was a warm brown from days in the mountain sun, and his brown hair was streaked golden. He had spent the summer working in the White Mountains National Forest, tending to the park's hut system, a chain of simple cabins dotting the wilderness where hikers could bunk for the night and get a warm meal. They'd spent a long weekend in the Whites as a family when Jimmy was eleven and Taber thirteen. Staring into the glassy waters of a secluded mountain lake, Jimmy had fallen in love. He was about to begin his junior year at Olden College, majoring in ecology and natural resources preservation.

"I helped this one freaked-out guy down from the shoulder of Mount Lafayette," Jimmy said. "He climbed above the tree line, took a look over his shoulder at the drop, and sort of froze."

"How did he get down?" Taber asked.

"Gripping my arm every step of the way," Jimmy said. "Here's this forty-year-old guy, a lawyer he told me, smart and everything, on a hike with his kids, and he's clinging to a tree trunk for dear life, panting like he's going to keel over."

"Sounds like a panic attack," Taber said. "My roommate has them."

"He tried to give me a tip, fifty bucks, down in the parking lot when it was over," Jimmy said. "I refused. I mean, helping people on the mountain is my job. He didn't owe me anything."

"Lucky for him you were there," Ellen said, a buoyancy lifting her. This boy of hers shone brighter than the sun. There had always been an affinity between them, a like-minded collusion.

"But the strangest part is he wasn't a new hiker," Jimmy said. "He told me he hiked all over the Whites back in college. He knew the trails. He'd just forgotten what it *feels* like to be up that high."

"To be that vulnerable." Ellen gave her children a weak smile. "To wonder why you ever placed yourself in such a position."

Jimmy's gaze met his mother's. "So do you guys need help with packing?" she asked.

When her children were in their rooms and the house was quiet, Ellen called Alice, whispering in Zach's old den with the door closed. "I think I'm having a crisis moment," she said. "I don't know what I'm doing. Who am I kidding? I'll never make enough money to hang on to this house."

"Whoa, wait. Where is this coming from? What happened to I'm-not-giving-up-this-house-until-I'm-ready?"

"I should get recertified and go back to teaching school, if they'll even have me."

"Is that what you want? To go backward?"

"Why are you whispering?"

"I'm, ah, in the middle of something. Can we talk in the morning?"

"Oh, I'm sorry. Sure. I'll call you." Ellen hung up. What was Alice up to and why the whispering? Not a good sign. Ellen went into the mudroom and pulled on a sweater.

Outside, a moonlit night, the sky above unfathomably dark. She stepped onto the soft welcome of the grass. The darkness beckoned, cloaked and soothing. Drawing near the woods, she could see the individual trees, standing resolute at the edge of the lawn, and beyond them, the huddled clusters of trunks and branches leading into the forest. Ellen glanced up at Arborview. She traced a finger over the rough bark and climbed the ladder.

Shadows filled the little enclosure, falling across the floor and walls. They were the shadows Ellen knew, the ones she had always known. A calm came over her, directing her to stop, to simply be still.

She had no way to explain this place she had landed—not to her children, or Alice, or anyone. This trembling ground beneath her feet was hers alone. It was where she had arrived, what she had earned and inherited. The uncertainty etched in her bones, her triumphs and despair, side by side. This entirely respectable, well-intentioned, middle-class life was hers to unravel. Why was she so fixated on keeping a house, when the problem was really so much larger? Confess your failures and your fears, the nuns used to say. You can't hide them from God.

Ellen went to the window and stared into the trees. A breeze moved through the branches, stirring whispery murmurs all around. She saw the flashing silver underside of the leaves, their sudden rise and fluttering collapse, the way they all shuddered as one. She could not see beyond this shimmering veil.

Chapter Eight

The classroom was a basement kitchen—not the same room she had learned in long ago, but a larger, updated space. It was a wide rectangle with a white vinyl floor and a bank of windows facing the ground level of a courtyard. A long stainless-steel prep table ran almost the length of the room. White ovens with range hoods lined one wall, and three industrial-sized utility sinks stood against the other.

On the day of the first class, Ellen tucked her purse in a cabinet above the sinks, along with a straw tote bag she'd designated for class materials, such as they were—a notebook, her laptop, sharpened pencils. Zach had bought her the bag ten years ago when they were vacationing in St. Croix. Ellen had rediscovered it three insomniac nights earlier, tucked in a corner of the attic.

She positioned herself now at the head of the steel table and glanced at the clock above the door. How melodramatic she was—how overboard—watching the clock like a death-row inmate praying for a last-minute pardon. Alice would have chuckled. It was the kind of image she would appreciate.

Ellen looked down at her hands with their short, stubby fingernails and the branching blue veins that seemed to be growing more visible lately. When had this begun?

The door clicked. Ellen turned, a half-smile on her

face.

Three, no, four students—a gaggle of sunglasses and backpacks—shuffled into the room.

"Hello, welcome," Ellen called. She cleared her throat. "You've got your choice of seats." She gestured at the row of wooden stools surrounding the steel table. "You can keep your bags under the table, if you like. But when we start cooking, they'll probably be a little safer up on the shelves."

The door opened again and again, until Ellen propped it open with a heavy chair. They'd need the fresh air anyway. Why hadn't she thought of this?

When the room was full, fifteen kids perched on stools around the table. Ellen took her spot at the head. It wasn't as bad as standing at a blackboard or podium, but her heart still skittered a bit. She swallowed hard.

"If you signed up for The Power of Pastry, you're in the right place," she said. "I'm Ellen Cahill. It's my first time teaching this class, so we'll be figuring this out together."

A boy in a Red Sox T-shirt yawned. A pair of sunglasses sat half-buried in the dark, wavy thicket of his hair.

"We're a small group this semester, which is great. It'll give me more one-on-one time with each of you." Ellen smiled.

A tall girl in too-dark lipstick and enormous gold hoop earrings glanced at the clock above the door. Counting the minutes already. Here for the easy A. Well, Ellen planned on being a generous grader. The focus would be on effort and attitude.

"I'm passing around a seating chart," Ellen said. "The seats you've chosen will be yours for the semester, so make any switches now while you still can. The seats are numbered and each one corresponds to a stove along the wall. You'll be cooking on the same stove all semester, and it matters, because you'll discover, if you keep baking, no two stoves are alike. What's three hundred and fifty degrees on one is more like three hundred and thirty on another—no matter what the dial says."

A girl with a long dark ponytail smiled at Ellen. She conjured Taber. A slender Hispanic girl with soft dark eyes, she perched delicately, almost tentatively, on her stool, as if she were wondering whether to make a run for it.

"First rule of baking," Ellen said. "You've got to develop a feel for what's taking place in the pan or bowl or pot in front of you. Gadgets and gizmos only get you so far. You've got to know your ingredients, know what's on the inside, and what happens when they come together. Temperature, pressure, time—all of these affect the magical alchemy, and sometimes in ways we can't predict."

A girl in a white peasant blouse, with a long auburn braid hanging over one shoulder, nodded. A skinny girl with dark boxy eyeglasses next to her scribbled notes. She stopped writing and looked up. Her eyes, wide with anxiety, met Ellen's. She raised her hand.

"Yes?" Ellen said.

"The catalogue said we don't need to have any cooking experience for this class. I hope it's true, 'cause I haven't got any."

"Your name?" Ellen said.

"Doreen Jones."

"Nice to meet you, Doreen, and don't worry. This

is an introductory course. It's a chance for you to discover baking."

Doreen stared uncertainly. "It sounds a little complicated already."

"Well, we're going to break the whole down into its parts." Ellen flashed a thumbs-up. "The complications don't start until we start putting the parts together. Kind of like with people." Ellen laughed, but not a single kid cracked a smile.

"I've got to get a good grade to keep my GPA up, or I could lose my scholarship." Doreen's eyes pleaded. "And I can't repeat any courses, no way. Paying for them one time is bad enough."

"You said it," mumbled a boy at the far end of the table—nineteen or twenty maybe, with penetrating dark eyes and hair buzzed close to his skull.

"Your name?" Ellen said.

"Javier Escamilla, and I'm outta here after this semester, got a college already lined up, so I don't need any baking troubles."

A few kids laughed.

"Well, that's terrific, but tell me, what makes you think you're going to have troubles?" Ellen asked.

Javier shrugged. "I'm no cook."

"No one is, right off the bat." Ellen forced a lightness into her voice. "I took my first class on this campus, and I've been baking ever since."

Javier's eyes narrowed. "You were a student here?"

"Yep."

"Must have been a while ago."

Snickering around the table.

It felt like a stinging dart had hit her. "My point

exactly. It was a while ago," Ellen said. "But I keep getting better. I've enjoyed my baking skills for years. A lifetime, you would probably say."

"Um, okay." The boy shifted on his stool.

"And," Ellen said, "did anyone ever tell you it's rude to reference a person's age in a derogatory manner?" She locked eyes with the kid until he glanced down.

"Yeah," he mumbled.

Ellen felt like she was back in Taber's and Jimmy's teen years, taking them down a peg when they went too far. It was good to know she still had it in her.

Another boy, a skinny pale kid with a dusting of whiskers along his jawline, snaked his hand into the air. Of the fifteen students, only five were boys.

"Yes?" Ellen said.

"Do men do this?"

"Do what?"

"Cook or, ah, bake. I mean, for a living."

"Oh, come on. You've seen them," Ellen said. "On the TV shows, all those chef shows."

The kid shook his head.

"No? How about Bobby Flay? Guy Fieri?"

Another shake.

"Some of the best chefs in the world are men."

The kid coughed.

"People—men and women—do make a living doing this. I swear." Ellen raised her hand as if she were taking an oath. "And other people make pastry just for the fun of it. Plus, they have a sweet tooth."

Ellen passed her syllabus around the table. She'd made twenty copies. Then she dove in, explaining each section in detail. She finished up by giving a simple homework assignment. Each student was to come to the next class with a Reach Recipe, a dish that exceeded, or they believed exceeded, their abilities. For the final project, they would create their recipes.

"Think big," Ellen said. "Not chocolate chip cookies, but Baked Alaska."

She got a few dubious looks, as the students rose and gathered their backpacks.

"See you next week. My email is on the syllabus if you have any questions."

A petite girl with a strawberry blonde bob smiled, passing Ellen. "Crème puffs," she said. "There's a reach, huh?"

"Now that's the spirit! Crème puffs—worth every ounce of labor you put into them."

The seating chart landed on the table in front of Ellen, placed there by the Hispanic girl with the ponytail. Ellen lifted it and scanned the names, noting the girl sat in seat nine.

"You're Rosa Escamilla?" Ellen asked.

"Yeah. Sorry about my big-mouth brother," Rosa said.

"Ah, Javier is your brother."

"Unfortunately." Rosa glanced over her shoulder. Her voice dropped. "But I like what you said about people making a living doing this. A good living, right?"

"In many cases, yes." Ellen smiled. "Are you considering it?"

"It's, um, something I'm thinking about." Rosa hoisted her backpack higher on her shoulder.

"Really? How excellent. I sometimes wish I'd considered going pro when I was your age. Any thoughts on your Reach Recipe?"

Rosa shook her head.

"Think big."

Rosa turned her luminous dark eyes on Ellen. A hint of a frown creased her smooth forehead. "How big is too big?"

She couldn't have been more than nineteen, a child really.

"You tell me," Ellen said, and for one absurd moment, she thought the girl actually might.

Rosa hesitated, gave a smile, and moved on.

The sun was fading in a rosy glow when Ellen made it back to her car in the lot. Evening classes were getting underway. New packs of students darted over the grass, throwing Frisbees in the dying light.

Ellen flipped up her sun visor and slid the key into the ignition. The wheel was warm and smooth beneath her hands. So good to be back in her car, doors locked, the click-click of the turn signal as she pulled onto the road, the spinning wheels carrying her home.

She stopped at a liquor shop—Morley's Package Store—in a strip mall before the highway entrance ramp. She had earned her glass of wine on the patio tonight.

The store was nearly empty. The ceiling lights shone over the aisles of glinting bottles. Ellen made her way to the "whites" section and selected a California Chardonnay; one Alice had introduced her to years ago.

An Indian man—Ellen assumed he was Indian—sat behind the counter, reading a newspaper, the radio behind him broadcasting a language that sounded like the rolling, the rising and falling, of Hindi. Ellen carried her wine to the checkout counter, as a man carrying his own bottle approached. They reached the counter together, and noting one another, each took a step back.

"After you," he said.

"Thank you."

He looked to be about Ellen's age, give or take a few years, brown hair graying at the temples, square chin, and deep-set eyes. "*Namaste*," he said to the cashier.

The man behind the counter smiled. "*Namaste*, brother." He bowed his head slightly.

They both chuckled, and Ellen snuck a look at the man next to her again.

He nodded at her. "I'm a regular."

"You speak Hindi?"

"Only a few phrases. I traveled in India. Years ago."

"Really? That's one place I always wanted to go," Ellen said. "I had the perfect opportunity. My college roommate was from India. Well, it's an old story now."

"But they're our specialty, right? Old stories?"

Ellen laughed. "Speak for yourself."

She could have been offended. Alice would surely have been. After all, what had this man implied other than that they were old—she was old? But something about him made it seem all right. His skin had a gently worn look. The lines along his mouth framed it elegantly, humorously.

The man behind the counter cleared his throat and tapped a few keys on the cash register. "Twenty-five plus tax," he said.

Ellen fumbled in her purse. She paid and collected the wine. "Have a nice evening."

On the patio at home, she felt the day drain from

her, all its needling concerns carried off by the evening air. She was safe, buffeted by the home she had built, even if she was here alone.

The straw tote bag with her class materials sat on the patio table. She closed her eyes and saw the long steel table in her classroom, the red cap perched on a lanky boy's head, sunlight filtering in from the quad, Rosa Escamilla's shy smile. *How big is too big?*

Ellen met Zach the summer she took her baking class at River Bend, and for the first time, she became a woman whom other women envied. Zach was sweet and attentive and bursting with plans. Her single friends had purred over her good luck. Did he have any friends?

"There'll be no stopping us," he said the night he proposed, as they lay together in a white-washed Cape Cod motel room with sand in the carpet and an oil painting of a fishing boat hanging above the bed. "We'll have an amazing life." Oh, the damp glint of joy, the certainty in his eyes.

"Will you marry Lydia?" Ellen had asked as they rode the elevator down from her attorney's office after signing the final papers.

"I can't imagine why it would be necessary," Zach had said.

When they parted on the sidewalk, twenty-two years of marriage behind them, the breeze of the spring morning moved over Ellen. It seemed to carry off pieces of her body, layers of the self she had become, peeling them away, leaving her not liberated as she had hoped, but smaller and more exposed.

The phone was ringing in the kitchen now. Probably Alice calling to see how the first class went.

There would be time enough tomorrow to tell the story.

Ellen stood. The blurry trill of the wine floated behind her eyes. In the corner of the yard, Arborview coaxed her to cross the lawn. She grabbed the tote bag and stepped off the patio.

Inside the tree house, the hush swallowed her. She dropped the straw bag, walked to the center, and sank down into the beanbag chair. The beans scuttled beneath her as the day faded to a whisper. Maybe she should change her last name, go back to her maiden name. Sanding was her real name. Only it didn't sound real anymore. What she needed was a new name. But what? Wasn't this something she should understand by now? What to call herself?

Ingredients. What had she told her students? *Understand your ingredients.* Well, she'd gotten her own mixed up, and now she was going to have to sort them. Arborview creaked. *You got that right.*

Ellen sat up, then struggled to her feet. It was almost completely dark, but she could make out the dull glow of her straw tote—Zach's Caribbean gift—against the wall. She grabbed the handle, reached inside, and pulled out her notebooks and laptop. She placed them in a pile on the beanbag. Then she went to the window and raised the empty bag overhead. With a heave, she hurled it into the dark woods. It crashed out of sight. Time for a new bag. A fierce thrill ran up Ellen's spine. She felt the breath enter, move into, and leave her body. "*Namaste*," she whispered, just to feel the word in her mouth.

Chapter Nine

Rosa filled the old steel pot with water and carried it to the stove. As she settled it on the burner, one of the handles gave out. She drew a sharp breath as the pot crashed to the burner with a clang. Water sloshed the front of her T-shirt.

"¡*Maldita sea!*" Rosa said. "This stupid thing."

Ah, the pot was ancient—how ancient? Who knew? Her mother's, before that her grandmother's. This crazy pot had traveled from Peru to Connecticut, fairly unlikely back in the days when Rosa's grandmother and her mother, only seven at the time, made the trip, but maybe not so unlikely now. The thing was ready for the dump.

Rosa lifted the pot, holding her arm beneath the worn metal weight, and dumped the rest of the water in the sink. Forget the rice. She'd have a sandwich for dinner. She had a lot of homework to get to. She'd make two sandwiches and put one in the fridge for Javier. He'd be hungry when he got back from campus, and by the time Mama returned from work, they'd both be asleep.

Mama was working the late hostess shift, which meant she'd be home after midnight. They'd see her in the morning, bleary faced, pouring coffee, wearing the faded pink bathrobe with the white flowers on the lapels and the fluffy slippers that slap-slapped across the linoleum floor. It had always been the three of them—Mama, Rosa, and Javi. Papi had died when Rosa was only two. She didn't remember him.

She took a loaf of bread, a cooked chicken breast, lettuce, and sliced cheese from the refrigerator. The history course wasn't going to be the easy ride she had hoped for. History of Western Civilization, part one. How many more parts were there? Greeks, Romans, who came next? And what did any of it really have to do with her?

Javier had aced the same course the year before, but Javier aced everything. And now that he had been accepted at the Niagara Institute of Technology, he was truly unbearable.

"*Mira*, Rosa, so what?" Mama had said. "This is no contest. Worry about your own hide."

Of course, Mama was helping Javi's hide. She was cheering him on—at least what passed for "cheering on" with Mama. She was encouraging and supportive, sentiments she had flatly refused to extend to Rosa for "cooking school." Rosa had tried to explain Seasons Culinary College was not a "cooking school." It was a full-fledged, accredited university that included the culinary arts.

"You don't need a school," Mama had said. "I will show you how to cook—for free. Then you can be another broke bum, hustling dinners and kissing butts."

Rosa was tired of trying to explain. She took solace in the fact that Javi was piling on the student loans, the same as her. Mama didn't have money for college. He'd graduate from Niagara with the debt pistol pointed at his head, too.

Rosa settled at the kitchen table with her sandwich.

The pastry teacher wanted a Reach Recipe. She looked like one of those ladies who hadn't ever had to reach for anything in her life. What did she know? Servants probably cooked her meals. The whole thing felt too much like a final exam, like something Rosa could fail—proving Mama had been right all along.

The truth was, Rosa had dozens of Reach Recipes, and not only for pastries. She dreamed of entire meals, dining experiences complete with fancy bone china plates and shiny silverware, wine glasses with delicate icy stems, and martini shakers rattling with promise as red-jacketed waiters shook them.

But first things first. Rosa bit into the cold chicken. Its clean simplicity calmed her. The lettuce crunched, sharp and fresh. Street sounds drifted through the open window. The hiss and bump of passing car tires as people returned home after work and the neighborhood settled in for the evening. Someone whistled on the stoop next door. Mrs. Esparza down the block called her kids in to dinner.

Rosa finished her sandwich and cleaned the few dishes. She turned off the light over the sink. What did Mama say about the last electric bill? "This has gotta stop. Nobody needs this much light." Wagging her finger at Rosa and Javier. "In Peru, Grandma had only lanterns, and she did fine."

Javier had rolled his eyes behind Mama's back. "So why not huddle around a match and call ourselves lucky?"

Rosa returned to the kitchen table and opened her history book. She forced her mind into the text.

An hour later, the deadbolt in the front door flipped, and Rosa heard Javier clear his throat in the little vestibule as he shook off his coat. The muffled throat clear always announced Javier. He did it when he entered a new situation, when he settled down to focus, and when he was nervous.

"I heard your signature rumble," Rosa called.

"*Hola, florecita*." Javier dropped his backpack on the kitchen table.

"Hey, be careful," Rosa said, pulling her book to safety.

"What are you eating? You got any for me?" Javier swooped to plant a kiss on top of Rosa's head. He smiled, flashing the rakish dimple in his left cheek.

"No Tilda tonight?" Rosa asked. Javi often brought his girlfriend home with him. Rosa never minded, but it seemed to irritate Mama.

"She's working late. Extra shift, overtime, couldn't turn it down."

"Any news on her squeezing me in? I'd love to work at Home and Hearth."

Javier smirked. "Beats hanging around with the dead and dying, huh?"

"You're so awful, Javi. The hospice isn't like that. I told you. It's kind of peaceful, actually."

Javi raised his hands. "Whatever you say. Anyway, Home and Hearth's not for you. You'd be playing with the dishes and forks the whole time. They've got cookbooks now, too. Tilda brought one home: *Summer Dining Al Fresco,* I think it was. You'd lose your mind."

"There's a sandwich in the fridge," Rosa said.

"Ah, I'm starved."

Javier got the sandwich and plopped himself down across from her.

"Chicken?" He raised an eyebrow. "Why not beef bourguignon? Come on, where's your Reach Recipe?"

Rosa laughed. "Where's yours?"

"In the frozen food aisle."

"Javi, you're crazy. This is your chance to learn how to make a really special dish."

"And then eat it? I don't get it. Who wants to work hard for something that'll be gone in a few minutes? I like my accomplishments to stick around a little longer."

"Spoken like a future electrical engineer."

"But you gonna be the Peruvian Julia Child. I can see it now." Javier raised his hands, bringing the tips of his thumbs and forefingers to touch, framing Rosa's face.

"I'd come out of Seasons Culinary College with a degree, Javi, like you. They help you get jobs. They've put graduates in the best restaurants and resorts and hotels in the world."

Javier raised an eyebrow. "But to Mama, it's cooking school, and you gonna be a cook."

"It's the hospitality industry, and lots of people make a living in it. You heard the pastry teacher."

"Yeah, I heard her. But Mama's gonna hear 'cook'." He winked. "I'll pray for you."

Rosa glared. "She won't even let me explain. She's never like this with you. It's so unfair."

"Fair got nothing to do with it. You'll never change Mama."

"I don't want to change her."

"Yes, you do."

Rosa wanted to smack him. "How do you know what I want?"

"Been living with you my whole life." He wiped his mouth with a paper napkin and looked at her. "You're an open book."

"Forget you, Javi."

He stood up. "Whatever. Figure it out yourself."

Rosa listened to his footsteps climbing the stairs to his tiny bedroom on the second floor. Her heart thudded. Mama had always favored him, and just because he was a boy. He was moving across the hall now to the bathroom over the kitchen. Rosa listened, alternately loving and hating him. The maddening thing was he was kind of right.

"You could at least tell her she's wrong," she called up the stairs.

Javi's room was across the hall from Rosa's. When they were little, she would sneak into his bed, and he would tell her stories until she was sleepy enough to return to her own room. Mama slept in a shoebox off the living room. This cramped cape house with its weedy postage-stamp yard and cracked linoleum floors was her crowning possession. It was a big achievement, Javi had once pointed out, when you make your living as a hostess, even at a swanky place like Sotto Voce.

Was there no way to make Mama understand what Rosa saw, peering into the dining room of a restaurant like Sotto Voce at night? She saw the possibility of transformation. It was in the wink of the chandeliers hanging above the whispery conversations of the diners, in the candlelight warming their faces, in the flash of a jewel tucked in a woman's hair, and in the white-coated waiters hoisting trays heaped with exquisite mystery.

Rosa wanted to be in the kitchen, bright and bustling behind those swinging doors, the nerve center making it all possible, transforming an overly large, too ornate room into an oasis of muffled sensuality, shutting out the world. Could such a place really exist, or was it only in her mind?

Chapter Ten

"So you're two classes down and twelve to go," Alice said. "I knew you'd like it."

Ellen sat in a patio chair, her feet propped on the edge of the red wheelbarrow next to Alice's flower garden. She had driven over on a bright Saturday afternoon to loan Alice a pair of gardening shears.

Alice was putting her rose bushes to bed for winter. In a wide-brimmed sun hat, pink lipstick, and matching gardening gloves, she knelt before the plants, clipping and fussing. She leaned back, cocking her head to one side, surveying the bushes. Then she snipped a twig. "Was I right or was I right?"

"You were, Oh Great One." Ellen pressed her hands together, as if in praycr. "Hey, I meant to tell you, Zach called again, woke me up this morning."

Alice turned. "You've got to be kidding."

"Nope."

"This needs to stop. Tell him to get lost. He left you for another woman." Alice poked at a branch. "And why does he always call so early? The illicit nature. The air of..." She snapped the shears, too forcefully. "Secrecy. It's not healthy."

"It has gotten a little weird." Ellen stiffened every time the phone rang now. His most recent call had been particularly annoying.

"You're up, aren't you?" he'd said, once again too

early in the morning, as she lay in bed. "I'm heading to the field office in Boston, but I wanted to catch you before I left."

"Zach, what is it? Is anything wrong?"

"No, everything's fine. I, ah, wanted to congratulate you on the River Bend course you're teaching. The kids filled me in. I never thought you'd teach again."

"Thanks. I appreciate it, but you didn't have to call just for…"

"You deserve a standing ovation."

Oh, he was nauseating. She *deserved* a lot more than he knew.

"I've got to get going," Ellen said. "I'm meeting Alice this morning."

"Alice…how is she? And Earle?"

"Fine, same as ever."

"Ah, well, good. I've got to run, too, but good luck. I'm…I'm proud of you, Ellen, if it makes any difference. Bye."

Ellen was grateful her old bedside phone still had an actual cord attached to a base, because it felt good to slam down the receiver. He was proud of her? Wasn't that a comment he perhaps could have made ten years earlier, when it would have mattered? When she was up to her eyeballs in Taber and Jimmy, and the car needed an oil change, and the bathroom sink had a leak, and she couldn't find the plumber's number?

"Get caller ID," Alice said now, pushing the straw hat back on her head so Ellen could see the hard glare in her eyes. "You're the only person I know who doesn't have it on their landline."

So Ellen did. On her way home, she swung into an

electronics store and bought a new tabletop phone with a digital display screen for incoming and outgoing calls.

And that evening the new phone rang, purring to life—it had a gentle trill of a ring, a big improvement over the last phone. Ellen was reading a copy of *Bon Appétit* in bed. She put down the magazine and turned to the phone. Ten boxy little digits stared out at her. Zach's cell, the numbers so familiar. Was he hiding in a closet this time, or was Lydia perhaps out of town tonight? Another ring. What could he want?

Ellen gripped the smooth plastic of the receiver. She had let him off too easy, all these years, coddled him. Easy Ellen. Look what it had gotten her. A hard-ass deal driven by a fast-talking lawyer, while Zach stared down at the table in that conference room. He had driven a merciless bargain, protecting himself, and only himself. She should have known he would. And now he was proud of her?

She released the phone. It rang two more times. Then silence. She couldn't trust what might come out of her mouth, and she didn't want to say something she might regret later. But she could feel a moment coming when she would let it all out, and soon.

Chapter Eleven

Ellen walked around the table as her students grated chocolate shavings to top the mini angel food cakes that were hopefully growing firm and spongy in their ovens.

"A little less pressure." Ellen passed the girl with the dark gelled hair rising in a slick wave over her forehead. "Push too hard and you get chocolate chips. Shavings should be paper thin. Think of them as cocoa flower petals."

The girl made a sound, half-grunt and half-laugh. She'd made the sound before. She grunt-laughed when her egg whites didn't stiffen, when her piecrust came out of the oven and crumbled, and when she dropped a pan of freshly sifted flour onto the floor. Her name was Lauren, but in Ellen's mind she was "Grunt."

Ellen stopped at Rosa Escamilla's station. "These are beautiful." She pointed to the tidy bowl of shavings the girl had produced. "May I?"

"Yes, please." Rosa stepped back.

Ellen popped one of the shavings into her mouth. "The percentage of cocoa fat makes all the difference in these, in all chocolate actually." She glanced around the table. "Some of you may have already realized this, but I purposefully gave you different kinds of blocks— bitter, semisweet, milk, various brands and fat contents. I know who's got what. When we taste test at the end of class, you'll get to appreciate the differences for yourselves. Some are subtle, others will slap you in the face, or the mouth, that is."

"Mrs. Cahill?" Rosa said. "Mine is super dark, right? It's almost bitter."

Ellen smiled. "And when you taste it on top of the angel food…"

"And it mixes with the sweet, it's all the topping I'll really need."

"The perfect complement." Ellen smiled. "That's what we look for in flavors, ones that bring out the best in each other."

"It's the point of the whole thing, isn't it?"

Ellen looked into the girl's bottomless dark eyes. "It is. Tastes, flavors, textures are one thing on their own, but the interesting—and tricky—part starts when you put them together."

"I love to cook," Rosa said.

"So I see," Ellen said.

The girl's voice was tentative, reserved. She glanced at the other end of the table where Javier had hacked his chocolate block into splinters. "My brother." She jerked her head in his direction. "Not so much."

Ellen laughed. "We'll see if we can change him."

When the class ended—and the angel food, the good and the bad, had been consumed—Ellen noticed Rosa and Javier packing up their bags together. She fiddled with her own papers, listening to them.

"Bring her a piece of yours," Javier said.

"Should I?"

"Why not? It's a midnight snack when she gets home."

"What am I gonna carry it in?"

"I can give you a container," Ellen called. "A plastic container for your angel food, if you want to bring it home."

"Problem solved." Javier zipped his backpack.

Ellen got a small plastic bowl with a lid from a cabinet next to the sink. "Here you go." She handed it to Rosa.

"Thank you," Rosa said. "For my mama, uh, my mother. She loves to try what we make."

"Is she a chef, too?" Ellen asked.

Javier snorted, and Rosa glared at him. "She's a hostess at Sotto Voce," Rosa said. "Do you know it?"

"I sure do. It's one of the best Italian spots around. Your mom could probably teach us all a thing or two."

Javier clucked his tongue. "The problem is, Mama's not so hot on the whole cooking thing." He slung his backpack over his shoulder. "I'll meet you at the car, *florecita*. Have a good night, Missus."

"You, too, Javier."

When he was gone, Ellen asked Rosa, "What does *florecita* mean?"

"Little flower. It's a nickname," Rosa said. "Brothers, one minute they torture you. The next they love you."

"I've got two myself," Ellen said. "I bet your mom is proud of you guys. You've got real talent, Rosa, a real sense of how things come together."

Rosa's eyes widened. "And I bet your husband loves your cooking, too."

"He did when we were still married." Ellen shrugged. "My kids love it now, and my friends."

"Oh." Rosa slipped her backpack straps over her shoulders. "Javi isn't completely full of it. My mom isn't crazy about baking, about me trying to make a living at it."

"Mothers worry. It's part of the job."

"Yeah, I guess so."

Ellen could tell she'd said the wrong thing, exactly what the girl didn't want to hear.

"Well, thanks. Javi's waiting." Rosa wheeled around for the door but paused in the threshold and turned back to Ellen. "Next time you go to Sotto Voce, if the hostess is a big lady, uh, heavy-set, I mean, not tall but big, with little gold hoop earrings, tell her chefs can have great careers. Tell her you know there's a lot of money in it."

Ellen couldn't tell if the girl was joking or not. "I bet she already knows. But I'll see if I can work in a word or two."

A smile, manufactured, spread across Rosa's face. She didn't believe Ellen. "See you next week." And she was gone.

Ellen turned back to the empty room. Her own mother would have pooh-poohed cooking as a career, too. And baking? Even more so. Trying to explain would have been futile. Was Rosa's mother as bad?

It only took a few minutes to wipe down the table and close up the cupboards. When Ellen stepped outside, evening was falling over the campus. The restless nudge of autumn moved through the cool air.

She followed the winding path, past squat campus buildings, across the courtyard where she had sat with Alice the first day, to the parking lot where her car waited. It wouldn't be long now—November, Thanksgiving would be upon her, and then the holiday season in all its dash and shimmer—her first as a divorced person.

This was how she had come to think of herself: a divorced person. She disliked "divorcée," which Alice liked to throw about suggestively. The word had the faint stink of misogyny, of finger-pointing, the whisper of failure—more so a woman's than a man's. Why was that? American men were simply "divorced," a neutral proclamation. No cutesy French name had been borrowed to designate their failed-marriage status.

And in truth, if Ellen had failed anyone, she had failed herself. This stinging little insight had come to her in Arborview, lying in dappled sunlight, where she was free to look at things and creep near the truth. The truth was she had fallen like a stone to the earth after all these years, and the voice she had learned to ignore had only grown louder. She had abandoned, or at least shelved, herself long before Zach worked up the courage to do it.

She really should tell Rosa: "Don't worry about what your mother thinks, or your brother, or anyone else. Choose, or the world will do it for you." This was what the girl needed to hear.

Ellen crested a small hill. A man was walking toward her, moving easily, dark trousers and blazer, shirt collar but no tie. A professor maybe, or an administrator. She glanced at his face as he approached. There was something vaguely familiar there, the humorous tic in the corner of his mouth, the curling ends of his graying hair.

He nodded at her. "Nice evening."

"*Namaste*." The word was out of her mouth before she could stop it.

He halted, broke into a wide smile. "*Namaste*," he

said, bringing his hands together in a prayerful pose beneath his chin.

Ellen stopped and did the same.

"Are you a yogi?" he asked.

"No, just a Chardonnay drinker."

He tapped his forehead. "I knew I'd seen you somewhere. Morley's, right?"

Ellen laughed, extending her hand. "Ellen Cahill."

His handshake was smooth and firm. "William Janssen. Are you taking a class here?"

"Teaching one. My first, actually, a pastry class. An 'enrichment,' I think is what they call it."

"Congratulations. Welcome to our little corner of the world."

His eyes exerted a soft pull, a need, but when she looked into them, there was no expectation, only curiosity and something else, a slippery shadow she couldn't quite name.

"I'm the director of financial aid, but I moonlight as a career counselor, too," he said. "Budgetary consolidation, they called it three years ago. Lots of us wear multiple hats around here now."

"Economic necessity." Ellen shrugged. "You do what you have to do."

"Helping these kids get ahead makes it all worth it, though," he said. "A lot of them go on to four-year schools, but it's always a scramble to scrape together the funding. My office is in full-scale panic right now."

"Wow, you are on the front lines. It makes pastry seem kind of superfluous."

He laughed. "Not at all. What's life without dessert, right?"

"I couldn't agree more." Ellen glanced up the path.

"I've got to run, but I'll see you around campus," he said.

Ellen smiled. "Have a nice night."

They parted, and he disappeared around a bend.

Later, the word came to her. Lying in bed, in the quiet dim of her house, she named the quality, the shadow, she had seen in his eyes. *Regret*. A sad submerged strain. It must be contagious at their age. No one was spared.

Chapter Twelve

Sarah was doing better. Rosa heard the hospice nurses talking. Sarah had surprised them all. She was perking up, looking stronger. One of the nurses said Sarah was a student at Yale.

Rosa wanted to meet this Sarah.

"It could be a final rally," the reverend said. "I've seen it before." He sat on the sofa in Mr. Janssen's little office.

Mr. Janssen was behind his desk, leaning back in his seat, a mug of coffee in one hand. "Who's the pessimist now?" he said.

"Just a realist." The reverend shook his head. "There's a difference. False hope doesn't help anyone."

Rosa emptied the trash can near Mr. Janssen's desk, dumping its contents into her cart.

"Thanks, Rosa," Mr. Janssen said.

"I got two of my aid applications filled out already." She gave him a big smile. He had found several scholarships and loans for her to pursue.

"Bravo, Rosa," the reverend said.

"Thanks." Rosa gave him a smile, too. He was sort of heavy-handed and dorky, but he was a nice man. "I'll catch you later," she said, wheeling her cart back to the kitchen.

The reverend wagged his fingers. He turned back to Mr. Janssen. "Of course, I'm hoping the best for the poor girl. To get hit with this type of cancer at her age—imagine what her parents are going through."

As usual, the reverend and Mr. Janssen were shooting the breeze in there, and Rosa had overheard more than she should. A couple of days earlier, they'd discussed their dead parents. Was death the only thing people thought about around here?

"My mom passed when I was in college," Mr. Janssen had said.

The reverend sighed. "Too young to lose your mother. How did it happen, may I ask?"

He always wanted the details, this guy.

"A generator. A freak accident. She touched a loose live wire on the outdoor generator. Our house was in the woods, you know, and people were always losing power during storms. There was a heavy snowfall, and she went outside to check the generator, to clear it off, and somehow… She was home alone when it happened."

"God rest her. I'm so sorry."

"Thank you. It was a long time ago."

"But that kind of thing stays with you."

Mr. Janssen was quiet a minute, and then he said, "When your mother dies—zap—out of nowhere, face down in the snow, her hand inches from the wires that stopped her heart with a single jolt, you've got to wonder—what difference does any of this really make anyway?"

Rosa couldn't recall how the reverend had responded. She went now to clean the visitor bathrooms. There a caddy with spray bottles and sponges and towels in the utility closet at the end of the hall, between the two bathrooms reserved for visitors.

Sarah's room was near the end of the hall, too. The door was open. Rosa hesitated before passing. Then she stepped forward and peeked into the room.

Sarah was sitting up in bed, reading a magazine. In the corner, mounted high, the television was on, minus the sound, one of those real estate programs where people go shopping for new houses.

"Hey," Rosa said.

Sarah turned her head. "Hi." Her long pretty hair was tucked behind her ears. Her eyes were large, the color of the ocean. She nodded, as if she were expecting something, or encouraging Rosa to continue.

"Do you, uh, need anything?" Rosa asked.

"No, I'm fine. Thanks." Sarah had a nice voice, gentle.

Rosa shifted from foot to foot in the doorway. "I'm Rosa. I work in housekeeping."

"I've seen you around." Sarah had the kind of eyes that really take you in when they look at you.

"You go to Yale, huh?" Rosa said.

"Yep, I do."

"You like it?"

"I wish I was there right now." Sarah smiled, and Rosa took a couple of steps into the room. She could see a wire, a thin tube, connected to Sarah's arm. But Sarah didn't look sick. A little tired maybe, like Mama after a long shift.

"I'm applying to colleges," Rosa said. "Culinary arts, that's what I'm going to study."

"Wow, sounds great. I'd love to be a better cook."

"Really?"

"Oh, yeah, definitely. What a talent to have. I may take up cooking, once I get out of here."

Rosa didn't know how to answer.

Sarah winked. "I know. I'm in a hospice, right? Nobody here gets out alive."

"Um, I don't know."

"But I've got a feeling they're wrong about me."

A wave of relief washed over Rosa. "My mother calls doctors 'quacks' all the time."

Sarah laughed. "The thing they don't tell you is miracles happen. They happen all the time. The records are full of them. I've been reading up on it."

"I totally believe it."

Sarah held up her palm, the tube dangling from her arm, and Rosa stepped forward and high-fived her. "I'm glad you're on my side," Sarah said.

Rosa glanced at the door. Were those footsteps she heard? "I better go. I don't wanna get in trouble. But I'll stop by again, if you'd like?"

"Please do? My parents are here a lot, but there's downtime. I've been feeling so much better lately, and it can get kind of lonely."

"Then I'll be back."

"Good. See you soon, Rosa."

Rosa hurried down the hall. It was hard to imagine someone like Sarah being lonely. She was even cooler than Rosa had imagined. The girl had cancer, in a hospice, and she was making plans. Maybe miracles really did happen, and they could happen for anyone. Rosa had always believed this. Sarah went to Yale, and she believed it, too, so there had to be something to it.

Lying in bed that night, waiting for sleep to come, Rosa remembered the baking teacher's words. "Real talent." "A real sense of how things come together." When she'd complimented the chocolate shavings, a tingly thrill had run up Rosa's back. This lady knew a lot about food. If she thought Rosa had talent, then maybe it was true.

Mama had urged Rosa to become a teacher. "It's like funeral homes and tax collectors. The world always needs them." She tapped her temple. "Think about it." Which meant Rosa would be crazy not to think about it. Nurses and secretaries were big with Mama, too. She saw them knocking back happy hour cocktails at the restaurant.

Rosa turned over on her side and pulled the blanket up under her chin. The house was empty. Mama was still at work, and Javi was out with Tilda. Rosa found it difficult to sleep in an empty house. She liked knowing other people were around. She liked having Javi across the hall. How was she going to sleep when he was in Niagara?

She sat up. Her laptop was on the desk across the room. She got out of bed in the dark and touched a key. The screen came to life. She opened her email, created a message, and typed: *Hello, Mrs. Cahill, I was wondering if you could suggest a good book about cooking? Not just recipes, but about why it all matters, why cooking is important in people's lives. Do you know what I mean? Thank you. Rosa Escamilla.* She tapped send. As she started to close the laptop, the ding of a new email message stopped her.

The teacher, already. Rosa clicked on the message.

Hi, Rosa, I sure do. I have the perfect book for you. I'll bring it to class. See you next week.

This woman stayed up late. *I sure do.* She probably had tall shelves full of books at her house. Rosa admired people who read. Mama did, too. Rosa got back in bed. Maybe she'd be able to sleep now. She closed her eyes. The quiet grew around her. If she went away to college, how would Mama sleep, all alone here, night after night?

Chapter Thirteen

"But he was good looking?" Alice asked again. "He had a certain something?"

Ellen shook her head. She had mentioned this guy in passing, and Alice had homed in like a guided missile. "Why? Do you want to date him?"

Alice gave an exaggerated blink. "I'm going to pretend I didn't hear that. I'm just saying good looks go a long way when the going gets tough, as it invariably does. I'm looking out for you."

"Yeah, well, this may be more help than I need." Ellen gazed up the street. The view from Alice's front porch was charming. Old Victorian houses and remodeled bungalows lined the street, flanked by flower beds. Tall trees shaded the sidewalks leading down to Main Street. The shifting sunlight of late afternoon filtered through the branches.

"Anyway, Zach is good looking, and it didn't do much for us in the end," Elle said.

"I said 'a long way.' Not all the way." Alice studied her hands. "I need a manicure. But he was *nice*, this man. I hate that word. It means nothing. His voice was soft, and he had a sad sort of look about him." Alice wrinkled her nose. "I've got to tell you—I'm not feeling it. Soft and sad? No thanks."

"I said he was interesting. And yes, okay, he was handsome."

"Why not bring him to my party?"

"I hardly know him."

Alice's annual "Halloween for Grownups" soiree was two weeks out. She always recruited Ellen for help with the menu. Alice had started the party after the kids had outgrown trick-or-treating.

"You'll need a date," she insisted.

Ellen stretched her arms overhead, yawning. "I'm staying in the kitchen. I'll be the hired help."

"Ah, you say that every year, and then when people get a load of the food, you're the guest of honor."

"Whoa." Ellen raised her hands. "Desserts are all I'm in for this time. You're doing the real food—the whole buffet—for this shindig, right?"

"Actually, Cuisine & Catering is. I'm ordering a precooked roast, a nice baked ham, and smoked salmon and laying it all out."

Ellen nodded. "Easy enough."

"Plus, salads and sides. Earle is bartending, of course. It wouldn't be a party without Earle behind the bar." At any sizable social gathering, Earle could be found mixing and stirring. He seemed to take great pleasure spearing olives and rattling a cocktail shaker. He always gave Ellen extra cherries.

Alice nibbled her lip. "Appetizers? How about stuffed cherry tomatoes, grilled lime shrimp skewers…"

"Not lime, too summery. We're going autumn, right? Braised beef on toast crisps, mini squash quiches in orange and yellow."

"Now you're talking! And you should bring him," Alice urged. "Mr. Sad and Soft, bring him."

"His name's William."

"William is welcome."

Ellen shook her head. "All the gossipy hens in this town will start wagging their tongues. It makes me cringe. And listen, a new man is the last thing I need right now. Unless he wants to pay off my mortgage and paint my house." Ellen stood. "I've got to get going. I need to do some shopping. I'm sending Taber and Jimmy a few Halloween treats from home."

"Send some to Caroline, from me? I'd screw them up." Alice chuckled. She stood and gave Ellen a quick hug. When she stepped back, she squeezed Ellen's hand. "You won't be the only single person at the party. You're not the only one in this town whose marriage has exploded."

Back in her car, Ellen turned the key in the ignition and gazed up the street. Crisp autumn air drifted through the red and gold treetops, over the dark shingled roofs and brick chimneys of these old homes, past the town's sole traffic light blinking on the corner of the green, and then over the farm fields and wooded hills. Ellen had driven these roads every day for twenty years, had taken her children by the hand to these schools, attended town meetings, voted on budgets, marched in the Memorial Day parade. Familiar faces greeted her everywhere she went. After all these years, the people here knew so much—and yet so very little—about her.

****

She found the old book that night, buried at the back of the living room bookcases. The spine cracked when she opened it, and dust drifted from the pages.

With Bold Knife and Fork by M.F.K. Fisher. Ellen had discovered Fisher early in her marriage, when she was pregnant with Taber. She had left her teaching job, due to unrelenting morning sickness, and Zach was putting in long hours, launching the version of himself he wanted to show the world. They were in the loft apartment in Hartford, and Ellen spent afternoons on the couch beneath the tall windows, nibbling saltines, as the ceiling fan whirred in the summer heat.

She had savored the book's words, dreaming of her own garden in the country, where she would grow herbs and spices and vegetables crunchy with sunshine and promise. Larger mysteries would then surely unfold. The sharp, fecund scent of the soil beneath her feet would call them forth. Zach would be amazed at the bounty she would bring into their life. Love would lead them.

That was a long time ago.

Ellen tucked the book beneath her arm and carried it to the kitchen. She left it near the coffee maker, where she'd be sure to remember it.

Upstairs, she got ready for bed. She left her clothes in a heap on the floor. She did laundry so rarely now— once, maybe twice a month. There was a time when she was doing three loads, twice a week. It seemed the machine was always sloshing and clicking in the mudroom. She had loved hanging the clothes out in the sunshine to dry when they first moved here. A sunny day proclaims the glory of God, the nuns used to say. Ellen would carry a burst of fresh air back into house, pausing to bury her head in a pile of towels or Zach's T-shirts before tucking them away into drawers and closets.

Then Alice told her clotheslines were low-rent. "Underwear and bras flapping in the breeze for all the world to see?" How young Alice was then—still in her headband phase. She liked the plaid ones with the little ribbon on top, all colors and shades. She gave them up in her thirties, as she said any self-respecting woman should.

"Nobody can see into our backyard," Ellen had argued. But Zach seconded Alice's opinion, and Ellen loaded the clothes dryer.

Zach had dismantled the clothesline, but maybe she'd put up a new one now, at the edge of the yard near Arborview, and show the world just how low-rent she could be. She knew the perfect spot where the ground was flat, and breezes rippled in from the woods. Ellen closed her eyes, smiling at the notion. A clothesline rebel. Why not? This house was hers alone now, for as long as she could hold on to it.

The cool sheet draped her body. Maybe she had turned away from her own sense of what mattered most, of what was possible, long ago. But there was so much rush and noise back then, so many others, their voices and need, their love, concrete and enveloping. Who could resist such love? Why had no one warned her that people sometimes go away? That time runs out, and unthinkable things come to pass.

Chapter Fourteen

William Janssen emailed her out of the blue—using her River Bend address—and asked her to have coffee with him. *How about three p.m. to break up the afternoon doldrums?* he'd suggested.

Ellen had hesitated before replying. But she didn't want to turn him down and spend the rest of the semester avoiding him, hurrying along the campus paths before he spotted her, or she spotted him. And of course, she was intrigued. It was only coffee, after all. A little chit-chat with a new colleague.

The Perk Up coffee shop was in the basement of the student center building. A single row of high, rectangular windows lined one wall, giving the room the feel of a funky, underground lair. A muted flat screen television sat high in one corner, and potted spider plants hung in macramé nets all around.

Ellen had forty-five minutes before her class, just enough time but not too much. She paused in the doorway, glancing around the shop—a scattering of tables and students, soft unintelligible conversations underway, the low gleam of the silver coffee urns behind the counter. The place made her want to take a nap.

Then she spotted William. He sat at a small, round table beneath the high windows, sun shining behind him. He wore dark trousers and a white button-up shirt with a pale green tie. Zach had favored red ties—reds and blues in bold, eye-catching patterns: "Or what's the point?" he'd say.

Ellen smoothed the skirt of the wool jersey dress she had slipped off the padded hanger in her closet that morning. A warm shade of ruby orange, the dress fell below her knees. She had paired it with her favorite chocolate brown suede boots and added shiny, half-moon silver earrings that curved stylishly toward her face. Alice would have cheered.

William saw her cross the room and stood. "You made it," he said, as if she had journeyed across the tundra.

Ellen smiled. "My class doesn't start until four."

"What can I get you? Coffee, or are you a tea drinker?"

She slid onto the seat across from him. "Try to guess." Playful, flirty. She sounded like Alice. Before he could respond, she said, "Coffee's fine, whatever's mild."

"Black?"

"Sure, I'll doctor it up with cream and sugar."

"I can't drink it black, either." He shrugged. "But you know, these days everyone is so discriminating. The world is suddenly full of coffee connoisseurs. I'm ashamed of my Maxwell House."

Ellen laughed, watching him cross the room to get the drinks. His chattiness made her think he was as nervous as she was.

She hung her purse on the seat back. Why had she been worried? He was simply a colleague at work. Up close, you could see his shirt was rumpled. His shoes were scuffed brown loafers. His graying hair brushed his collar. He was the kind of guy who had to remember to schedule a haircut. Zach had been on a strict, trim-every-four-weeks regimen. He never missed an appointment.

William returned with two mugs of coffee, sugar packets, and creamers.

"Just what I need," Ellen said. "I let myself have two cups a day now. I used to have three."

"Ah. Doctor's orders?"

"No, a friend said my teeth are getting yellow, and I refuse to put those bleaching strips in my mouth. My friend does it every month, along with her bikini wax."

William cleared his throat.

Ellen felt a blush climb up her neck. She'd walked the planet for almost half a century, and yet she apparently thought it a good idea to tell this man she hardly knew that her teeth were yellow, and her bikini line was in need of tending. She swallowed hard.

"Friends," William said. "Can't live with them, etc., etc."

"I'll drink to that." Ellen lifted the coffee to her lips.

"I had a weird encounter recently with a guy from Massachusetts I grew up with. Nice guy, working class sort of family from Worcester. His dad was a plumber, off and on. There was some kind of problem there. They always seemed to be short on money, but super nice people.

"This summer I found out he was living in town, so I called him. We went for a few beers. It was great to see him again and kick around old times. So we got together again and went to a Red Sox game, where apparently I committed a cardinal sin."

"What did you do?"

"I ate a hotdog."

"So?"

"He looked at me like I was eating cyanide. You could see the disgust on his face. He's a vegan now. This is a guy who grew up eating canned SpaghettiOs, but he wouldn't have bitten that hotdog if you'd held a gun to his head. He needed to lecture me about it, too. He wasn't the person I used to know."

Ellen nodded. "People have a way of doing that—turning into a fuzzy version of the original you knew, and then you're left with…"

William studied her.

"Well, I mean they change. And not always for the better, or at least it looks that way when you're on the receiving end."

The air moved slowly between them, and Ellen sensed the weight of his wondering stare.

"You've been on the receiving end?" he said. "Dumb question, right? At our age, who hasn't been?"

Ellen raised her eyes to meet his—these cool gray eyes, not in the least surprised. When he smiled, the outer corners of his eyes ticked down, and made her think, *he is just like me.* Someone who has seen a bit of life and has no delusions. "Tell me more about your last trip to India," she said.

"It was in my wild youth."

"At least you had one."

They laughed together, and Ellen's shoulders relaxed. She hadn't realized how tense they were.

"India," he said. "I won't tell you about my most recent trip. I'll tell you about the first time, when I saw it all through fresh eyes, as you will when you finally get there."

Ellen wrapped her hands around the smooth warmth of her mug and listened.

William took her to Mumbai, on his first trip when a woman named Liv and he, in their mid-twenties, slipped away together. He took Ellen into a steamy morning in a jumbled port city, the brine of the sea in the air, the streets teeming with honking horns and lurching bicycle rickshaws. Liv and he took walks, weaving through the crowd of bright saris, a riot of color everywhere: screaming yellows, pinks, blues, and oranges.

One day, they braved the blistering sun of the city; the next day, the cool, shadowed mystery of a temple—the hush and play of light across the ceiling; how "only a whisper felt appropriate." At night, a gleam sparked in the dark eye of the large, determined lizard scampering across the wall in their hotel room.

"On our second trip, we visited the Taj Mahal," William said.

"The famed monument to love," Ellen said. Because it had happened so long ago, she thought it okay to ask, "What became of your girlfriend?"

"We actually broke up in front of the Taj Mahal." He chuckled, shaking his head. "She was expecting me to propose, and I didn't. My third trip to India was solo."

Ellen nodded.

"Liv eventually married someone else."

"At least you didn't have to call in the lawyers."

"When was your divorce final?"

"About seven months ago." Ellen sipped her coffee. "How long have you been with the college?"

"Coming on ten years now. Hard to believe. They run into each other. When you're young, everyone warns you how quickly the years will fly by, right? How really short life is, but you don't believe it."

"Of course not." Ellen didn't want to go any further down this road. "It's what youth is for, right? Dodging the truth," she said.

"Until it runs you down. What I would like is a do-over," he said.

"Who wouldn't?" Boy, he moved into deep waters fast. Ellen glanced at her watch. "I'm sorry. I've got to run. My class."

He stood as she did. "It was a real pleasure."

She took his hand, holding it a moment and placing her other hand on top. "It was," she said. "Let's do this again?" She had to say this. It was what everyone said.

He smiled. "Definitely."

Ellen turned and strode across the shop. She pushed open the door, stepped outside into sunshine, and headed down the campus path. He was nice. Alice would hate hearing this, but it was true. He was easy to talk to, too. His narration of India had transported her there. He noticed so much. He remembered so much, and in such evocative detail. And yet he was alone now. He wasn't even "shacked up," as Alice liked to say.

Chapter Fifteen

She discussed eggs in class. The many roles they play and the artful power these little pouches of protein and fat have to change whatever they touch.

When class ended, she waved over Rosa. "How would you like a job?" she asked, as students streamed around them.

Javier stood by the door, head bowed over his phone.

"A job?" Rosa cocked her head to the side. A bright pink headband held back her cascade of dark curls, shaving years from Rosa's face. If someone said the girl was fourteen, Ellen would have believed it.

"How much does it pay?" Rosa blurted. Her face reddened. "I'm sorry. The thing is, I do need work. I found this part-time cleaning job at a hospice, but I need more hours than they've got, and I'm running out of time."

"How would you like to do a little baking? I have a party coming up."

"Are you a caterer?"

Ellen pursed her lips. "Not a professional. But every year I make the desserts for a friend's Halloween party, and this time I could use a little help. It's only a one-day gig, but I'll pay you in cash."

"Do I go to…where will we do the baking?"

"How about right here? Plenty of space and we can

fire up as many ovens as we need."

"Awesome."

"How about $200 flat? It'll be an afternoon's work. Four hours, I think."

"Fifty bucks an hour." Javier whistled from the doorway. "Not even Mama gonna complain about that."

"When?" Rosa nearly whispered.

"Next Friday afternoon. The party's Saturday."

"I'll be here. I just hope you don't regret this."

"Why would I?"

"I've never baked *for money*. I mean, I'm not a professional."

"Ha, you got that right," Javier cracked.

Ellen waved her hand at him. "We invent ourselves, Rosa. Someone told me that once. I should have listened."

It had been Zach, back when he was interviewing for director of his department, a position which would put him a heartbeat away from the chief marketing officer job of his dreams.

Ellen had tried to reassure him they would be fine even if he never advanced one rung further up the corporate ladder.

He hadn't responded. He had squeezed her hand, kissed her mouth, and bolted off to his interview. He got the job.

Rosa pulled on her backpack. "See you next week," she said.

"Wait, this is for you." Ellen took the M.F.K. Fisher book from her bag. "Ever heard of her?"

Rosa studied the cover. "No."

"Give it a try."

"It's long. Can I get it back to you in a couple of

weeks?"

"Keep it. I've had this book longer than I'll admit. I wasn't much older than you when I first read it."

Rosa tucked the book under her arm. "Thanks, Mrs. Cahill." She drifted toward the door, still looking back at Ellen, until she disappeared into the hall.

When the classroom was empty, Ellen sat down. Her feet ached. Would Rosa's mother approve of this baking job? Did it matter? Rosa needed to make her own choices. That was the bottom line, and putting a few dollars in the girl's pocket in the meantime couldn't hurt.

Ellen rubbed her temples. It had been a long day. Maybe she'd get a bottle of wine on the way home. She'd pick one up back in town, at The Angry Grape wine shop on the green. She liked its jingling door chime and the black cat who sat in the window. And she didn't want to risk running into William again. Those cool gray eyes had stayed with her.

Chapter Sixteen

When Mama got home from work, you needed to give her time to herself. "Reentry," she called it. Javier called it "decompression."

Night after night, Mama smiled and took coats and led diners to their tables. She stood in for busboys in a pinch, filling glass tumblers with ice and lugging stacks of dirty dishes back to the kitchen. If they were down a waitress or waiter, she took drink orders to get things rolling. Her feet hurt, and her voice grew hoarse by the time the conversations in the dining room reached full force. For all its elegance, the place was loud.

"The part that amazes me, even after all these years, is how entitled these people are," she said. "They think they were born to have their butts kissed."

"Mama, you been saying this for years." Rosa stood at the stove, stirring a pot of hot cocoa, homemade—she'd selected the chocolate herself, based on what Mrs. Cahill used at home. "A nice, hot cup of this will put it all out of your mind."

Mama sighed at the kitchen table. "You're the cook." She leaned back and put her feet up on the chair next to her. "Killing me. Last week I wore those flats, remember?"

"The black ones, sure. They were perfect with your outfit."

"Not perfect enough. They weren't heels. And the

manager, I see him giving me his fishy eye all night. And you know the next day—bam—he hands out a memo to everyone. Formal dress is required for all employees in the dining room, blah, blah, blah. Spiteful little bastard."

Rosa laughed.

"He's a jerk." Javier's voice floated down the stairs. He was studying in his room. Tilda was up there with him.

Mama raised her eyes to the ceiling. "They both up there?" she mouthed silently.

Rosa nodded.

"*Hola*, Tilda!" Mama called. "I hope you two are doing homework, and not making me a grandmother."

"Mama." Rosa whirled around from the stove. "Shush."

Mama glared. "The last thing I want is Javier can't go to Niagara because he's gonna be a daddy. Like so many of you kids. Drop out and get a lousy job. All this hard work—all my hard work—for nothing."

"Javi's too smart for that." Rosa carried a steaming mug of creamy cocoa to the table and placed it before her mother.

"No man's too smart," Mama said. "You'll see. Every woman finds out in time."

"Drink," Rosa commanded.

They sat in silence. As Mama sipped, her expression softened. "How are your classes going? You look into the nurse's aide course? Genevieve, the waitress, has a daughter who's finishing and already has job offers—three." Mama raised three fingers. "Good jobs, Rosa. Real money."

"I know."

The heavy makeup Mama wore had blurred on her face, leaving faint rosy swipes on her cheeks and mascara shadows beneath her eyes.

"Listen," Rosa said, "I got a job." She slid to the edge of her seat.

"Home and Hearth called?"

"No, it's my pastry class. The teacher is catering a party, just desserts, and she asked me to help make them."

"What's she paying you?"

"Two hundred dollars. But it's an honor, Mama, and a chance to learn. Mrs. Cahill is very good. She gave me a book about a famous writer who cooks. The book is famous, too."

"You getting robbed," Mama said. But she reached out with one hand and cupped Rosa's chin. "Ah, money is money, right? And at least you got the hospice, too. I know you'll have a good time doing this baking."

"I love it." Rosa struggled to keep her voice on an even keel.

"Make a cake for your brother before he leaves us."

"Javi will never leave us."

"You say that now, and I love my boy, God knows I do, but he's still a man."

"We're not going there tonight." Rosa glared at her mother. "Why would he leave when he's got you as a cheering section?"

Mama raised an eyebrow. "You got anything more you wanna say?"

"I just said it." A nervous bird flapped inside Rosa's chest. Not now, not yet. But she couldn't stop herself. "It's not right," she said.

"Ah, the baking school."

"College."

"Life ain't about 'right'. It's about being smart," said Mama, who had never made one smart decision in her life, as far as Rosa could tell.

"I am smart. I know what I'm doing." Rosa's heart pounded.

"Is that so?" Mama sighed.

Rosa opened her mouth to bite back, to snap Mama's head off, but then she stopped. It was as if Mama had aged right before Rosa's eyes. Rosa saw the puffy flesh of Mama's face, the pale patches of scalp peeking through her thinning hair. And the sigh? There was something heavy, final, in it. Defeat.

"Sign up for the nursing," Mama said. "Be smarter than your old mother. Don't break her heart."

The words pierced Rosa. "I'm not trying to break your heart, Mama."

When Rosa was little, she saw a picture of a real heart in science class at school. Was it third grade or fourth? The heart looked nothing like a valentine. Rosa imagined her mother's heart, all pink and lumpy like the picture, beating away, day and night. Mama yelled so much back then, Rosa was afraid her heart would simply give out. Some colossal shock or outrage would blow it up. And then where would they be? Every night, Rosa had asked God to keep Mama's heart beating. On her knees, before her bed, she had prayed. *Please, God, please.*

****

On Friday morning, Rosa showed up early and was surprised to find the classroom empty. She shrugged off her backpack and stuck it in a corner. She hoped they'd use all the prep space, firing up multiple stoves, chopping, mixing, scraping, the scents of sugars and spices rising all around them. Maybe Mrs. Cahill would let her handle a few recipes on her own from beginning to end. She wanted to show what she could do.

"You're gonna be a glorified dishwasher," Javier had teased, before urging Rosa to bring home any leftovers. Mama had chuckled. But Rosa let it slide off her back. She couldn't take on both of them at the same time.

She took a sponge from the deep utility sink and wiped down the prep table. A habit, she was forever wiping the kitchen counters at home and at the hospice.

She perched on a stool before the table and drummed her fingers against the cold steel. Mrs. Cahill wouldn't be late. She seemed like the kind of woman who was never late, who had never missed a single important thing in her life. Why hadn't she become a chef, if she loved cooking so much? She could have opened a restaurant of her own. She must have kids. Maybe her husband had been a real bastard, as Mama would say, *el diablo* come to curse us.

The door opened. "Hey there," Mrs. Cahill said. "You beat me." She carried two large shopping bags and dropped them with a thud onto the table.

"Let me help." Rosa hopped off the stool.

One bag was loaded with Tupperware containers of every size, and the other with ingredients: flour, eggs, blocks of baker's chocolate, heavy cream, fresh apples, canned pumpkins, chopped nuts, honey, and pastry shells which must have been made days earlier.

Mrs. Cahill looked flustered, like she was having one of those mornings that made Mama curse God and anyone else she came across. Mrs. Cahill brushed the flyaway hairs back from her face. She pulled a water bottle out of her purse and took a drink. "The market was jammed."

So this teacher got wound up over little things, too. It wasn't just Mama.

"I'd have waited for you," Rosa said. "No big deal. My day is open."

"You cleared your calendar?"

Rosa paused. "Uh, yeah."

"Well, this is going to be a lot of fun," Mrs. Cahill said, as if she was determined to make it so. "And maybe we'll learn a few tricks along the way."

"A baking party," Rosa said. "My kind of gig."

"Okay then, here's the menu." Mrs. Cahill pulled a pad from her purse. "Nothing too fancy, just a few fall favorites—all finger foods. My friend doesn't like cleaning up."

"Who does?"

"It's one of the first things you learn," Mrs. Cahill said. "Cooking isn't just about what people will eat, but *how* they'll eat it, and how much work it's all going to take. From experience, I can tell you simpler is better, especially by the time the dessert tray rolls around."

"Yeah, when the cocktails have been flowing all night."

Mrs. Cahill laughed. "You've picked up a tip or two from your mom."

"The restaurant business. Mama says you see every mess under the sun and then a few you never imagined."

"I bet she's right. So here we go: chocolate chip cookies, French apple tart, pecan shortbread with chocolate drizzle, caramel pecan bars—yes I love pecans—and upside-down pear gingerbread."

Rosa bit her lip. "Shortbread and anything upside-down I don't know too much about."

Mrs. Cahill dug through the bags. "No biggie. There's not much to know. And I'll be right here."

"Learning by doing." Rosa echoed one of the refrains repeated in class.

Mrs. Cahill smiled. "Looks like I'm not just talking to myself in here."

Standing across the table from each other, they set up stations for the different recipes and got to work. Mrs. Cahill sliced apples for the tart, while Rosa measured and mixed the flour, sugars, and eggs for the cookies.

"The college is okay with us using their stuff?" Rosa asked.

"I got approval," Mrs. Cahill said. "We're calling this an out-of-class exercise for extra credit. Facilities doesn't mind as long as we clean up."

"Extra credit?" Rosa swallowed.

"Extra credit, in the form of cold, hard cash." Mrs. Cahill winked.

Phew. Rosa looked down at the table and rearranged the bowls.

"How's it going at the hospice?"

"Okay, you know. It's not the job I want, but it's all there is right now." Rosa poured a half-cup of packed brown sugar into a mixing bowl.

"You know there are financial resources at the school?"

"Oh yeah, I know. And I've got savings. Next year…I just need to get my plan straight."

"Your plan?" Mrs. Cahill swept a pile of freshly peeled, sliced apples into a bowl. Then she sprinkled little brown bursts of powdered cinnamon over them. "And what is the plan?"

Why not spill it? Mrs. Cahill might have something to say that could help.

"I have something to show you," Rosa said. She walked across the room to her backpack and pulled out the catalogue, glancing at the bright, promising cover: Seasons Culinary College.

"I'm applying." She slid the catalogue over the table.

"Seasons Culinary College?" Mrs. Cahill opened the catalogue. "It's one of the premier culinary institutes in the country. Bravo, Rosa."

"If I get in, I can start next fall. I'll have enough money to begin, and if…"

Mrs. Cahill's face was all lit up, waiting for her to finish.

"The problem is, Mama doesn't want me to go."

"Oh." Mrs. Cahill paused. "Well, I can kind of understand that. Both you and Javier will be gone then."

"It's not the distance," Rosa said. "She's fine with Javi going to Niagara. You know, Javi can do no wrong, in her eyes. It's my school. It's what I want to do."

"Does she know you're applying?"

Rosa shook her head. "She doesn't want me to cook, to become a chef or a pastry chef, any kind of chef…"

"Ah." Mrs. Cahill put down the wire whisk she was about to use on the eggs.

"Mama hears 'cook' and she's done. She hates the food business. She hates her job."

Mrs. Cahill pulled up a stool and sat. "How about your dad?"

"He's dead."

"Oh, I'm sorry."

"It was a long time ago. I was just a baby." Rosa had, in fact, no memory of her father at all, though she'd heard the story of his death. How he'd been on the highway outside Hartford, in a cold, driving rain, how the Datsun he was driving was struck head-on by a driver who'd fallen asleep and drifted across the median. Rosa didn't tell Mrs. Cahill the accident occurred at two o'clock on a Saturday morning or that her father's mistress—the stinking whore, as Mama referred to her—died in the passenger seat next to him.

"Javier and you must have been a big comfort to your mother," Mrs. Cahill said.

"Yeah, I guess we were." Rosa remembered the nights when Mama would scrunch up next to her in her little girl bed, and they would fall asleep together. Rosa would wake, in the pink glow of her ballerina nightlight, and hear the soft sniffles of her mother crying.

"We mean everything to her. That's what makes it so hard." She wasn't going to cry in front of Mrs. Cahill. Rosa held her breath.

"Try to help your mother understand Seasons Culinary College is a terrific school, and it will open all sorts of possibilities for you."

"Mama thinks it's all slinging hash and kissing butts."

Mrs. Cahill laughed. Rosa couldn't stop from

cracking a smile, too.

"Point out you'll be a trained chef, and who knows? Maybe one day, you'll own your own business," Mrs. Cahill said.

"Won't matter."

"You can never tell what's going to matter. It might take some time, but stick it out, if this is what you want. Look at Javier. He's doing it."

"And with Mama's blessing." Rosa swallowed over the lump in her throat. Mama would have died if she knew Rosa had told this woman personal things about the family. But something compelled her to go further. "It's not fair," she said.

"No." Mrs. Cahill shook her head. "It's not."

"They're not going to stop me," Rosa said. "I'm working with the financial aid man here, Mr. Janssen. This guy knows all the angles."

"Ah, yes, I know him."

"He works at the hospice, too. He volunteers."

"Really?"

"Yep, and he thinks we can scrape up the tuition and room-and-board. I told him I was baking with you today. This is Seasons Culinary College application money I'm earning."

"Ha, well I'm glad I can contribute," Mrs. Cahill said. "And listen, my husband—ex-husband—had a number of colleagues who worked in the hospitality industry. There are a lot of opportunities in the field. You might want to tell your mom."

"They made a lot of money?"

"Some of them did. After they had—you know—worked their way up and established themselves."

Rosa flipped open the catalogue to a dog-eared

page and pointed. "Baking and Pastry Arts and Food Service Management. That's my major. So I'll learn how to manage the business side of things, too."

"Smart girl."

Mrs. Cahill thumbed through the smooth, glossy pages—photographs of smiling students in white chef's coats and tall hats, colorful delicacies laid out on gleaming trays, a lecture hall packed with eager faces before a professor with bushy white hair.

"How exciting." She closed the cover. "I wish I had gone this direction myself."

"Why didn't you?"

Mrs. Cahill held up her palms. "Another story for another day. Show your mom the catalogue and…"

A knock at the door, and they both turned. Mr. Janssen stood in the threshold. "Sorry to interrupt. Rosa told me she'd be here today, and I wanted to drop off financial aid forms for her to sign."

"Hey," Rosa said.

"William, come on in," Mrs. Cahill said. "Rosa just filled me in on her plans."

"Keep your eye on this one," Mr. Janssen said. "I'm predicting big things for her."

He handed a stack of paper-clipped forms to Rosa. "I hear you're prepping for a big party. I don't want to get in your way."

Mrs. Cahill shrugged. "Well, I wouldn't say 'big'. It's more of an open-house, a neighborhood thing. And it's not mine. A friend is throwing it. I'm—we're"—she nodded at Rosa—"making the desserts."

Funny. Rosa had never seen Mrs. Cahill so…what was it? Jumpy? Rattled?

"Thanks for the forms." Rosa nodded at Mr.

Janssen, but he was looking at Mrs. Cahill.

"Sounds like a fun party," he said.

"It's a lot of work." Mrs. Cahill rearranged the bowls on the table.

Rosa thumbed through the papers. "Where do I sign?"

"Halloween was my favorite holiday as a kid," he said.

Rosa perked up. "Mine, too!"

"I'm helping a friend," Mrs. Cahill said. "You'd be surprised how often people call on you when you can bake. Everybody wants dessert."

"Best part of the meal," Mr. Janssen said.

"You think so?" Mrs. Cahill asked. "My ex-husband always said the best part was the first round of drinks."

They both laughed. Rosa shifted from foot to foot.

"Well, don't let me hold you up," Mr. Janssen said. "Looks like you've got a full plate here—no pun intended."

Mrs. Cahill glanced at the clock over the door.

"Enjoy your party," Mr. Janssen said.

Mrs. Cahill blinked fast. "You can, ah, come by the party if you'd like. It's Saturday night. You're probably not free, though, on such short notice."

"I happen to be free." A big smile from Mr. Janssen.

"Oh, then I'll email you the address." Mrs. Cahill gave a really pretty smile. "You'll be able to sample our handiwork."

"Yeah, you will," Rosa blurted. "And I'll stop by your office Monday. I've got this all figured out."

Mr. Janssen flashed a thumbs-up, but he wasn't

looking at Rosa.

The rest of the afternoon, Rosa helped Mrs. Cahill mix and stir, then bake, and finally clean up. She watched with a new fascination. The desserts they made ended up looking like little works of art, beauty on every plate. But it was what she'd seen come to life between Mrs. Cahill and Mr. Janssen that amazed her most.

Chapter Seventeen

Ellen reached into the pocket of her jacket and drew out the letter that had arrived the day before, the one she'd been putting off reading. Why hadn't Zach emailed? Or better yet, texted? Why all this stagey formality? A handwritten letter, so unnecessary. She opened the single sheet:

Dear Ellen,

I hope autumn is fulfilling your every wish and your return to the classroom has been a runaway success.

Her every wish? He must have had a bottle of gin in front of him when he wrote this. Zach liked his gin dry and straight up.

Thanksgiving approaches, as I'm sure you're aware.

No kidding. Ellen smirked.

The kids will be returning, and if you can find it in your heart, Ellen, I would like us all to be together for dinner.

If she could find it in her heart? What did he know about her heart? What had he ever understood about her heart?

Lydia will be visiting her elderly mother in New Hampshire, so I will be on my own.

He wasn't invited? Strange. Maybe the elderly mother didn't want to know her single, middle-aged daughter had broken up a marriage and was now shacked up with the guy. Alice would have a good take on this bit of information.

Ellen, I'd like us to be together, as a family. Is this possible anymore? I will accept whatever decision you deem best. I await your response. Zach.

Ellen's stomach actually turned. It quivered and flopped. She balled up the paper and tossed it across Arborview. It landed in a corner full of cobwebs. He would accept whatever she deemed best. That would be a first.

Why had it taken her twenty-two years to realize how tepidly she had moved through her own life? She could have gone back to work when Jimmy and Taber started school. Or even gone to a cooking school then, full-time, gotten another degree. Why not? Connecticut had a couple of fine culinary schools. She could have met someone new before Zach ever laid eyes on Lydia. She never would have actually done this—"You're not the type who runs around," Alice had said—but it was nice to think about.

She dropped onto the beanbag. The ashy shadows of evening were building. November was only a week away. If only she could stay, curled up here, suspended above the expectations and demands. The public schools were next on her job-hunt list. Teaching one course at River Bend wasn't enough. She needed to be smart about things, practical, for once in her life.

What she didn't need was added pressures, like William, rocking her boat. "Encumbrance," was the word that popped into her mind when she thought of him. Maybe he wouldn't show up at Alice's. She never should have invited him. But the way he had stood there, face full of expectation. She had cracked.

She needed to be careful with Rosa, too. Who knew how this could blow up in her face. But why should old Mama be allowed to screw up Rosa's life, like Ellen's own mother, and then her husband, had helped screw up hers? Though this wasn't entirely fair. Ellen had done a fair amount of screwing up all on her own.

She imagined taking Mama out for a drink, maybe to one of those little wine and tapas bistros Alice raved about: an open kitchen with the chef in clear view, moving ably between stovetops and prep tables, the scent of seared meat and garlic in the air.

Ellen would lean over the corner table toward Rosa's mama and say…what? "Back off, you miserable shrew, and let your daughter live her life?" That's what Alice would say. Ellen—the old Ellen—would listen and smile and perhaps gently suggest Rosa was a big girl now and able to choose for herself. And the new Ellen, now, what would she say?

A wisp brushed her face, tickled her lip. A cobweb? She struggled to her knees and stood. She pulled her hair back away from her face.

What she needed to do was focus on herself. She zipped her jacket. Let Zach come to Thanksgiving and then be done with it. With any luck, she'd be able to dodge him entirely at Christmas. It had come down to this: dodging her ex-husband during the holidays. A spark of anger broke loose in Ellen. He was the one who should be dodging her. Her mother had been right about one thing. Ellen was too mousy.

She had noticed a few new gray hairs popping up along her temples that morning. The truth was, she liked her grays. They gave her a touch of gravitas she'd never had. Distinguished, people would say, if she were a man. Alice would wrinkle her pert little nose. "Don't gray in your forties, Ellie, even your late forties."

Why not? So Ellen could fool the world into believing she was someone she wasn't? This was the goal? To trick everybody? To go on tricking herself?

Dusk reached into Arborview in somber warning tones. *It's getting late*, they seemed to whisper. *What are you waiting for?*

Ellen stepped to the opening in the floor and half-slid down the ladder. She hit the ground with a hard jolt. Everything was so hard, so unforgiving. But she was still strong enough to slide down and hit the ground and keep going. She strode from the edge of the woods onto the sweep of her lawn, her arms pumping at her sides.

Then she took off running. She burst into a sprint, legs scissoring, up to the patio and then around the house, her heart thudding into high gear, her breath coming hard and fast. She circled the house over and over, passion powering her legs, surging forward. She leapt over a pail full of birdseed. She could have run all night.

Chapter Eighteen

It had grown dark beyond the kitchen windows, and Mama was still hunkered down in her chair, arms crossed in front of her chest. Rosa sat at the edge of her own chair, hands resting on the kitchen table between them.

"I know I can't stop you, but you're not gonna change my mind," Mama said. She raised her hands over her head. "God forbid your mother interfere, but I don't have to like it. You can't make me like it."

"Nobody's trying to make you do anything." Rosa's voice came out more a growl than a plea. "I'm asking you to wait and see what happens."

"I don't need to look over the side of a cliff to know jumping off isn't a good idea."

"But the girl's got a point," Javier said, sauntering into the kitchen. "Why not hear her out?" He leaned against the counter next to the sink, folding his arms across his chest.

"You, Mr. Stupid-Taking-Your-Girlfriend-To-College, keep out of this," Mama said. "I don't know where I went wrong with you. How you gonna study with Tilda sprawled across your bed every night?"

"None of your business, Mama, okay? And I told you Tilda will be working and taking cosmetology classes, doing her own thing."

Mama snorted. "She gonna be doing your thing,

Javi. And you better be careful."

"Oh, not again." Javier shook his head.

"I bring you kids up the best way I know—on my own, with no help from anyone else."

Rosa cringed. The "on my own speech." How many times had Javi and she heard over it the years? Too many to count. Mama never let you forget she was a single mother.

"Now, you're grown," Mama said. "Your mistakes are your mistakes."

"Why don't you let us make them first?" Javier asked.

Mama pushed her seat back from the table.

"Let's agree to disagree." Rosa watched Mama's face. "I try Seasons Culinary College, and we just leave it alone."

"You can always say, 'I told you so,' and I'm sure you will, Mama," Javier said.

Mama glared at him. "And I pick up the pieces when this one"—nodding at Rosa—"falls flat on her butt."

"Enough." Rosa slammed her hands down on the table.

Mama jumped.

"I don't need anyone 'picking up the pieces.' I'll handle whatever happens." Rosa caught her breath. "On my own."

Sparks of flint coming from Mama's eyes, sharp as daggers, but Rosa wouldn't look away. Not this time.

Mama raised her eyes to the ceiling, as if imploring God, her lips moving soundlessly.

"Stop," Rosa snapped. "This isn't some tragedy you gotta pray over."

A flashy show of surrender from Mama: hands raised high over her bowed head. "Just don't come crawling back to me."

"Like anyone would," Javier muttered.

"Javi, please." Rosa bit her lip.

"Nobody asked you to be here." Mama glared at Javier.

"No, but it's a good thing I am."

"Go, run away to Niagara." Mama made a scatting motion with her hands. "You kids. Things gotta be to your liking. They gotta be fair. Listen to me. There ain't nothing in this world that's—"

Rosa jumped up, grabbed her coat off a hook in the foyer, and barged out the door into the cold night.

"Where you going?" Mama called after her.

The tears Rosa had managed to hold back broke loose. She stumbled down the front steps and onto the sidewalk. The streetlights threw a pool of light. She headed for the highway.

Behind her, the door slammed a second time, and a minute later, Javi grabbed her arm. She spun to face him.

"What are you doing?" He was wild-eyed. "You've got to back off her about this. You hear me?"

"All I want is to be left alone."

"Is that so?" Javier scoffed. "You're not fooling anybody. You're pissed she's okay with me going to Niagara, but she won't give you the time of day for cooking school."

Rosa shoved him then, a hard thrust with both hands. Javi stumbled back.

"You're nuts, you know that?" he said.

A wave of fury, seething and scarlet red, tore

through Rosa. "Don't you see? I want to matter." More tears flowed, and Rosa couldn't stop them. "You're the important one, the one who…"

"I don't have to listen to this."

"Yeah, you do."

Javier grew still.

"You're taken seriously. I work as hard. I'm smart. I can do all kinds of things. The baking teacher says I have real talent. But do I get credit from anyone?"

"I don't make the rules."

"They aren't rules. They're a bunch of bull." Rosa twirled a finger at her temple. "Other people don't live like this. They don't believe this crap."

Javi looked down at the sidewalk. "Yeah, Mama's old-fashioned. The stuff she's got swimming around in her head died a long time ago for most people. She's still got a lot of Grandma in her."

Rosa glanced back at the house, half expecting to see Mama at a window, watching everything, shaking her head. Fighting in the street like animals, she'd say.

"Look, you're just gonna have to leapfrog the old lady." Javi gave her his loopy smile.

"I'm going for a walk."

"If you're not back in fifteen minutes, I'm coming after you."

Rosa waved him off, but she knew he would come after her.

She had fallen through the ice on a pond one winter when she was eight, and Javi was nine. Mama had taken them into the woods to try ice skating, a thing Mama knew nothing about in an environment she knew even less about. The pond was frozen, but in a small cove, where pine branches hung low over the water, the ice had thinned. Rosa broke through into water so cold, it burned. She plunged up to her waist, her legs stabbed by fiery pins, her arms splayed to the sides. Javier raced over. Rosa couldn't get any words out, only gasps, but she saw something on her brother's face she would never forget. Mama on the bank reaching out to Rosa, praying and cursing in Spanish. Javi skating to the bank, crawling along, the blades of his skates winking in the sunlight. A branch in his hand, held out to Rosa. "Grab it! Grab on!" Rosa's flailing hands closing around the branch. Javi and Mama pulling together. Straining and slipping, and Rosa sliding across the ice like a slick, wet seal.

The thing she had seen in her brother's face was this: His sister drowning under the ice at age eight would simply not be permitted. Their story would not end like this. "Keep walking," he commanded as Rosa's frozen legs wobbled down the trail to the car, and Mama cursed the heavens.

A sliver of icy moon hung over the street now. A handful of battered cars parked along the curb, fenders splattered with rust, oversize fuzzy dice hanging from a rearview mirror, a pickup at the end of the block jacked up on enormous tires. A little white cat sat on a front stoop watching her with wary eyes.

Rosa had an urge to keep walking, up the street, across the intersection, and onto the highway. She could disappear. Who would care besides Javi, and Mama? Maybe her giggling, longhaired girlfriends stuffing themselves into too-tight jeans and push-up bras. Maybe Mrs. Cahill and Mr. Janssen? And Sarah? Rosa visited her at the end of almost every hospice shift now. What would Sarah think?

But they'd all forget. Everybody forgets. Rosa had forgotten her own father. She never really knew him, and it didn't make any difference now.

At the end of the street, she could hear the whir of highway traffic in the distance. All she had to do was follow the lights, a string of hazy beacons winding into the unknown. And as Mama had always warned, danger lurking everywhere. Car jackings and muggings, home invasions where you wake to find a shadow moving through your bedroom, rapes, murders—people shot for drugs or money, or sacrificed to the rage burning at the edges of their lives.

She turned into the driveway of an abandoned house on the corner. The upstairs windows were broken. Torn sheets of plastic stretched over them. Rosa walked to the peeling porch and sat down.

A photo from the Seasons Culinary College catalogue came to her—a gleaming prep table with white-coated student chefs and trays of exquisite, creamy pastry laid out before them. Snowy white cupcakes dotted with cherries like rubies, coconut sprinkled like snowflakes on the tray; lacy confections, four or five layers high, cakes topped with blooming flowers, rosebuds of yellow and pink; dark rich bowls of chocolate sauce. She could smell the sweet, privileged indulgence of that photo.

Her grandmother's funeral was to blame for all of this. Mama didn't know that. The parish priest sent a towering plate of pastries wrapped in shiny red cellophane to the funeral reception. Rosa, at eleven, couldn't take her eyes off them. How did the cream bend and stand up straight without toppling? She bit into a white dollop of cake, and it dissolved in a puff of pure bliss in her mouth. What magical alchemy had created these things?

Her grandmother was long dead now. The porch step was hard, and Rosa was cold. There was nowhere to go but home. She stood. An air of sour, mocking defeat followed her off the porch and down the street. It covered the houses and the rusty cars. It permeated everything.

"I am going to Seasons Culinary College." Rosa's cold fingers curled into fists at her sides.

Her house came into view, a light glowing on the porch. Mama had turned it on. She always left the light on when Rosa or Javier was out at night.

Upstairs, another light shone in Javier's window.

Rosa looked up to see him, watching her make her way down the street. She couldn't tell if he realized she saw him. But she could sense his thoughts coming to her in the night air. It's a grim job, taking control of your life. There are those who will not understand, those who will not be able to hear over the ghosts in their own heads. Hearts will be broken. Maybe your own. There is always a price to pay.

Chapter Nineteen

Alice towered over Ellen when she opened the door. A clingy black tank dress hugged her body, and sheer stockings glimmered on her legs. Alice had good legs, trim and toned. Five days a week at the gym and a personal trainer does that for you. A silk orange wrap across her bare shoulders, and black pumps with a three-inch heel and daring peep toe, completed her ensemble.

"Earle, we're saved," she called over her shoulder. "Dessert is here!"

"What happened to casual?" Ellen demanded. "You look like you just stepped off the Red Carpet."

"Casual-chic," Alice said, winking.

"You might have told me." Ellen wore a dark green knit skirt that fell below her knee, black tights, and ballerina flats. She had topped it off with one of her favorite sweaters, a lightweight cashmere knit— gossamer to the touch, with three-quarter length sleeves and a softly draped neckline that showed off her good collarbones. Three silver bangle bracelets Taber had given her for Christmas decorated her right arm.

"Oh, Ellie! You look absolutely spiffy, and dignified, too. The kind of girl you want to take home to meet Mom."

Ellen rolled her eyes as Alice ushered her inside. "I left my pastry trays on the patio, at the back door."

A fire crackled in the ancient fireplace as they walked through the living room. The flames and soft, recessed lighting in the ceiling cast a gentle glow. They found Earle in the kitchen, and Ellen stepped into his arms for a bear hug. "Dessert lady's here," Earle said. "The party can officially begin." He wore dark brown wide-wale corduroys and a creamy button shirt, tasseled loafers on his feet, and black suspenders decorated with silhouettes of witches on broomsticks

"You've got the Halloween spirit." Ellen laughed.

"Earle, will you bring the desserts in from the patio?" Alice asked.

"At your service, ladies."

Alice moved past Ellen into the dining room. She left a faint sweet floral scent in her wake—gardenias, Ellen thought. "The rest of the food is already out," she said. "Desserts are going on the buffet."

Ellen followed her, seeing again how much she loved Alice's dining room—its pale yellow walls with white molding and trim, the elegant cherry table in the center, and the matching buffet along the wall. A truly impressive array of finger foods filled the table tonight. Deviled eggs, smoked salmon, sliced onion, capers, cream cheese and toast squares, bowls of olives, mixed nuts, and a crudité platter. A bean dip surrounded by a fan of yellow, dark blue, and red tortilla chips. Stuffed mushroom caps—you could smell the garlic and butter—and sliced beef tenderloin. A cheese and cracker display—sprigs of parsley tucked among the cheeses, little dipping bowls of honey and olive oil—sat next to a crystal punch bowl filled with something purple.

Ellen peered into the bowl. "What's in the punch?"

"Earle's latest concoction. Eye-Ball Brew. Claims he found the recipe online. I couldn't talk him out of it."

"And what's this?" Ellen pointed to the corner where a lifelike wooden bat perched atop a stool, staring at the table through penetrating amber eyes.

"I couldn't talk him out of that either."

"Where's your holiday spirit, sour puss?"

The doorbell rang. Earle's footsteps moved across the entrance hall, and then the front door opened. "Come in, come in. So glad you could make it." A murmur of voices, punctuated by laughter. No one did gracious better than Earle.

"It's the Mayfairs," Alice said, straightening a platter on the table. "I'd know that woman's laugh anywhere."

Heather Mayfair barked like a seal when she laughed, emitting a series of hoarse cries ending in a snort. Ellen had once heard her three aisles away in the grocery store. Heather and her husband, Bob, were the team behind Mayfair Realty, the agency everyone used to buy or sell homes in town. "Local folks making local deals," was their slogan.

Guests trickled in regularly, in pairs or solo. Alice's speech therapist colleagues arrived, June and Carol, two squat little brunettes, one widening in the rear—an ass like a Mack truck, as Alice put it—the other, a stringy rack of bones with a strangely small head.

Ellen greeted Anna Colangello, the high school principal who had survived a nasty coup attempt by the Board of Education, fueled by rumors of an extramarital affair with a woodshop teacher. The rumors cost the teacher his job and Anna her marriage, but she was still the principal.

"Anna," Ellen said, reaching for her hand.

"Ellen Cahill, you look fantastic. How is Jimmy? And Taber? She must be what? A junior now?"

"She's so glamorous, I hardly recognize her," Ellen said.

Anna gave the satisfied smile of someone who has spent her life helping children make their way in the world. Her shiny dark hair was swept up in a casual bun, with loose tendrils framing her face. Her wedding band had been replaced with a large cocktail ring, a deep emerald set in gleaming silver.

"You look fabulous, Anna," Ellen said. "You know, I miss having kids in the schools. I miss dropping by, volunteering. I'm going to look into substitute teaching."

The lines around Anna's mouth softened. "The empty nest is brutal. What you need is someone new to fill it." She placed one hand on Ellen's shoulder and winked. "And I don't mean children."

And Ellen realized of course Anna knew about Zach and the divorce. By now, the whole town knew. Well, so what? People get divorced every day. Ellen winked boldly back at Anna. She had not called for Anna's scalp when the righteous hordes were clamoring. She had actually found the whole episode inspiring, daring.

Ellen made her way to the dining room, where Earle was describing the technique he had used to create the bat's snout. Anita and José Pérez were nodding. They owned the Honda dealership on the highway.

"The trick," Earle said, "is to whittle it down in the smallest increments possible. You need a very light touch on the face. Mere shavings of wood—paper thin."

The doorbell rang again and again. The totter of heels across hardwood, a burst of laughter, and the French doors to the living room creaking open. Music, a dreamy, brooding medley of cello and piano, came from a stereo tucked in a bookcase. Ellen sensed the room vibrating around her, separate and yet also tied to her. She felt a rush of warmth, of deep, nodding affection for this house and the people here. At the center of such a web of belonging, anything seemed possible.

"I'm not a big classical fan, but maybe I should be."

Ellen turned.

"The finer things in life are lost on some people." William smiled. "The harp, though, I do like the harp. It always makes me think of angels."

Ellen took a step back. "And do you believe in angels?"

"Sometimes yes, sometimes no."

Ellen laughed. "Fair enough. Hey, I'm glad you could make it. Did you find the house easily?"

"GPS never fails. And I met your friend, the hostess. She's quite a talker."

"Oh please, don't let her corner you, and don't mention me too much. She's like a bloodhound."

"Too late."

Ellen gave in to the strength of his pull. In the soft lines framing his mouth, at the corners of his eyes, she saw an unspoken kinship. His clothing gave him a youthful, easygoing air—khaki pants, brown suede lace-up shoes, and, what Ellen really loved, a deep, ruby-red flannel shirt. She could almost feel the softness of the fabric.

They made their way to the table, and William handed her a plate.

"What kind of music do you like?" Ellen asked, reaching for a slice of tenderloin.

"Classic rock, a little jazz, and, lately, I've discovered the charms of country."

"Really? I can't picture you with a cowboy hat and boots."

"It's so much more. Every song is a story, a tale of bad luck, or broken hearts, or flat beer."

Ellen laughed. So he was funny, too. "Try the mushrooms," she said. "This caterer does a really superb stuffing."

William spooned a few onto his plate.

"My son likes country music, too," Ellen said. "I used to hear him singing all over the house: cheating lovers, bad hangovers, trucks that won't start—every sorrow known to man."

"How old is he?"

"Jimmy's twenty. He's a sophomore at Olden College."

"Olden College. I'd bet it's a pretty tuition bill."

"You'd bet right." They moved on to the salads. "And my daughter, Taber, is at Empire Fashion Academy, so we've got two at the same time."

"Ouch. Sorry, I'm talking shop, aren't I?" William shook his head. "It seems tuition is never far from my mind, and what a sorry statement, seeing as I don't have any kids. It's sort of a vicarious parenthood for me."

"I bet it has its perks." A bright flash on Ellen's

left—Alice's gleaming hair.

"You two look cozy." Alice beamed.

Ellen shot her a look, but Alice gave her sunniest smile. "Any friend of Ellen's is a friend of mine. And she never mentioned how dashing you are, William."

"Oh, you're too kind."

"Not at all. I'm simply stating an empirical truth when I say—"

"Try the salmon." Ellen pointed to a platter at the far end of the table.

"I was going to." William coughed. "Excuse me a minute?"

Ellen turned to Alice. "Are you crazy? Tone it down. Way down."

Alice widened her eyes in feigned innocence. "He's not the sad sack I was expecting."

"Shh! How much have you had to drink?"

"Not enough that I can't recognize the look of love."

"Go away." Ellen gave Alice a little push. "Go mingle."

Alice moved out of the room as William returned.

"How long have you two been friends?" he asked.

"Seems like my whole life. Alice is, well, an original. There's no one like her."

In the corner, Earle rattled a cocktail shaker. William surveyed the buffet where Alice had laid out the desserts. "I'm saving room," he said.

"I hope you won't be disappointed."

"Not a chance. How did the baking go with Rosa?"

"She's talented, and a great girl, a hard worker. She's in a bit of a pickle though, isn't she?"

"Her mother? Yes, I know. I'm still hoping they

can work it out."

They turned together to the living room, where they found a couple of armchairs near the fire. William went to get wine. Ellen rested her plate on her knees. They'd have a nice chat by the fire, enjoy the food, and call it a night. No big deal.

He returned and handed her a glass. "To Alice. The best friends are the ones who keep us on our toes."

"I'll drink to Alice any day." Ellen took a long sip. The wine slipped down her throat and rolled through her in a warm, reassuring wave.

"This house is amazing," William said. "You can tell the owners really love it."

"They did it over, Alice and Earle, a total renovation about five years ago."

He nodded. "It shows."

"Alice dumped a fortune into this house." Ellen waved her fork. "My ex and I never renovated. I didn't want to change it. I loved it the way it was. I still do."

"Everything about it?"

Ellen looked into the fire. "Maybe not everything, but it is home."

"I'd love to see it sometime."

Ellen smiled. A little forward of him, maybe, but so what? They chatted comfortably while they ate, a discussion of the River Bend students, campus, and administration, punctuated by Ellen identifying the other guests circulating through the house.

"What if I get us a few of those fabulous desserts?" William finally asked.

Ellen offered him her glass. "And a refill?"

"Absolutely."

She watched him cross the room. He was the sort

of man who caught her eye, no point denying it. Zach cut a dashing figure, in his fine wool suits, with the elegant breaks in the trouser legs, silk ties like bright slashes, and polished shoes. She had sometimes felt like his little sister tagging along. William was not as sleek, not as polished. But he exuded an air of—what would Alice call it? Shabby chic—battered elegance, like a lake cottage with aging flowerboxes in the windows, peeling paint on the kitchen table, scuffed floorboards.

When William returned, he placed the pastry plate on the small table between them.

"Rosa's cookies." Ellen lifted one from the plate. "They're beautiful."

She tasted the crumbly, buttery shortbread, imagining Rosa's situation solved, wrapped up with a tidy bow, and Rosa moving forward with no misgivings, no chorus of naysayers in her head. They had stopped Ellen, those voices.

She placed her wineglass on the table. "Will you excuse me a sec?"

"Sure."

Ellen stood, and the room followed her up. She needed to slow down on the wine. She hadn't eaten much all day.

The lights were dimmed in the entrance hall. Ellen moved over the ivory runner lining the floor to the half-bath beneath the staircase, outside the kitchen. She closed the door behind her and brought one hand to her forehead. In the mirror above the white pedestal sink, she appeared vibrant and bright-eyed. Young. A warm glow flushed her face.

She turned to use the toilet. The party would break up around eleven. They usually did. She would wish

William good night and help Alice clean up. In the morning, Alice would call, and they'd do a postmortem on the night. Alice would of course want every detail about William—not that Ellen would have many to share.

She washed her hands at the sink and took another look in the mirror. A fresh swipe of lipstick would have helped. Still, good enough. She closed the bathroom door behind her.

Laughter from the dining room, and the sweet, mingled scents of warm bread and pumpkin spice floating down the hall. The food was a hit. They'd made good menu choices this year.

Ellen turned to the kitchen, deciding to peek in and see how much was left. Earle might be there, too. He was known to take time-outs during parties.

But the kitchen was empty. A half-full tray of celery and carrot sticks sat on the island next to a basket of cold dinner rolls. Ellen glanced around at the counters—a bottle of ginger ale, a few wine glasses next to the sink, a bowl of burnished red apples near the refrigerator.

She walked to the sink. The window above looked out on the backyard. The moon was full, high above, washing Alice's yard in a ghostly, preternatural glow, just right for the season. William struck Ellen as the sort of man who would have astronomy as a hobby— books about the galaxies on his shelves, a long slender telescope pointing into the heavens in one window.

"*Oh, oh, ahh.*"

The sound came from the narrow laundry room off the kitchen.

"Earle?"

The laundry room was dark. Ellen walked over and snapped on the light.

Alice gasped. She was pressed up against a man's chest, his arms wrapped around her. Ellen didn't recognize him—about their age, dark hair, navy blazer.

Ellen stepped back. "I'm sorry. Excuse me." She spun around and headed for the hall.

"Ellen?" Alice was beside her in a heartbeat. Her sleek hair stood out in little tufts at her temples. Her ruby lipstick was smeared.

Ellen raised her hands. "It's none of my business."

"Oh, come on. Please listen."

"Sshh!" Ellen glanced at the kitchen doorway. "Go pull yourself together. Earle could walk in any minute."

Alice's eyes pleaded, but Ellen also saw a hint of frost forming in them: *Don't judge me. Don't you dare judge me.*

"I can't believe you," Ellen hissed. "With Earle in the next room, and all these people here? What is wrong with you?"

"None of your business, huh?" Alice glared.

"You've got a way of making your dirty business my business." Ellen turned away.

"Wait…"

But Ellen was gone, into the hall, away from the kitchen and the moon and Alice, standing wild-haired on the hard tile. She passed the dining room where she heard Earle saying, "…my favorite time of year, when they roost in numbers…" Her heart thudded.

William had left their spot by the fire. Ellen went to the coat closet to collect her purse, and she saw him through the window, standing on the front porch, gazing into the night sky.

"Full moon," he said, as she stepped onto the porch.

"It's lovely. I'm sorry, I didn't mean to abandon you in there."

"Ah, I'm a big boy. I know how to mingle."

Someone else might have been offended. How forgiving he was.

"Happy Halloween," he said, bending toward her. Was he going to kiss her?

Ellen took a step back. "Trick or treat." She gave a weak laugh. Her heart pounded.

She closed her eyes. She imagined Earle at his workbench, gluing on a blue jay's wings; Zach and Lydia holed up in an impossibly white bedroom with ruby flower petals strewn across the floor; and Alice and whoever this guy was, breathing fast, their desire barely containable, in the dark laundry room.

"Ellen, are you all right?"

She sniffed hard and swallowed. "I'm sorry. Maybe a little too much wine. I think I might call it a night."

"Can you make it home?"

"Yes, I'm fine." She hadn't said any goodbyes, but Earle wouldn't mind. He always gave her the benefit of the doubt. It was an unspoken pact they shared, to see the good in each other, even when—especially when—their respective spouses did not.

"If you're not feeling well, I wish you'd let me drive you home," William said.

Ellen sensed William scrambling for a way to extend the evening, to stretch his time with her. He was part of the moonlight, part of the dark stirring in the trees. Maybe a little company would help. "Chivalry isn't dead, after all, huh?" she said. "Thanks."

"I'll make my good nights and meet you in the driveway."

"Please don't mention this?"

"Not a word." He crossed his finger over his heart and smiled a sweet, moonlit smile.

A vibrant chill had crept into the air, the kind of autumn ping Ellen had always loved. She made her way down the walkway to the driveway. "You can breathe better this time of year," Jimmy had said when he was maybe ten, and she was waiting with him at the school bus stop. How could it be that Jimmy was now hundreds of miles away, deep in the hills of Maine, planning a future all his own? Ellen drew a deep breath. Jimmy in Maine, Taber whirling through Manhattan, Zach…God only knew, and Alice making out in the laundry room.

And yet here she was, scrambling to hold on to what she had. She wished she could blast off—a new Ellen, a new future. To seize her desires, and damn the consequences, like everyone else was doing.

"Ellen?" William calling. "Everything okay?" He carried a foil-covered plate heaped with food.

"The air helps." She touched the foil. "Doggie bag?"

"Earle wouldn't let me leave empty-handed."

They reached his car, a gray sedan with leather interior, so clean, so spotless, she knew immediately neither children nor pets had ever ridden in it. The car came to life and moved onto the road, solid and heavy, the dashboard glowing like a cockpit on a bumpy night flight.

Chapter Twenty

He guided the car down Main Street and then, following her direction, onto the side roads winding back to her country lane. The woods grew darker, the trees dense.

"You are a little off the beaten path," he said.

"We bought this house when Zach got his first big promotion." Ellen's gaze followed the road. "It seemed such a towering extravagance, and then it became, you know, home—kids, dogs, nonstop noise, cars and bikes and baseball bats in the driveway. It seems like we've always been here."

"Must be nice to feel so connected to a place. To have a sense of history with it."

"It's the one thing from my marriage I'm determined to keep."

Ellen was glad he didn't respond. She wasn't asking for input. She'd already spent too long soliciting advice instead of simply doing what she wanted.

The car rounded the sharp bend before the driveway. Had Alice realized yet that Ellen had left? Had her new boyfriend scurried out the door, too? Or maybe they'd returned to the laundry room to pick up where they left off. Alice had broken the rules, time after time, but still she had love.

"Very nice," William said, as they turned into Ellen's driveway. The headlights picked up the house's sunny shade of yellow. He put the car in park. "My favorite color."

Ellen turned to him. "You're putting me on? It's mine, too." It seemed so significant, a little a-ha moment when she needed one. Zach had never quit grousing about the color, yet here was a man who loved it.

Ellen unclicked her seatbelt. "Well, Alice sure knows how to throw a humdinger, doesn't she?"

"Thanks for inviting me."

The air crackled with expectation. And Ellen thought, why not? "Do you want to come in for a nightcap?"

If he was surprised, he didn't show it. "Sure. Will you give me the dime tour of this beautiful house, too?"

"You got it."

She was suddenly overcome by the need to have him in her house. To see him at the refrigerator or sitting on the couch. She wanted him to leave a mark, to inject an essence of himself into the air, so the place would never be the same.

She took him in through the garage. In the kitchen, she dropped her purse on the counter and turned to him. "I've got a couple of nice cabs in here, a chardonnay, if you like."

"Cabernet is fine. What a great kitchen."

Ellen grabbed a bottle of wine from the metal rack in the corner and two glasses from the shelves above it. A little more wouldn't hurt her either.

He was studying the magnets and lists stuck to the refrigerator door. "So cooks really do keep shopping lists on the fridge," he said.

"Doesn't everyone keep lists on the fridge?"

"You're talking to a man with no domestic life."

"None?"

"No kids, no ex-wives."

Wasn't it a teeny bit weird that he had always lived alone? Alice would think so. "Have you ever lived with a, you know, partner?" Ellen asked.

"I lived with a woman once, long ago. It didn't last long."

Ellen filled the glasses. The ruby wine gave off its subtle, luxurious wink as she handed one to him. "Let me show you the house."

She led him around, first into the dining room, with the long Shaker-style ash table and matching chairs. "Simple, classic," he said. He ran his hand over the smooth top. It looked deft and solid on the wood, practiced, at home. It thrilled Ellen.

She took him next to the little study at the end of the hall near the front door. She snapped on the light. Zach's old desk in the corner, the bookshelves lined with photos and novels—he'd never read any, as far as she knew—the leather loveseat against the wall, all seemed washed in a startled glow.

"Very cozy," William said.

"We always wanted to install a wood-burning stove. Never got around to it."

She led him across the hall to the living room. "This is my favorite room, after the sun porch."

He walked over to the fieldstone fireplace, silent and cold now. "I bet you've had great roaring blazes in here, huh?"

"We have. And seven-foot Christmas trees." She pointed to a widescreen television mounted at the far end of the room, before a burgundy and cream-striped sofa set. "And terrific movie nights."

"This is a lot of space for you alone."

Ellen stiffened. "So I've heard."

He turned to her. "I'm sorry. I didn't mean to overstep. I sometimes speak without thinking first."

Ellen shook her head. "No, no, it's all right. Friends have urged me to sell, but I can't. This has been my home for a long time. I don't want to lose it now, too."

Ellen shut her mouth. She'd sounded foolish. *...lose it now, too.* Whiny, like an angry child.

William watched her with quiet, sober attention. "You don't need to explain. Anyone in your position would feel the same way."

"Anyone impractical."

"Anyone with a heart."

Ellen couldn't think of a response. A warm gratitude filled her. The little gold clock on the mantel above the fireplace ticked. "Come see the sunroom," she said.

In the sunroom—her haven—William truly fit among the wicker furniture and potted plants, the dog-eared magazines and half-finished *New York Times* crossword puzzles strewn across the floral pattern couch.

"I wasn't expecting guests tonight. You'll have to excuse the mess," she said.

"You never have to spruce up for me." He walked to the sliding glass door overlooking the patio and the moonlit backyard. Shadows cloaked Arborview.

Ellen joined him. "I've loved this yard since I first laid eyes on it. I wish it were daylight, so you could get a better look."

"I've got a pretty good idea. What a place. Private, a little enclave of your own. Who'd want to leave this?"

He got it. She had been heard. Understood. She was not alone. Maybe this was the feeling that had driven Alice to other men. Maybe Ellen had judged too harshly.

She reached for William's hand. Her fingers brushed it tentatively, and she kept them there. He didn't move at first, and it occurred to Ellen he might be surprised. She had perhaps read everything wrong.

Then his fingers closed around hers. They turned to each other simultaneously. His face was half in shadow. All year, Ellen had been crawling and grasping, seeking anything to pull her from the alien place she had landed.

Alice seemed never to crawl. She seized what was before her. She didn't wait for things to get going. Here, now, was something before Ellen, something real and warm and alive that she could seize.

She gave a tremulous smile, and when he kissed her, she returned the kiss. She leaned into him, and the sunroom, her bright kitchen, the house where she had loved and struggled and grieved for so many years, fell away as he pulled her closer.

Later, she woke in the night, not at all startled to feel him beside her. She retraced everything that had happened, each step that had led to this: an Ellen no one would recognize—not Zach, not her mother, not Alice, and certainly not the old nuns.

In a way she had always been moving to this night, to this place. Ellen sometimes imagined the world—the earth—as a big cloud-shrouded ball suspended in the vast expanses of space, untethered, rotating through the millennia with generation after generation swarming over it, clinging, striving, and at last, inevitably, dropping off. Charades only last so long. Maybe now she had stepped beyond her own—the charade of who she was supposed to be.

****

Ellen opened her eyes. "Good morning," she said.

William stirred beneath the white sheets. His face was puffy with sleep. "Good morning." He rubbed his eyes. "It's the morning after, isn't it?"

"I'm afraid so." Ellen sat up. She wore a long white T-shirt, an old one hanging nearly to her knees. She had grabbed it from her bureau in the dark. "How did you sleep?"

"I have to say pretty darn well." He smiled. "How could I not? Next to a beautiful woman in a beautiful house."

"Ha." Ellen plucked at her T-shirt. "You know, this is a first for me. I mean, going home with someone and…" She took a breath. "I've never been the kind of person who does things like this."

"Well, my dear, I'm glad you are now."

My dear. How long since she had been called that? She had a sudden ache, saw a flash of a very young Zach beholding her with such tenderness in his eyes, what a prize he had once considered her.

William got out of bed. He had put on his boxer shorts at some point in the night, just as she had scrambled for the T-shirt. He crossed the room to gaze out on the backyard, streaming with morning sunlight. "A tree house," he said, tapping on the glass.

"My kids," Ellen said.

"I had one, too. I loved it."

"I go out there to think, and sometimes to pray." The words were out before Ellen could stop them. "I guess you could call it that—praying."

He turned to her. "What do you pray for?"

She wondered if she would regret this later. "Clarity, I guess, a way to understand what's happened..." Her voice drifted off. "Solace." She looked away from his eyes. "Do you know what I mean?"

He turned back to the window. "Intimately."

Ellen released her breath.

"I tried that route, too—praying, church," he said. "Never got any traction. Only the Indian traditions made sense. The Eastern traditions—Hinduism, Buddhism especially. All suffering is caused by desire. The greatest meditation is a mind that lets go."

"India," Ellen said. "So that's why you kept returning?"

He shrugged. "You may be onto something."

They shared coffee in the sunroom, wrapped in bathrobes, a bond of spent exhilaration and grateful connection between them. A plate of Ellen's cinnamon rolls sat on the wicker ottoman.

"There's another thing I pray for," Ellen said. "Money. Don't take this the wrong way, but I can't hold on to this house without generating new income."

"So you've returned to teaching?"

She nodded. "And I'm going to go back to the public schools. One class at River Bend won't cut it. I thought I could tutor, too, but honestly it's not going to be enough."

"These rolls are incredible." William licked his lips. "Your own recipe?"

"I've been making them every Sunday morning for twenty years." Ellen laughed. "Old habits do die hard."

William gazed across the yard to where the morning sun was falling over Arborview. "Well, I'll tell you what you should pray for," he said. "A shop of your own."

"A shop?"

"A pastry shop, a business. A place filled with you—your sense of beauty and, what was it? Solace, right? Your own creation."

Ellen fell silent, but the notion of a space set aside, sanctified, a retreat from the bruising world, took hold inside her. It wasn't as if the thought had never occurred to her. But it had always seemed like a fantasy.

"I know nothing about business," she said.

"You can learn. People open small businesses every day."

"A lot of them fail."

"And some of them make it."

She sipped her coffee. "Well. I *can* bake."

"My cautious queen of understatement." He reached for her hand. "Prayer works, isn't that what they say?"

Chapter Twenty-One

Inside Mr. Janssen's office, the reverend was saying how he had to take it easy on the sweets. He'd put on a little weight. Mr. Janssen grunted, like he understood.

Rosa hadn't noticed. The reverend was such an unremarkable man, walking the hospice halls, entering patients' rooms with an apologetic clearing of his throat and a small nod before easing the door closed. He always wore the same clothes, too, a white turtleneck or dress shirt and gray or brown slacks, sometimes a sweater, red or navy blue. He always carried a leather briefcase-type bag and a clipboard.

Rosa knocked tentatively on Mr. Janssen's open door as she stepped in to empty the trash can.

"*Holá*, Rosa!" The reverend's feet were propped up on a wooden milk crate. He gave her a big smile. He liked to throw a little Spanish around with her. His accent was atrocious, but Rosa knew he meant well. He was endearing in his goofy way.

"Hey," Mr. Janssen said.

"Sorry to disturb," Rosa said. She pushed her wheeled trash cart to the desk and dumped in the contents of Mr. Janssen's small metal floor can.

The reverend jumped up and helped her push the cart back across the room, even though it wasn't heavy. "*Gracias*," he said, smiling.

She smiled back. "*De nada*," she said. "Thanks a bunch."

She wheeled the cart into the kitchen so she could empty the tall plastic trash containers along the wall. She heard the reverend settle back in his chair again.

The kitchen trash was a little nastier. Rosa wrinkled her nose, heaving the plastic container and dumping its contents. Brown banana peels, expired yogurt scraped into the trash so the little plastic cups could be recycled, wilting carrots, and splotchy tomatoes. Such waste. It would have driven Mama crazy. Why did the hospice buy so much food in the first place? It's not like dying people eat a lot.

"So I'm watching carbs," the reverend told Mr. Janssen. "I'm not cutting them out totally. I don't think it's considered healthy anymore, is it?"

"I don't know," Mr. Janssen said. "When I need to drop a few pounds, I just cut back on everything, you know, across the board."

"Makes sense."

"And I don't drink beer anymore. I gave it up years ago. I kind of lost my taste for it."

Rosa decided to take a breather. She flopped down in a kitchen chair and stretched.

"I never liked beer, myself," the reverend said.

"Neither does the woman I'm seeing."

"Oh? Someone new?"

Rosa could tell the reverend was tamping down the curiosity in his voice.

"A handful of dates." It sounded like Mr. Janssen was holding back, too. "We're taking it slow."

"Smart."

"At our age, is there another option?"

They both chuckled. Rosa rolled her eyes. If they thought they were so old, why did they bother? Trying to lose weight and going on dates—why didn't they relax and take it easy? It seemed old people could never stop worrying. Mama certainly never did.

"You know, I feel like I've crossed into new territory," Mr. Janssen said.

"Really? How so?"

Mr. Janssen's voice dropped. "I've made my share of mistakes, of, you might say, failures…"

"Who hasn't?" The reverend, a little softer now, permissive and confiding. Rosa had heard him use the same tone with patients.

"One time—with a terrific woman—I really dropped the ball." Mr. Janssen cleared his throat. "The woman has since, ah, passed—died. This was a few years back."

"Oh, I'm sorry. A few years, not a long time when you've loved someone."

"No, I guess not."

Rosa sighed. When he talked to the reverend, Mr. Janssen could sound depressing. He was a bit of a drag actually.

"And this, now, feels like another…feels like I've been given another chance," he droned on to the reverend.

"Second chances. The Lord knows we all need them."

Mr. Janssen chuckled, but Rosa could hear the nervous dip in his voice. "Well, this may be my last."

Rosa had the creeping sensation she shouldn't be hearing this.

"Listen, these situations—relationships ending

badly—are never solely one person's fault," the reverend said. "I used to counsel couples, and I can tell you it is never the case, so don't be so hard on yourself."

Silence, then Mr. Janssen saying, "The problem is I haven't been hard *enough* on myself all these years."

The reverend whistled. "Oh, *mea culpa*. None of us is perfect. We learn, we move on."

Rosa had heard enough. It was time to take her break. She grabbed her backpack and headed down the hall. She had something for Sarah, a copy of *Gourmet* magazine. The issue was old, but recipes never expired, and there were lots of good ones in it. Plus, the photos were gorgeous. Sarah had said she liked cooking.

The smell of Sarah's fruity candle hit her as she approached the room. Everyone tried to make the rooms smell better here. Fresh flowers perfumed the air. Patients lit scented candles, the ones Mama claimed gave her a headache, heavy and dripping with the candied scent of vanilla or the cloying reach of lavender that tickled Rosa's throat. But people died in these rooms. Getting rid of the smell of death isn't easy. The sharp scald of bleach was what Rosa would one day remember most. It reached her now, a slip of it, beneath the candle's scent.

Sarah looked tired today. Gray half-moons hung below her eyes. She rested her head back into the pillow. Rosa almost scrapped the magazine idea when she knocked at the door, but Sarah seemed to brighten upon seeing her.

"Hey! I was hoping you'd stop by."

"I wanted to bring you this." Rosa stepped inside and handed her the magazine.

"Oh, thank you." Sarah immediately began turning pages, then stopped at one. "Oh, wow. Can you make this, Rosa?" She held up a photo of a lovely *Croquembouche*, the delicately stacked tower of caramelized crème puffs also known as the French Wedding Cake.

"You know," Rosa said, "I actually can. I copied this one. It came out a little lopsided. The caramel was too runny, but it tasted pretty good."

"You'll have to teach me."

"That would be so much fun," Rosa said. "These French desserts are, you know, pretty hard. I've always wanted to try a Napoleon, but all those layers, ack."

"Intricate," Sarah said. "I wish I could have minored in a culinary field."

"What are you studying?" Rosa asked.

Sarah's gaze drifted to the window. "Political science and history. I'm going to go to law school."

"You must be smart."

Sarah laughed. "Shrewd is more like it."

"But law school, wow. My brother's going to be an engineer."

"An engineer and a chef—you'll both be creating things. I admire you." Sarah studied Rosa a moment. "I'd like to meet your brother."

"Javi? No, you wouldn't. He can be such a jerk. Do you have any brothers?"

Sarah shook her head. "A sister. She's already in law school. We're going to go into practice together."

Rosa imagined Sarah's family—a mother and father beaming with pride over their daughters, two lawyers working together, these smart, hard-working, much-loved girls.

The elevators at the end of the hall dinged. Sarah's parents were downstairs getting coffee. This could be them. A nervous rush came over Rosa. She didn't want to meet them, not in her hoodie sweatshirt and old sneakers. And they might not like her being here, bothering Sarah, especially when she looked tired. "I should go," Rosa said.

"Don't feel like you have to." Sarah looked surprised.

"My break's almost up." Rosa stepped back from the side of the bed. "I'll try to pop in again before I leave."

Sarah gave her a thumbs-up.

Footsteps in the hall, coming closer. "We'll bake something soon," Rosa said. "Amazing things happen in the kitchen. Things come together. Miracles even, like you said." She headed for the door but turned back once. "Do you still believe that?"

Sarah smiled. "Of course I believe it. Don't you?"

Chapter Twenty-Two

The light was dying in Arborview. Ellen had to get going, but she wasn't ready. Descending the ladder meant reentering her life. The time she spent here, suspended among the branches, did not banish the uncertainty that crept back when her feet hit the ground, but it did give her reprieve.

The stillness, the silence, slowed her mind. *Be still and know that I am God.* She used to love that old Psalm. This must have been what it meant. Her thoughts unraveled in Arborview, exposed in a cool, piercing light, a calm glow giving her hope.

It had been a week since she'd heard from Alice, and the memory of her guilty laundry-room face lingered. Perhaps Ellen had been too harsh, too judgmental. That was a big thing today, wasn't it? Judging. Nothing was supposed to be off limits, nothing truly wrong, or shameful. Ellen had broken down and left a voicemail, but Alice had not returned the call.

The warm impression William had left in her bed, the faint whiff of his cologne on the pillows, had stayed with Ellen, too. He was coming to take her to dinner in an hour.

William had struck a chord with his pastry shop idea. It had taken root and grown all week within Ellen, its tendrils reaching into her heart. She could see it: a little storefront place, a jingling bell on the door, cakes and pies in the window, a soft wash of light on the gleaming display cases inside.

The Sweet Spot? No.

Daily Desserts? No.

Just Desserts. Ellen paused. The pun, the *judgement,* appealed to her. *Just Desserts: The Endings We All Deserve*. She could picture it in swirling red letters across the shop window.

A slip of breeze came through the cracks in Arborview's walls. Who gets what they deserve? Who finds peace? *The peace of God, which surpasses all understanding*. The nuns used to say this. It seemed such a quaint notion now.

Ellen closed her eyes. She felt the growing cold, the first stirring of winter when snow would blanket these woods, quieting all strife and yearning, until the spring rains washed them clean. Year after year it would go on, carrying away all traces of what had been here.

She rose from the beanbag chair, a little stiff, her hips achy. Were cold afternoons starting to put a "crick" in her bones, as her mother used to say? It was almost four o'clock, which meant another thirty minutes of daylight.

"Ellen?" A voice in the yard, calling. A woman's voice. *Alice*.

Ellen scrambled for the opening and started backing down the ladder.

Fading daylight, the house in shadows, and Alice moving across the lawn.

Ellen dropped to the ground, but she was too late. Alice hurried, trim legs in blue jeans covering the lawn in bounds. "What were you doing up there?"

Ellen brushed off her hands. "Looking for something."

"Up there? What?"

"Taber thought she might have left a sweater."

Alice stared up into the branches. "The whole thing looks like it could crash to the ground at any minute."

"It's still pretty solid actually."

Ellen turned abruptly to the house, motioning for Alice to follow. The light over the kitchen sink glowed in the gathering dark. "You've been lying low."

Alice had confessed her other affairs early on to Ellen, sharing her angst and her titillation, crying one day and giggling the next. Not so this time.

"I need to explain," Alice said.

Ellen didn't want to come on like a heavy. "You don't owe me an explanation."

Alice took Ellen's arm. They stopped, but Alice looked at the ground. "I don't know if I even can explain."

"How long has it been going on?"

"Late February, March, around then."

"February? Zach had just left."

"What's Zach got to do with it? Let's not drag him into this."

Ellen stepped back. "What happened? I thought you were done with all this?"

"If I could answer, I wouldn't be in this mess, would I?"

Ellen couldn't stop herself. "You'd find another mess. You'd create one."

"Please." Alice raised her hands. "No tough love today, okay? I can't take it."

Ellen climbed the steps at the deck. In the kitchen,

she patted a stool at the island. "Sit." She turned on the burner beneath the teapot on her stove. "It's not my place to judge you."

Alice hunched over, propping her elbows on the hard marble of the island top, dropping her head into her hands. She needed a color boost; Ellen could see grays around her part.

Ellen pulled up a stool across from her. "Look, I'm worried about you." Alice seemed fragile, undone. "This secrecy this…I don't know. It feels different this time."

Alice nodded.

"Does Earle know?"

"Of course not. He's as oblivious as ever."

"I thought you were going to try counseling with him?"

Alice lifted her chin. "It wouldn't make any difference. You don't know Earle the way I know Earle."

Ellen couldn't argue. "I wish I'd never found out this time."

"That's why I didn't tell you." Alice sighed. "And I was too embarrassed. I know how much you care about Earle, but Ned…"

"His name is Ned?"

"Yes, and I won't tell you any more, except to say he's divorced, so I'm not breaking up anyone else's marriage."

"But during the party? With everyone in the house? With Earle *right there*?"

Alice sniffed. "Look, I feel awful about it, but Ned gives me something I can't get from Earle."

Ellen had heard a version of this before, but she bit

her tongue.

"He sees me for who I really am, and he understands." Alice's eyes misted. "He approves of me."

"Earle doesn't understand or approve?"

The teakettle whistled, and Ellen went to the stove. She poured the hot tea into two mugs. Slips of steam rose from them as she placed one before Alice.

"Ned makes me feel vital and…and needed." Alice paused. "I know it sounds pathetic."

"No, it doesn't sound pathetic." What had Zach said? *She thinks like me. A better match.* Ellen closed her eyes.

"I'm sorry you had to find out," Alice said. "There are things I keep to myself these days. I've learned the hard way. They're secrets, Ellie, not lies. Strategic little secrets, and they hurt no one, as long as no one finds out."

"You're scaring me, you know that?" This didn't sound like the Alice Ellen knew. Something had taken hold in her. A knotted braid of defensiveness, a cold thread of calculation.

Ellen put down her mug. "I hate to see you go through this again, and you're getting reckless now. You've never been so bold, almost flaunting it at…"

Alice raised a palm, like a police officer stopping traffic.

Ellen stopped. "Enough for one day?"

Alice nodded. "Tell me something good, okay?"

"William's taking me to dinner tonight."

"I knew I saw sparks flying between you two. Lucky you. You can have a lover now."

"Well, good, because I do."

"Are you serious?" Alice's eyebrows shot up.

"Please don't call him my 'lover.' We're friends."

Alice didn't argue. Ellen suddenly wished she wasn't going to dinner. "You know what? I'll cancel. Let's you and I have dinner tonight," she said.

Alice gaped at her. "Are you crazy? You've got a date with a new man, and you want to sit around with me?" She glanced at her watch. "He's coming to pick you up? Then you've got to get ready."

"Can you come for coffee tomorrow?"

Alice stood. She ran her hands through her hair. "I didn't choose to be in a marriage this lonely, you know."

"No one does. But you need to make up your mind and come clean."

"Easy for you to say."

"Are you kidding me?"

"I'm sorry. What a crumby thing to say. I'm not…not myself today."

Ellen let it go. There was no point in pushing when Alice was like this, and the real Alice—the one Ellen loved—was still in there somewhere.

"Come tomorrow? We'll talk," Ellen said.

Alice reached out and squeezed her hand. "I'll try." At the door, she called back, "Where's he taking you for dinner?"

"Sotto Voce."

"Very nice, very nice," Alice half-whispered, hurrying out. "Good luck."

Chapter Twenty-Three

Sotto Voce hadn't changed since the last time Ellen had been there. She had taken Taber for a mother-and-daughter dinner before Taber left for her freshman year at college.

Taber had sat in the candlelight, a fresh-faced girl who had pulled her hair up into a chignon and stepped into a satiny slip dress with rhinestone straps. To Ellen, though, she had still looked far too young to head off to New York City alone. The world was ready to claim this girl, though she was still a child.

William looked more at home in the candlelight. "I haven't been here in years," he said.

"I was thinking the same thing. I brought my daughter before she started college."

"The fashion major?"

"Yes, Taber, fashion merchandising."

William sliced through one of his tenderloin tips. "Empire Fashion Academy—she's in the right place, from what I've heard. We had a girl transfer there a few years back."

"Taber's amazing," Ellen said. "Right from the start, she knew what she wanted, and she went after it. We are so different. It amazes me."

"I'd like to meet her."

Ellen smiled, but she hadn't told Taber or Jimmy she was seeing someone. Dating? What did they call it now? She didn't know him well enough. This whole thing could end at any moment, and she'd never see him again. There was no reason to ruffle feathers.

They stuck to the safe stuff. During the appetizers, splitting clams casino and prosciutto-wrapped scallops, they discussed Alice's house. William said he'd never been able to find the "arts and crafts style" bungalow of his dreams. "When I do, I'll snap it up in a minute, and there I'll stay."

"A house is a big commitment." Ellen twirled her fork in her plate of fettuccine alfredo. They did it right here: not overloaded with the heavy sauce, but rinsed in it, smooth and sweet with sprigs of fresh parsley dotted throughout. "But there are bigger ones."

"For those brave enough."

"Or young and foolish enough."

"To the young and foolish." William raised his wine glass. "To the delusions of love."

Ellen clinked her glass into his. "You know, the food here hasn't slipped. Usually restaurants are uneven. Chefs come and go, or the place changes hands. The quality or the service starts to slide."

"See? You already talk like an insider. I hope you're seriously considering the pastry shop idea."

"It's percolating." Ellen tapped her temple. "There would be the startup costs to get over first. But I think I could manage, for a short time. I'd have to hit the ground running."

She didn't tell William how the notion of the pastry shop came to her now, invading her thoughts at all hours of the day, and once when she woke to a night sky of black silk with a brilliant white slip of moon hanging outside her window.

Just Desserts. She pictured a sunny seating area: tables and chairs sprinkled about, coffee, fragrant and brewing in the corner, soft instrumental music—the harps and cellos she loved—in the background. She imagined transporting the calm clarity of Arborview, the silence that did not condemn, that simply took you in and urged you onward.

"Do you know anything about starting a business?" she asked.

"I do, but I don't think you want my advice."

"Why not?"

"Years ago, I opened a wine and cigar bar outside Boston. It was a total flop, and truth be told, I was the reason."

"That's hard to believe." He seemed so competent and thoughtful, cautious, too—which must be a good trait in business.

"I thought my finance degree equipped me to take on anything," he said. "But I knew nothing about marketing or advertising, or weak, oversaturated markets. In other words, I was an overconfident jerk, and I got what was coming to me." He took a sip of his red wine.

"It was a learning experience, though, right?"

Ellen saw a grateful glint in his eye. "Do you always see the glass as half full?" he asked.

"Oh, I'm not as upbeat as I may seem."

"Moments of doubt and uncertainty?"

"More like years."

He reached over the table and took her hand, so their fingers rested, entwined, on the smooth, white tablecloth. "Any way I can help with the shop, just ask. I'd be happy to take a look at your books."

Ellen felt a surge of new protectiveness. She wanted this shop, if it ever saw the light of day, to be hers alone, at least for now. "How sweet of you. But I'm still in the mulling stages."

"It's our secret then," he said.

Ours. As if they were already a couple, a fused entity, jointly experiencing what came now, so there would always be more than one side of the story. Ellen slid her hand away from his. Maybe she needed to slow things down.

The hostess passed, leading a couple to a table in the corner. She was tall, Hispanic, not heavy but not slim either, stocky, wearing a billowy white blouse and a black skirt that looked—and must have felt—too tight. Her ankles wobbled with each step in her pointy high-heel pumps. She seated the couple, gave them a tight, perfunctory smile, and handed them menus. Turning away, she brought one hand to her forehead and closed her eyes.

When she passed again, Ellen saw the dull sheen of too much sticky spray in her dark, upswept hair and the shadowy half-moons beneath her eyes. There was something distantly familiar about her, an echo of someone Ellen had seen before. And then it hit her. "That's Rosa Escamilla's mother."

William's fork stopped in midair.

"Rosa mentioned her mother is a hostess here. I'd forgotten. You can see a resemblance, kind of, a little."

"Yes, I can see it, too. Did I tell you? It looks like Rosa could get her financial aid," William said. "We put together a package, provided Seasons Culinary College agrees."

"But she hasn't been accepted yet."

"This is preliminary, but going over the projected numbers and the available funding, it could work."

A shiver ran up Ellen's spine. "I'll write her a recommendation." She could feel William's curious gaze. "I like to see good kids get a break."

If Rosa could tune out the naysayers and hear herself, then one morning far in the future maybe she would wake, look in the mirror, and know exactly who she was and where she had arrived. Maybe Ellen could, too.

She looked into William's eyes. "Why did you never marry?" she asked. "I'm curious."

He looked surprised for an instant, then he shrugged. "It's a fair question. I wish I had a better answer."

"Give it a shot."

He swirled the dark wine in his glass. "There's so much senseless tragedy in the world." He sighed. "Tying yourself to anyone—to anything—believing in permanence never made sense to me."

It occurred to Ellen he might think she was vetting him out as marriage material. That was the last thing she had meant to imply. "Permanence doesn't have to mean marriage," she said.

"But love still means commitment of some sort, doesn't it?"

She couldn't disagree. "Yeah, I guess it does. Sticking around—through thick and thin—all that. I guess it does."

William cleared his throat, made a show of it, as if to change the subject.

"Ah, maybe you're right." She cracked a smile. "It's not like it's guaranteed. I'm living proof. I could never regret my kids, but I do think I messed up along the way."

It was the truth. Why not tell it like it really is? For once. Say the things she should have said, when she was barely out of girlhood and Zach appeared, the answer to a prayer—as everyone had told her—she had never prayed.

"You're in good company," William said. "Tell me more."

So she did. Sitting before his admiring eyes, Ellen let years of brittle denial slip away, along with the last remnants of her guardedness with William. Nothing she said seemed to surprise him, so she let the whole story spill out: the quiet dignity of the sisters at Mercy High School; her mother's sharp-tongued insistence on teaching; meeting Zach in the dreamy days when she was first living on her own; and those cozy, cossetted nights in the nursery, rocking baby Taber—and then Jimmy—in the dark hours while the rest of the world slept.

He ordered another round. They talked into the night, until the last lingering patrons trickled out and busboys cleaned the tables, until the parking lot sat still and empty and Rosa's mother had long since gone home.

Chapter Twenty-Four

"Your Reach Recipes," Ellen told the class, "are so inspiring. I'm surprised how bold and adventurous you guys are."

A few appreciative nods from the students seated around the prep table, as Ellen lifted the list before her. "Should I share a few?"

"Go ahead!" said Tim, a skinny freshman whose blue jeans hung off his hips. He'd shown little aptitude for baking, but Ellen had grown to appreciate his weird brand of enthusiasm.

"We'll start with yours, then, Tim," she said.

"Feel free, Mrs. C." He pushed the cap back on his head.

"Yorkshire curd tarts," Ellen said.

"Yep."

"Turds?" Rosa's brother, Javier, laughed. "Where'd you get that?"

"Curds!" Tim sneered. "My English grandmother eats 'em with tea. She loves them. I'm gonna surprise her."

"What a great idea," Ellen said. "I bake for the people I love, too. I think a lot of people do." Tim would never be able to pull off the complex little tarts alone, but she'd convince him to let her help.

"You're gonna poison your grandma, dude," said Anthony, a lanky boy with acne scars on his cheeks.

"Hey, no grandmas are getting poisoned on my watch," Javier said.

"And you, Javi." Ellen turned to him. "Let's see." She glanced down at the paper and then peered over her glasses at him. "Brownies? Your Reach Recipe is brownies?"

"These aren't your everyday brownies, Mrs. Cahill," he said. "I got a secret recipe."

"Yeah, Duncan Hines," Rosa said.

Everyone laughed.

"That's jealousy talking," Javier said. "These brownies are gonna knock your socks off."

"I hope so," Ellen said. "Okay, let's talk ingredient lists. Come on, everyone."

It was dark when class ended. Early evening, but the sun was long gone in mid-November. The trees across campus lifted bare arms and crooked fingers across the sky. Only the pines bristled, brave and alone.

Rosa stayed in her seat while Ellen was packing up. Something in the girl's expression, excitement battling fear, betrayed her. Ellen waited until the last student had left before she asked, "You want a recommendation for Seasons Culinary College?"

"How'd you know?"

"I can read minds."

Rosa smiled, but she looked a little doubtful. "I'll send you the link. It's super easy."

"Of course. I'm happy to do it. You'll be a shoo-in."

The girl still looked skeptical.

"How is your mom?" Ellen asked. "I saw her the other night at Sotto Voce."

"You did? She never said anything." Rosa

frowned. "How'd you even know it was her?"

"You told me she works there, remember? I saw her from a distance, but I could tell she was your mom. We didn't get a chance to talk."

Was relief crossing the girl's face? "My mother and I had it out," she blurted. "I told her I'm going to Seasons Culinary College, if I get in, and there's not a single thing she can do about it."

Ellen sat down on a stool across from her. "So you threw down the gauntlet, huh?"

A stony resolve stiffened Rosa's jaw. "I told her what the deal is. She can either accept it or shut up about it."

"Whoa." Ellen spread her fingers across the counter between them. The bitterness jarred her.

Rosa glanced away. "I'm sorry."

"You don't have to be sorry. I'm just surprised. I thought your mom would come around."

"You don't know her."

Obviously, Rosa's mama was a more formidable foe than Ellen had imagined.

"Hang on a minute." Ellen went to the refrigerator in the corner. She reached in and brought out a sheet pan full of brown cakes in small porcelain-white ramekins. She crossed the room and set the pan on the table before Rosa. "I brought these to share today, but we ran out of time. My Reach Recipe, once upon a time."

Rosa studied the little cakes. "Soufflés?"

"Not just any soufflé. They're Julia Child's Six-Ingredient Chocolate Ganache Soufflé Cakes."

Rosa's interest was piqued. "Oh, yeah? Too bad we didn't get to try them."

"Help yourself." Ellen grabbed two spoons from a drawer. "These were a reach for me when I first got married. I hadn't been baking long, and soufflé seemed very exotic. So I made them for my husband as a surprise one night."

"Mmm." Rosa licked her spoon.

"Only the recipe flopped," Ellen said. "I took it out of the mold too soon, or it never jelled right. It was lumpy pudding, a runny, brown mess. Looked like diarrhea. Sorry, not an image you welcome when you're eating."

Rosa laughed. "Javi would have loved this story."

"But I kept on baking. Now, I could make this soufflé in my sleep, and…"

"It's perfect," Rosa whispered.

Ellen tasted a spoonful, the chocolate draping, smooth and rich. "My husband's gone now, but you know what, Rosa? I'm still baking."

The girl took Ellen in, her dark eyes still and deep. "What did you think of my Reach Recipe?"

"French Napoleon. Very impressive. You're brave, tackling all those layers."

"It's my mother's favorite. She had it on her honeymoon, a long time ago. I've been hearing about that cake my whole life."

Ellen dug into the ramekin, savoring the sweet silkiness, the subtle bite of bitterness. She wanted to let Rosa talk, let her get it all off her chest.

"I know this girl who goes to Yale," Rosa said. "She's into baking, too. Not as much as I am, but she's really interested. She admires me, you know?"

"I'll bet."

"She's been sick, but she's doing better now."

Rosa nodded. "I've got a feeling she's going to be fine."

"Introduce her to your mom. Maybe you can all bake together?"

Rosa glanced away. "The thing is, I bet Sarah's parents were crazy about her going to Yale."

"Probably."

"I bet they're the kind of people who would support anything Sarah wanted."

"Maybe."

Rosa looked down at the little soufflé. She swallowed hard.

"Do you want to take these home?" Ellen pushed the tray toward Rosa. "I made so many."

Rosa looked up. "Do people in families really forgive each other?"

Ellen saw the fear in the girl's eyes. "What do you mean?"

"I mean, if things gets really bad, like ugly, are things ever the same again?"

Oh, at eighteen, at nineteen, how set in stone the world seemed. The absolute truths of childhood, the foolish exaggerations of adolescence.

"Maybe things aren't meant to stay the same," Ellen said. She put her hand on top of Rosa's and left it there. If only she could help the girl understand that it's better to gamble with this pain now, and not years later, when regret would make it so much worse.

Chapter Twenty-Five

"I'm going to end it," Alice said. "I don't see any other way."

The golden tones of late afternoon threw shadows over the sidewalk. They walked through Alice's neighborhood, toward Main Street, along the streets of cozy bungalows and colonials with their sense of permanence and business-as-usual calm.

Ellen placed her gloved hands into the pockets of her coat. "What does Ned say?" she asked.

Alice gave a hard laugh. "He wants to marry me."

"You're kidding."

"He's getting clingy. He's making plans, asking me to leave Earle. He even found me a lawyer."

"And Earle has no idea." Ellen grimaced. She saw a flash of Earle's scholarly spectacles as he squinted at the intricate wooden feathers of one of his birds.

"I don't think so." Alice sighed. "Though maybe it would force the issue."

"But you are ending things?"

"I don't want to get married again. Ever. If Ned would leave things the way they are, we'd be fine."

A car passed. Ellen listened to the engine fade. "You'd still be lying to Earle."

"Leave Earle out of this. I'm trying to figure out what *I* should do."

"I can't leave Earle out."

"Then why are you here?"

The two stopped walking. "What an asinine question," Ellen said. "What is wrong with you?"

Alice bowed her head. "I'm sorry," she said, walking on again.

"Look, I'm not claiming the high ground. But maybe Ned's right. You can't stay on the fence forever."

Alice picked up her pace, and Ellen knew it was best to back off for now. Red leaves skittered across the sidewalk. The faint whiff of smoke from a distant chimney drifted over the rooftops. Such a pretty neighborhood, Ellen thought. Maybe she should move down here and be in the center of things. But how she would miss the woods surrounding her yellow house, and the great, dark silence of the night.

"Tell me more about William," Alice said.

"There's not much to tell."

"You're sleeping with a new man, after twenty-plus years of marriage, and there's not much to tell?"

"Okay. He's great actually. But we're not, you know, set in stone or anything. We're enjoying each other's company."

"I'll bet."

"And he's been a big help with my shop. He owned a small business once, and he put me in touch with this volunteer group called SCORE—stands for Service Corps of Retired Executives. It's a nonprofit. They're great mentors, and they've walked me through everything—business plan, customer base, financing, competition."

"Your shop." Alice shook her head. "And all these years, I'd never thought of you as a businessperson."

"Well, it's more like a creation. It's a business, yeah, but it's based on something I love doing, and something I love giving."

They reached the village green. The branches of the oak in the middle were bare now, the fountain that burbled all summer still. The American flag hung listlessly from its pole high above the War Memorial plaque.

They crossed the street as the sun ducked behind a blanket of cindery gray clouds.

Alice looped her arm through Ellen's. "Well, it sounds like you've got it all figured out," she said.

Ellen sighed. "You know that's not true. The grass is just looking greener to you right now."

They walked toward the fountain, out of habit, a light drizzle dotting the pavement. "Remember all the times we brought the kids here to play when they were little?" Alice asked. "Those were good days."

"They were. You just need to figure out now what you want." Ellen wasn't sure Alice was listening anymore. "I know it's easier said than done."

Alice's gaze followed the passing cars.

"You owe it to yourself and to Earle," Ellen said.

Alice smirked. "I owe all sorts of people all sorts of allegiances, and I haven't been very good at fulfilling them. Truth is, I'm a deadbeat."

"Ah, what a load of crap."

"Such a foul mouth." Alice winked. "You know, I think William must be having a good influence on you."

****

He called later that night, as Ellen was lying in bed, his voice husky and tinged with longing. Her insides lurched with expectation at the sound. It was like being twenty-four again, watching from the window as Zach's shiny silver coupe pulled up at her apartment building.

They discussed Thanksgiving, and the planned dinner with Zach.

"At least his girlfriend—Lydia?—isn't coming," William said.

"A small blessing," Ellen said. "But all of us around the Thanksgiving table. I'm not sure I'm up to it."

"I wish we could zip off to Vermont and rent a cabin. Picture it: roaring fire, little turkey in the oven, bottle of wine, and just us."

Ellen groaned. "Don't tempt me. I need to see my kids. This is big for them, the first holiday after the divorce. They need to know we're still here for them." Ellen rolled onto her back. "Do you ever wish you'd had children?"

He didn't hesitate. "I would have screwed it up."

She laughed. "Please. I can't picture you as anything but kind."

"Kind isn't always enough."

After they'd wished each other good night, Ellen lay in the dark for what seemed a long time. Maybe in the spring they could go to Vermont. Stowe was beautiful then, with the mountains ripening into green and the swollen streams flowing fast and deep with run-off. Alice would enjoy picking out a few nice outfits for Ellen to pack. She could nail the right outfit for any occasion. Hopefully, by then Alice's situation would be sorted out. Ellen couldn't recall ever having seen Alice at such loose ends. What was different this time?

The phone rang again. Had he forgotten to tell her

something? Ellen reached for the receiver.

"Hello?"

"I hope it's not too late."

Zach.

"No, it's not." Ellen grimaced.

"Your line was busy, so I figured you had to be awake."

"You were right."

"Are the kids okay?"

"Fine, as far as I know."

"You weren't talking to one of them?"

"No, I wasn't. Zach, what's up?"

"Thanksgiving. I don't want to pressure you, but…"

"Yes, it's fine. We'll eat together."

"Really? Okay, good. I mean, great. I'm looking forward to it. What can I bring? Dessert. Ha! I guess not. That's you, right?"

"Not this year," Ellen said. "We're eating out. I'm making a reservation at the inn."

"You're not cooking?"

Was that shock in his voice?

"No, I'm not." The words resonated within Ellen. "I'm not hosting dinner, but I'll attend. We'll all attend."

"You're such a great cook…"

"But that isn't the point, is it?"

Zach coughed. "No, it isn't."

"This is for Taber and Jimmy."

"Yes, being together for them."

Being together. The words made her stomach turn. Hadn't they been together enough? "I'm sure we'll have a nice time," she said.

"I'm sure we will." He hung up without saying goodbye, and in her head, Ellen heard Alice say, "Screw him."

Chapter Twenty-Six

The night before Jimmy and Taber arrived, Ellen stayed at William's. She wouldn't see him again until the weekend was over, when everyone would be gone, and her life could swerve back into its newfound path.

"And this is for you," she said, placing the pumpkin pie she'd made the night before on his kitchen counter.

"Ellen, you're too much." In low-slung blue jeans and white button-up shirt, tails hanging, stocking feet, and rumpled hair, William was undeniably sexy. And why should she deny it? Ellen was drawn to him, captivated by him. She hadn't felt this way in years. The arc of his lips, the smooth, easy strength of his hands. He was more than Zach with the sharp edges sanded down. He was something completely different. New worlds wait around every corner. Who had told her this? Alice, in one of her pep talks in the numb days after the divorce was final.

"Your Thanksgiving dessert is on me," she said. "I wish it could be the entire meal."

"Next year." He bent to kiss her neck, then put his arm around her and steered her toward the living room.

She liked his townhouse. It was part of a small development, fifteen units off a winding road in a residential suburb. "All the benefits of home ownership with no grass to cut, no leaves to rake, or snow to shovel," he had said the first time she visited.

There was a small gas fireplace with a ceramic log that left no ashes; a big bay window; a whitewashed galley kitchen, and two bedrooms upstairs.

William flipped the fireplace switch, and flames appeared. He sat at the end of the couch, facing her.

"I could get used to this," Ellen said.

"I hope so." He lifted one of her feet and began rubbing it.

His hands were so warm. Ellen groaned. "I'll be glad when this weekend is over. I wish I could hide out up in the tree house. The kids named it 'Arborview' back in the day."

He laughed. "I'd like to climb up there and see it."

She smiled, but Arborview was her refuge, her private retreat. The sacred stillness, the softly filtered light. She wasn't ready to share it.

He started on her other foot. "Have you thought any more about selling your house?"

"No. I'm hoping my shop will solve that problem. I don't want to be forced out."

He nodded. "I've got a good feeling about it."

"From your lips…"

"Put in a request the next time you're up in your Arborview."

Ellen smiled. "What do you think I've been doing?"

Chapter Twenty-Seven

Rosa cooked Thanksgiving dinner, the whole thing. There was a golden turkey breast marinated and roasted in a sauce of garlic, cumin, lime, and aji peppers—like her grandmother had always done. For a starch, the purple potato salad Mama loved, and for Javi, mac and cheese, his favorite.

She had spent days assembling the ingredients. She started the meal with hot bowls of *Sopa de Camotes a la Arequipe*, a Peruvian sweet potato soup that packed sweet, spicy, and smoky into each spoonful. She threw in green beans, candied yams, and pumpkin pie, too, because it wouldn't be Thanksgiving without them. She dotted the kitchen table with little bowls of nuts and olives.

"You put the hotshots I work with to shame," Mama said, scooping potato salad onto her plate.

"The girl's a natural," Javi said. "Born to do it."

Mama cleared her throat.

"How about you, Javi?" Rosa said. "When you making your Reach Recipe? The morning it's due?"

"Why not? It's brownies. Maybe I'll buy some and put them on a plate."

Rosa laughed. "Don't you dare."

"Your head's getting bigger every day." Mama wagged her fork at Javi. "Maybe this Niagara business isn't such a good idea after all."

"Too late," Javi said. "Come January, this boy is gone. Happy New Year!"

Mama might have been scolding, but she was smiling, and in her eyes, Rosa saw the tender pride she had always reserved for Javi. He was her saving grace. Rosa had always known this. She had always worked around it. Even now, when the Seasons Culinary College application had been sent, Mama said nothing. Rosa knew better than to keep bringing up the subject. Javi could hammer way. Rosa had to nibble at the edges of things until she reached the center.

"You keep your head in your books and your hands off Tilda," Mama said.

"Not on Thanksgiving, Mama." Javi shook his head.

What if Rosa got into Seasons Culinary College and wanted to take off for Rhode Island with a boyfriend in tow? What would Mama do? She'd have two heart attacks and a stroke. The good-girl double standard was alive and kicking in this house. Shouldn't Mama know better? What had believing all that crap gotten her in life?

Rosa stabbed at the turkey on her plate.

****

"I don't know why you're even doing this," Alice had hissed when Ellen told her about the Thanksgiving Day plan. "Let him sit home alone. And isn't it weird, darling Lydia's old bat of a mother didn't invite him? Maybe the bloom's coming off the rose."

Sitting now at a corner table, Ellen wasn't sure why she was doing this either. Zach sat across from her, with Taber and Jimmy at their sides. The meal was not what Ellen would have typically prepared for

174

Thanksgiving. But this wasn't a typical Thanksgiving.

"Turkey's not as moist as yours, Ellen," Zach said.

"But they've redeemed themselves with the gravy—not a sodium bath—and the scalloped potatoes aren't bad," Ellen said.

"A restaurant is never as good as home on Thanksgiving," Taber said. In a cotton candy-pink cashmere twinset and pearls, which Zach had given her an hour earlier, Taber had taken a hard fashion turn to the traditional for the day. "But we're going to have coffee at the house after. Right, Mom?"

"Sure, only Daddy has to run, remember?"

Taber shrugged. "Of course." The hint of bitterness in her voice made Ellen and Zach exchange a glance.

"Maybe we can take the bikes out on Saturday if the weather holds up," Jimmy said.

"Absolutely." Zach glanced at his watch. "Let me…check my schedule first, but it should be fine. I hear the state park trails are nice and clear."

Zach had given Jimmy an early Christmas present: an off-road mountain bike with a bright blue paint job and fat black tires. Zach had an almost identical bike. The two had mountain biked together since Jimmy was in middle school. It was the only time Zach ventured into the forests Jimmy loved so much.

The bike was out on the rack on Zach's car. He was going to drop it off at the house after dinner.

The "drop off" reference had pleased Ellen. She didn't want him coming inside for coffee, or for anything else. She wasn't going to wind up the evening playing hostess to Zach. She wanted to get in a call to William tonight. She hadn't told any of them about William. She kept him to herself, carried him around like a warm, glowing secret protecting her from whatever the day would bring.

But she could tell them other things. "I do have a little news," she said.

All eyes turned to her.

"It looks like I'm going to become a businesswoman. I'm toying with the idea—more than toying actually—of opening a pastry shop. There's a vacant store on the green right now, on the South Street side, I've got my eye on. It's the perfect size, great morning light, big windows."

"On the green?" Taber said. "What was there before?"

"Zelda's, the yarn shop."

"Oh, I didn't know Zelda went out of business."

"She retired."

"You rock, Mom," Jimmy said. "You'll have customers lined up out the door and down the street."

"Ellen, what inspired this?" Zach eyes were wide. "I've never heard you mention…"

"I wish I'd done it years ago."

"You came up with this on your own?" Zach asked. "I mean, no one suggested it?"

Ellen put down her fork. "You find it hard to believe?"

"Not at all. I'm just surprised."

"These are surprising times."

In the moment of silence that followed, a new force built within Ellen, a shield—no, a sword—a way to clear a path, an incipient hardness pushing forward, refusing to acquiesce, refusing to look away.

"I think it's awesome," Jimmy said. "Congratulations, Mom."

Ellen laughed. "Why the heck not, right?"

"Yeah, why the heck not," Jimmy said.

"Taber?" Ellen turned to her. "I'm counting on you to come up with a design scheme for the shop. I need to 'brand' myself, I've been told. I need colors and a logo, and who knows what else."

"I can take a look, too, if you'd like," Zach said. "Branding is right up my alley."

"I think a woman's touch is needed." Ellen reached to squeeze Taber's hand. "And that woman is right here."

"I'll do a bang-up job for you, Mom," Taber said. "Who can capture your essence better than me?"

"No one," Ellen laughed. "No one ever has."

Zach refilled his wine glass.

An unexpected wave lifted Ellen. She had thrown him for a loop. She still had a few cards up her sleeve. "You know this dinner really is pretty good," she said. "We should keep it on the list for next year."

They drove back to the house afterward, Zach's Subaru wagon following Ellen's old Audi, as the sky grew dark around them. The motion sensor lights above the garage doors glowed to life when the cars pulled up.

Jimmy wrestled the bike from the rack and gave Zach a high-five, their hands meeting in a clap.

"See you Saturday, Dad."

"You're on," Zach said.

Jimmy wheeled the bike into the garage.

"Good night, Daddy," Taber said, sweeping in to kiss Zach's cheek. "Thanks for the pearls. I don't know how you knew I needed a short strand."

"Your old man's got a good memory."

When the door to the house closed behind their

children, Zach and Ellen stood alone in the spotlight of the driveway. Zach looked different, altered somehow. There was the same structure, the features, of the man she knew, but some foreign, nascent force had emerged, making him alien to her.

"It went well, don't you think?" he asked.

"I do."

"Taber is a bit off."

"A bit."

"Their grades held up well this semester, so that's a good sign," he said.

"It's an adjustment. I'd say they're doing remarkably well."

Zach plunged his hands into his pants pockets. "And you, Ellen, this shop, wow. You must be pretty excited."

"I don't want to count my chickens, you know, but, yeah, things are looking up."

"Good, good." Zach took his hands out again, cupped them in front of his mouth and blew to warm them.

If he was angling for an invitation inside, he wasn't going to get one. Ellen glanced toward the backyard and thought of Arborview. She turned to face Zach. "I hope you enjoy the holidays. We'll talk about Christmas later?"

He nodded. "Thanks. How, ah, are Alice and Earle? Do you hear much from them?"

"I've been hearing much from Alice for twenty years. Nothing has changed there."

"I ran into her in Hartford last week. She was on an errand, having lunch with her accountant, a guy named Ned."

The name jolted Ellen. "Yes, Ned. He does her books. Alice says her business is growing. There must be a lot of speech-impaired people in this town."

"She's probably sleeping with him."

Ellen stopped cold. "What?"

"Ned—Alice is probably sleeping with him."

"Why would you say that?"

Zach shrugged. "It wouldn't surprise me."

Ellen pushed down the stir of the old antagonism. Had she forgotten already how maddeningly smug he could be, with his preachy absolutism, his predictions and pronouncements?

"But maybe this will surprise you," he said. "Lydia wants a baby."

Ellen's mouth dropped open. She forced it into a smile. "How terrific. I wish you both the best."

"Ellen?" A tremor of exasperation crossed Zach's face. "I've done all this already. I don't want to go through it again. I don't know if I can."

Ellen stepped back. "Isn't this something you should discuss with Lydia? It has nothing to do with me." Her heart quickened, a jerky thump-thump tickling the back of her throat.

"She says she understands if I want out," Zach said. "She's willing to go it alone."

"Then the ball is in your court."

Lydia must have already seen she could do without him. The woman rose a notch in Ellen's estimation.

"She says there's a hole in her life." Zach grimaced. "Why are people always worried about holes? Why can't they focus on what they have?"

The irony of the question coming from him was too big for comment. Ellen brushed off her hands. "I can't

179

tell you. But I do think you moved too fast. You ricocheted into…"

"Maybe so."

Zach looked at the ground a moment and then stared up at the house. The windows upstairs—Taber's room, Jimmy's room—glowed.

Ellen looked away. He could turn his bleary longing gaze elsewhere. It wasn't only that he had left her, which might have happened anyway and would have been painful enough. But he had replaced her first. He must have believed he couldn't possibly be at fault if another woman could love him so readily. Zach thought like this even in matters of the heart. X cancels out Y.

What would not have occurred to him is that grieving honors the dead, even the living dead. He had not planned on any grieving. He simply intended to move on.

Ellen sighed. "Go home, Zach."

Was he wincing or just getting cold?

"I'm sure it will all work out," she said.

"I'm glad someone is sure."

"Good night."

Ellen turned and started toward the door, but Zach said, "Ellen?"

"Yes?" She stopped to face him.

"I'm sorry."

"I am, too," she said, and she found a smile to give this man, her one-time friend and dream of love, standing before her now, growing cold and seeking something she no longer had to give him. "There's plenty of sorry going around these days."

He nodded.

"Good night," she said.

"Good night."

Ellen watched his car retreat down the driveway and head up the road until its red taillights disappeared around a bend. Then she lifted her gaze. The sky above soared so far, and was so dark, so unfathomable, it was impossible to know what lay beyond. The astronomers are only scratching the surface, she thought. We don't know. We don't really know anything.

Chapter Twenty-Eight

Mrs. Ciccarino had died overnight. Rosa took a peek at her chart, which someone—who was going to be in a lot of trouble—had left on the sink in the staff bathroom. Mrs. Ciccarino was eighty-nine. Well, that was pretty old.

Rosa squinted at the chart—lots of numbers, the doctor's scrawled handwriting she couldn't even read. She shouldn't leave the chart in the bathroom. This medical stuff was private, top secret.

Rosa washed her hands and took the chart. She'd bring it back to Mrs. Ciccarino's room and leave it on the bed she'd just finished stripping. She still had to wipe down the furniture. Hopefully, a nurse would stop by, see the chart, and take it where it belonged.

She passed Sarah's room. The door was open. Sarah sat at the small table before the window, writing in a little red book. "Hey," Rosa said, stepping into the room. "How was the pie?" She'd given Sarah a slice of leftover apple pie Mama had brought home from Sotto Voce. *These people waste food like nobody's business.*

"You got me on a good day." Sarah turned around, smiling. "I'm feeling pretty peppy. I ate the whole piece."

A surge of joy warmed Rosa. "There's nothing like food to make things right. I mean, to make you feel like everything's gonna be okay."

Sarah sat back in her chair. "On days like this, I know I'm getting out of here." The metal pole with the plastic bag, full of a clear fluid, was parked next to her, a thin tube connecting the bag to a patch of bandages on her hand. "The literature is full of amazing stories, of people who defy the doctors, and beat the odds."

Rosa nodded, her ponytail bouncing on her back. "There's a TV show all about this. *Medical Miracles*, it's called." Mama liked to watch the program with Rosa, but only to snort over the tearful surprise cures, the new beginnings. *They all getting paid to say this. Enough money and—bang—you got a miracle.*

"I'm keeping a record of my journey." Sarah lifted the red journal. "I'm going to write a book when this is all over."

Rosa's heart jumped. "Good for you. You gotta take control of things." She watched Sarah's face for a reaction. "We can become whoever we want to become."

"You got it." Sarah sat up straighter. "I'm a fighter. I'm not giving up, not ever." Her voice dropped. "I made it out of here two nights ago. Did you hear?"

"Made it out?"

Sarah giggled. "I've been craving pizza all week. I mean, *really* craving. They won't let me have it, for some asinine reason. So last night I waited until the coast was clear. Then I pulled on clothes and caught the bus across the street." She pointed out her window. "It pulls up at 7:20 every weeknight. From there, it was easy. I got off when I saw the first pizza joint on the boulevard."

Rosa started breathing again. "But what if something had happened?"

Sarah waved a hand. "It did. I ate three huge slices of pepperoni and felt like crap the next day. I couldn't get out of bed. But it was worth it."

"Were you caught?"

"Oh, yeah, they were frantic here. My parents were beside themselves. I feel bad about it, but it's my life. I can't live it, or end it, the way they want. I've got to do what's right for me."

Rosa shook her head in disbelief. "An authentic life," she said. Where had she heard that phrase? Her literature class last semester?

"Exactly!" A tired, yet undeniably content, smile spread across Sarah's face.

Rosa was a fighter, too, but Sarah's ferocity and daring were amazing. "Not everybody thinks this way," Rosa said. "Some people give up, and they want you to give up, too. They want you to accept, or be, something you're not."

Sarah sniffed. "The haters. They break your heart."

A twinge of guilt hit Rosa. Mama wasn't a hater. "Maybe they don't know any better."

Sarah shrugged.

"Hey, I'm going to see if we can make a Napoleon together," Rosa said. "I'm making one now for a class project, so hopefully I'll get the recipe down."

"Can we do it here?" Sarah's eyes widened. "I'd love to."

"I'll find out."

"My parents will back you. Which means a lot around here."

Rosa glanced at the clock on the wall. "Crap, I gotta run. Sorry. But get a little rest, okay?"

"Sure."

"Promise?"

"Cross my heart." Sarah traced a finger over her chest once, twice, then closed her eyes.

Rosa beat it down the hall to Mrs. Ciccarino's room. The last of the daylight was slipping through the windows as Rosa dropped the chart on the bed. She pulled on fresh rubber gloves, the heavy yellow ones that made her feel safe, insulated, from the things happening in this place. Cleaning the rooms after patients died was the part of the job she liked least. An eerie stillness hung in the air when the rooms were suddenly vacated. The bed was like an empty stage, stripped bare, no family members sniffling, crumpled tissues in their hands, no doctors hovering at a respectful distance. All the bottles and cups and basins gone from the tabletop.

Rosa would never let Mama die in one of these places—hater or not. When Mama got old and sick, Rosa would take her to her own house. She'd have one by then, a big one with a long dining room for all the parties she'd throw and carpeting upstairs and one of those deep bathtubs with the Jacuzzi jets.

"You must be planning to bake a lot of cakes," Javi had said when she once confessed this dream to him.

Rosa took a sponge and the spray bottle of the strong, bleach stuff they told her to clean the rooms with after clients had "passed." She sprayed the table and was wiping it down when a knock came at the open door.

"*Hola.* I don't want to disturb you." The reverend, standing in the threshold, a soft smile on his lips. "Sorry."

Rosa smiled. "You're not disturbing me." His

goofy apologies were one of the things she liked about him.

"I forgot my glasses." He pointed at the window, where his glasses sat on the ledge. "Left them last night when I was with the family." He crossed the room. "I don't want to hold you up."

"You're not holding me up." Rosa spritzed the tabletop.

"I can see you're busy." The reverend sat down in the armchair near the window, making himself at home. "You know, I admire young people today. It seems times are tougher than when we were kids, my generation. Everything is more expensive, more competitive, difficult in so many ways. You've got to work harder, be smarter."

"It's true," Rosa said. "I'm working my way through school."

"How admirable, Rosa!"

Her name rolled off his lips. She liked the way it sounded. She realized she probably had a little crush on this guy, old as he was.

"I'll bet your family is proud of you."

"Well, it's just me and my mom. And my brother."

"I bet they're proud, then. Especially your mother."

"Oh yeah. She tells me all the time how proud she is."

"Because she knows how lucky she is, having you for a daughter." The reverend leaned back in the armchair, stretching his legs.

Rosa gave a little smile. Her lying was ridiculous, but he was so kind, and she wanted him to think good things about her, to think she was a nice girl from a nice family. "My brother is going to the Niagara Institute of

Technology in January," she said.

"Two ambitious kids in the same family? Well, your parents did something right."

"Yeah, they did." Her parents. Whatever. Rosa gave the reverend a sideways glance. He was sitting still, lips pursed, considering the next helpful thing to say. That's the way he was. She would have liked him as a father. A hollow pang. A tickle in the back of her throat.

Another rap at the door. Mr. Janssen, in his black overcoat, car keys dangling from his hand. "You still need a ride home? Hey, Rosa."

"Indeed, I do." The reverend stood. "Car's in the shop." He nodded at Rosa.

She spritzed hard and whipped the sponge across the table.

Mr. Janssen glanced at the stripped bed. "The family settled their account today. That chart shouldn't be here. I'll get someone from medical to pick it up. "

"It's late," the reverend said. "Are you almost through, Rosa?"

"Yep, I'll be able to catch the five-twenty bus."

"On the corner of Hull Avenue?" Mr. Janssen asked. "That's a hike. Would you like a ride home?"

Rosa stopped. "Uh, you don't have to do…"

"It's no problem. We're heading out that way," Mr. Janssen said.

Of course he knew where she lived, her town, from all her financial aid papers. "Thanks," Rosa said. "I need a few minutes to finish here and get my stuff. Can I meet you in the parking lot?"

When they were gone, she gathered her cleaning supplies and stashed them in the hall utility closet. She snapped off the light in Mrs. Ciccarino's room. It was always awful turning off the lights the last time after a patient died. Rosa felt like she was erasing them.

Back in the kitchen, she pulled on her coat and gathered her backpack and umbrella. It had been raining when she arrived, but the skies had cleared. Still, it was cold. The bus ride home was a grinding, stop-and-go, forty-five-minute haul. She was thrilled to get out of it.

Rosa stepped out into the cold shock of the night. The wind was picking up, she could see a riffle running through the pine trees shielding the asphalt lot.

Mr. Janssen had a dedicated "staff" parking space on the side of the building. He and the reverend were sitting in the front seats. Rosa slid into the back and closed the door. "Nice car."

"Thank you. I cranked the heat." As if reading her thoughts, he added, "It'll warm up quick."

It was a nice car. Leather seats, glowing dials, quiet and smooth when he pulled onto the road and then onto the highway, a lot nicer than anything Mama—or anyone Rosa knew—had ever driven. What kind of money did professors make?

"Godspeed, Mrs. Ciccarino," the reverend said, looking out at the passing night. "You ever notice how frequently it happens overnight? The sun goes down, and souls depart."

"She hung on for a long time," Mr. Janssen said, switching into the fast lane.

"Lots of family were here last night." The reverend sighed. "I've never seen so many people packed into a patient's room."

"A lot of people must have loved her," Rosa said.

She had cleared eleven paper cups half-filled with water from the room, and trash cans overflowing with wadded-up tissues.

"My definition of a life well lived." The reverend raised his index finger, making his point. "In my business, of course, death isn't the end, anyway."

Mr. Janssen grunted. "Nice business. But you do make a good point. My friend, the woman I told you about, died in the night. It was at a hospice, too. I wasn't there when it happened. It's always bothered me."

The reverend turned to Mr. Janssen. Rosa studied his profile in the dashboard light. He was probably kind of handsome when he was younger. His nose was straight, and the outer corners of his eyes ticked down ever so slightly, giving him a thoughtful air. "The end can catch you off guard," he said. "Even on the final leg, the timeframes vary. Hours to days to weeks. It's very hard on the family, and on the friends, too, of course."

So Mr. Janssen's girlfriend had died, and he wasn't there to say goodbye. That was the thing bothering him, the thing she sensed lurking behind his eyes? It probably happened every day. What about people who drop dead, out of nowhere, with heart attacks or get hit by a car? Nobody says goodbye to them.

The reverend shook his head. "People put too much emphasis on the final moments. What matters is all the time before."

"I'll take your word for it."

"Good man."

The car heater blasted now. Warmth filled the space. It washed over Rosa, melting the chill that held her. The headlights of an oncoming car shot a beam through the windshield.

"Rosa tells me she's got big plans." The reverend turned to smile back at her.

"She sure does." Mr. Janssen guided the car into the middle lane, spotty traffic passing them, a tractor-trailer lumbering behind. Rosa could see Mr. Janssen in the rearview mirror, the restless movement of his eyes, his downturned mouth. He was not a happy man, no doubt about it.

The reverend was so different. There was a lightness to him. The things she heard them talking about: getting old, people dying, how screwed up the country was, the reverend seemed to have a place to put these things. He reminded her of Javi.

Mr. Janssen caught her glance in the mirror. She looked away.

"The waiting is the hardest part," the reverend said. "But I have a good feeling you're going to land in the right place, Rosa. You'll find your way."

"You do?" Rosa's voice sounded thin and little girlish. Stupid, she was almost twenty.

"Absolutely, and your mother will be doubly proud."

"Oh, yeah, she's gonna be proud."

"Is this your exit?" Mr. Janssen asked.

"Yep, right here." Rosa sat up straighter.

The road narrowed heading into her neighborhood. Mr. Janssen's nice car was going to smash through the potholes he wouldn't know were there. The reverend would see the stolen orange traffic cones Mrs. Quitto's crazy son had all over their front yard. Two doors down, he'd see the bed-sheet window curtain with the big Bugs Bunny face on it. And on the corner, old man Cerralto's dog would rush the fence and bark like crazy until someone yelled, "Shut up" or worse.

"Turn here," Rosa said.

"Evergreen Terrace." The reverend read the street sign. "Got a nice ring."

"Yep." But Rosa's house was not on Evergreen Terrace. It was two streets over. Evergreen was the last "good" street in the neighborhood. "The edge of the zone," Javi called it. There were no boarded-up windows or cars propped on cinderblocks, sheaves of parking violations tucked in their windshields. There were flowerpots and front porches and neat squares of lawn people watered in summer.

"This is it." Rosa chose a house right in the middle of the block, a white one with a red front door and a little picket fence around the yard. She glanced at the windows. No faces peering out.

Mr. Janssen pulled up to the curb. "Here you go."

"Thanks so much." Rosa gathered her backpack and opened the door. "I really appreciate the lift."

"See you on campus." Mr. Janssen smiled.

"Good night." The reverend waved.

Rosa closed the door with a solid thump and watched them pull away. Then she let out her breath. When their taillights had disappeared and she estimated they had to be approaching the highway ramp, she started walking home.

She thought of Mama in her bathrobe and slippers, tired after a long day, turning on the porch light, and Javi up in his room, reading in bed with a little scowl on his face. The house was locked tight against the night, a humble boxy fortress smack in the middle of the zone. Mama and Javi would think she got off work early when they heard her key in the lock, and she would let them.

Chapter Twenty-Nine

Ellen steered the Audi into her regular spot across the parking lot from William's office. She cut off the engine and sat for a moment. Today was the last class, the Reach Recipe feast. Only four months ago, she had determined teaching was her ticket back to the workforce and the way to hang on to her house. And now she was bidding the classroom goodbye. She was taking a sudden leap into the pastry business. Her mother would have called her "flighty."

Ellen closed her eyes. She tried to detach, to find a still center within her. But it didn't work. She didn't pray anywhere but Arborview, the only place she didn't feel ridiculous doing it. The only place where it seemed like reasonable, healthy discourse and not desperate grasping, or groveling.

She unsnapped her seatbelt. She had moved into unchartered territory now, no doubt about it. There was a sizable bank loan in her name alone, and no Zach to shield her if the creditors came calling. Her mother would have also called her "reckless."

Alice, the night before, had called her "courageous."

Alice had called late, but Ellen had answered, relieved to see it wasn't Zach. They had talked for more than an hour, Ellen propped up on pillows, and Alice's voice small and tinny like a broadcast bouncing off a remote satellite. Alice kept stopping and starting over, backing up, rephrasing. It sounded like she was sitting on a fence, on the verge of toppling off. Finally, Ellen had said, "What is with you, tonight?"

A weirdly long pause and then, "I'm in over my head this time."

Ellen stifled a yawn. It was a little late for drama. "This will pass. We'll find a way through it."

"I've boxed myself in, Ellie." Alice's voice, morose. "I don't see a good way forward."

The nightstand clock read 12:15 a.m. Ellen's eyes burned. "Let's talk more tomorrow?"

Alice took the cue, but Ellen had a hard time falling asleep anyway.

Today she'd felt heavy and slow-footed all day. She took her purse and two canvas bags from the passenger seat, stepped out of her car, and locked the door. The picnic table where Alice and she had sat that hot summer morning stood in the courtyard. What a formidable place this campus had seemed then. How absurd she'd been with her angst, her damp-palmed anxiety. She grimaced. She was as dramatic as Alice sometimes.

The students were already seated around the table, a hodgepodge of tinfoil-covered bowls and pans before them, when Ellen hurried in. "You beat me," she said, shrugging off her coat. "And the funny thing is, I don't think I've been late all semester until today."

"The best day of all," said Doreen, the grade-point obsessed girl who scribbled notes every time Ellen spoke, and who was getting an A. Rosa was getting an A, too, of course, as were a handful of others who had truly applied themselves and achieved a level of skill.

Effort was what mattered. Mostly Ellen planned to award B and C grades. No one would fail.

"I have a bunch of paper plates and forks here." She lifted her bag onto the table. "Let's pass them around. I'd like to make a few brief—very brief—comments, and then we'll dig in."

"Woo-hoo," said Javier. "My brownies are gonna rock your world, Mrs. C. They gonna…"

"You are so unbelievably lame, dude, making brownies," said Henry, who, beneath the visor of his ever-present baseball cap, had carved out the role of sardonic class critic. He'd gotten a B.

"How would you know, with your—what was it? A peach cobbler?" Javier stuck a finger in his mouth and made a gagging motion. "Sounds like summer food, man. You way off, way off."

"Come on, get those plates passed around, pull off the foil," Ellen said. "A pleasing visual display is part of the gourmet experience, right? Our food should look as good as it tastes—and it's doubly true when it comes to pastry."

"You in trouble already," Javier cracked to Henry, "because that thing looks like a pan of cement."

"Hey, big mouth," Rosa called from her end of the table, glaring at Javier. "You talking mighty big for a man with a plate of brownies."

Snickers around the table.

Ellen clapped her hands. "Cut it, Javi. And Henry, I love cobbler year-round. I have a couple of announcements to wrap up the semester. One is how much I enjoyed working with all of you. And the other—I don't know if you're aware—is I won't be teaching this course, or any course, next semester."

"You're retiring, Ms. C?" Henry's eyes were wide.

"Not quite. I'm opening my own pastry shop in the spring, and all my time will go into it."

"Woo-hoo!" Henry's eyes narrowed with interest.

"Onward and upward, huh?" Javier said.

"It feels like it. Not that I'm ruling out teaching again." Ellen shrugged. "Maybe when the business is up and running. In the meantime, I'll need help, some part-time workers—counter help, cleanup crew. If you're interested, send me an email. It'll be a skeletal staff to start, but who knows where it'll lead."

"Go, Mrs. Cahill." Rosa began applauding. The other students joined in, and a ripple of clapping rang out around the table.

"You're heading for the big-time, Mrs. Cahill. You go kick ass." Henry pumped his fist.

"Kick pastry ass," Javier said.

Ellen held up her hands to quiet them. "And with this somewhat disturbing image in mind, let's eat," she said, laughing.

The Reach Recipes, aside from a few barely recognizable mishmashes, turned out fairly well, given the kids' experience levels. Rosa's Napoleon was superb for a first attempt. Henry's cobbler had a nice balance of sweet and savory. Even Javier's brownies were passable. They spent an hour eating and laughing as a group, passing plates around and critiquing each dish. No one complained, and no one was cruel. Javier kept flashing a thumbs-up as the fork traveled from his plate to his mouth.

When the class drew to a close, they dumped the paper plates and napkins in the recycling bin near the sink and wiped down the long steel table until it gleamed.

"I'll miss you," Ellen called as her students began packing up. "Keep in touch?"

A few threw her smiles, several kids high-fived her on their way out the door. But she knew she would never hear from most of them again.

"Good luck in Niagara, Javier," she said as he passed.

"Thanks. I enjoyed your class. Despite everything."

"Everything?"

"Well, me having no interest in baking."

"Then I take it as a huge compliment. Take care of yourself."

Rosa joined him at the door. "I'm gonna email you, Mrs. Cahill, about a job at your shop. It's so amazing. I knew what was hers to keep and how to find true solace."

"I'll look for it."

Rosa stepped forward and in one graceful sweep embraced Ellen. She was such a bitty thing. Her head came to Ellen's shoulder. Her hair smelled like strawberries. "You taught me a lot," she said.

"Oh, Rosa. It was my pleasure."

"Yeah, and not just baking, you know. I'm reading the book you gave me."

"It's been a delight having you in class." Ellen didn't want to lose this girl. "I'm expecting great things of you."

Rosa gave a secretive smile and nodded. Then she dashed through the door, her footsteps retreating down the hall.

Ellen stood a moment. The room—bursting all semester with loud voices, clattering pots and pans, and stovetop drama—was suddenly still. The sky hung dark beyond the windows. It was December twentieth, the eve of the Winter Solstice. Tomorrow would bring the longest night of the year. The finality shook Ellen. She had crossed a bridge. She had moved into a new space, and it suddenly seemed everything that had once been was now further away and more lost. It frightened her.

Maybe she could spend tomorrow night at William's. The two of them, holed up together, and in the morning, she would wake to the new web of dreams she had spun—her own pastry shop, William at her side, sunny days slipping into sweet, cocooned nights. She would move through this new world with assurance, with ease, as she became someone who didn't need to climb into a tree house to find solace, someone who already had it within her.

She packed her bag, wiped a tear from her eye, and turned off the lights.

****

"So the lease begins January first?" William stepped around leftover cardboard boxes. It was his first visit to Ellen's shop.

"I've already paid the first month's rent," she said. "All systems are go."

The shop in the evening—even empty and with half-soaped windows—was as cozy as she had hoped. Maybe she'd start a Saturday night coffeehouse type event, if things went well.

"This atmosphere," she said, turning in a circle, "is exactly what I wanted. It's going to be such an oasis. Can't you see the tables clustered around? The lamps in the corners? Wait until the display case is filled with cookies and cakes. And the music—harps, I'm going heavy on the harps. I should have named it 'Ellen's Escape.' "

She liked sharing these details with him, laying out her vision. He seemed to enjoy it, too. He had become her new confidante, especially with Alice in the state she was in.

William turned the front doorknob. "Get a dead bolt installed. In fact, get an electronic security system. Ask your landlord to put one in."

"This is a pretty safe town. I can't remember the last time there was a break-in."

"Well, you don't want to be the first. You're going to have a lot of people coming in and out of here. You'll be attracting attention. It's better to play it safe."

She couldn't argue with that. "I'll call the landlord tomorrow. But what I can't wait to do is paint." She raised her arms. "Robin's egg blue and buttery yellow. Picture it."

"It'll look great." William buttoned his coat.

Ellen turned to him. "Hey, want to spend the night? I've got leftover lasagna, and the wood's all set in the fireplace. All we've got to do is strike the match."

"I've got an early morning tomorrow." He coughed.

"There's hardly anyone on campus. The whole place is shutting down."

"Not my office." He coughed again. "And I think I'm coming down with something."

Ellen's heart sank, but she understood. She went to get her coat from the counter. "Taber and Jimmy will be home soon, but I'll be able to sneak away." She joined William at the door. "They spend so much time at their friends' houses, I hardly see them when they're home. And of course they'll be at Zach's, too. How is Friday looking for you?"

William stared through the window, watching the lazy beams of headlights move around the green.

"William? Friday?"

"I'll call you."

She watched the glow of headlights passing in the street.

"You've got something special here." He pulled on his gloves. "But get a security system, okay? The world is full of creeps." He turned and wrapped his arms around her, pulling her close.

Chapter Thirty

Gauzy sunlight flooded the windows as Ellen carried her coffee, laptop tucked beneath one arm, to the breakfast nook overlooking the backyard. It was too cold for the sunroom, which wasn't heated and on winter days was only bearable in midafternoon when the sun was strongest.

She checked her email first thing each morning now, either on her phone or on her laptop. With the shop set to open in four months, it seemed there was always a minor crisis brewing. A snag in the insurance policy; then the ovens had to be special ordered and were, of course, delayed; the town building inspector determined the front steps and railing weren't to code. Every day it seemed more money was flying out the window. William said it was all part of what he called "entrepreneurial jitters."

Ellen slid onto a stool, propped her elbows on the table, and logged on. There was only one message in her inbox. It was from Rosa.

Dear Mrs. Cahill,

I'm sorry we couldn't talk more after class. I really am hoping I can work for you at your new shop. It's so exciting. Congratulations! I would be honored to work alongside you. So consider this my official application, okay? Maybe I can even come back when I'm on breaks from Seasons Culinary College. Ha-ha. I haven't heard

from them yet. Hope I haven't jinxed it. I hope you have
wonderful holidays!

    Your friend,
    Rosa Escamilla
    Ellen typed a quick response:
    Rosa,
    You're hired! I'm hoping to open the shop in May,
so please leave some room in your schedule. That is,
until you head to Seasons Culinary College, or the
Coastal Culinary Institute—another school you could
look into. I am so proud of you and all your work this
semester. Let me know when you get news?

    Merry Christmas to you, Javier, and your mom.
    See you in the New Year!

    Ellen signed off and closed the laptop. She folded
her fingers around the warm coffee mug. Jimmy and
Taber were arriving that night. The house was stocked
with food, and William had helped her put up a
moderately sized Christmas tree, not the brushy,
sparkling tower of their childhood, but a respectable,
lovely little tree. A red-ribboned wreath hung on the
front door, and a couple of ruby poinsettias sat on the
mantel above the fireplace.

    But Ellen hadn't yet brought out the traditional
trinkets and flourishes that had always meant
"Christmastime" in the house. She had to set out the
crude, wooden reindeer with the green scarf around his
neck and tealight candle dishes attached to his antlers;
the manger scene of course, though the baby Jesus was
missing an arm, and the shepherds had lost most of
their sheep; the ceramic caroler dolls who stood in the
bay window; and the crystal snowflake candy dish she
kept stocked with chocolates all month. They all had to

be in place before the kids arrived.

Ellen hoped to sneak off to see William when the kids were at Zach's. He had been so odd last night in the shop—edgy, worrying about deadbolts. He had emailed her later, apologizing for his "grump attack." It was signed—for the first time—"With Love, W," which had lit a hopeful flame in Ellen. Against her better judgement, she had begun to imagine a future with him. She had shut out the cynical whispers and started to believe.

She placed her coffee mug in the sink and swallowed a few spoonfuls of cottage cheese from the container. She had a lot to get done. Upstairs she slipped on a pair of Olden College sweatpants Jimmy had given her for Christmas last year. Alice would have shuddered, but Alice wasn't here, and Alice had enough in her own life to shudder about now. Ellen made a mental note to call her and check in.

She pulled a red sweatshirt over her head and tied her hair up in a loose topknot. In the bathroom, she brushed her teeth, then she returned to the bedroom to turn on the nightstand radio—a relic, Taber called it— and tune in the Christmas music station. "Winter Wonderland," spilled out. Ellen hummed along.

They kept the decorations—organized, boxed, and labeled, at Zach's request—in the guest bedroom closet, tucked at the back, behind the ironing board and Jimmy's old hand weights.

Ellen lifted the board out of the way and carried the three cardboard boxes, one at a time, into the master bedroom—which, thanks to William, she had begun using again. After sleeping there with him, hunkered down together amid the crisp new sheets she'd bought, the room was hers again.

She placed the boxes on the bed and started unpacking: ornaments of glass and ceramic, strands of tree lights coiled neatly in paper bags, velveteen red bows, the well-worn red stockings with "Taber" and "Jimmy" stenciled across the snowy trim at the top.

Here was the Winter Solstice snow globe Taber loved. Ellen shook it, and a tiny flurry of white engulfed the golden star emblazoned with "Shortest Day of the Year" inside. She would put it in the middle of the dining room table tonight, a centerpiece Taber would be sure to notice. She'd place the sterling silver candlesticks Jimmy had given her on either side, a robin's egg blue taper—his favorite color—stuck in each. She had selected this same blue as one of the shop's primary branding colors. Her "signature shades," the marketing specialist she'd consulted said. She'd paired the blue with a dreamy, sunny yellow. These colors would be stamped throughout the shop—on the front door, on her business cards, the menus and napkins.

William had nodded approvingly when she'd described the colors to him.

"Transcendent," he'd said. He got it.

It would've been fun to have him here, unpacking the Christmas stuff. She wondered what he was doing right now. Sipping coffee at his desk, walking across the blustery campus? She could squeeze in a visit tonight, a quick early dinner. Or maybe he would show up on her porch, unannounced, with a bottle of wine, as he'd done a few weeks back.

Ellen lifted the old gingerbread house from its box, marveling that the candy Lifesavers were still stuck to the sides. A desiccated corner of the cookie roof chipped and fell on the bedspread. This might be the last year for the gingerbread house. She brushed off her hands. She'd carry the items down in batches and put them in place. Going up and down the stairs was good exercise.

But what was missing?

The angel. For the top of the tree, of course. The white-robed angel with the feathery halo and translucent wings had sat atop their tree for what? Twenty years? Zach hadn't taken her, or any of the trinkets of their life together. Maybe Lydia didn't want them. If they had a child, they'd have to get all new things and weave another history. And Zach was fifty. The thought made Ellen weary enough to weep. Good luck to him.

She walked back to the guest room. In the closet, she spotted the angel box on the back shelf. Clothes hung on the rack beneath, a couple of Zach's old dress shirts and his blue blazer. He must have overlooked them.

Ellen took the angel box from the shelf, tucked it in the crook of her arm, and pulled the shirts and blazer from their hangers. Back in her bedroom, she dropped the clothes on the bed. She'd mention them to Zach. If he didn't want them, the Salvation Army would.

It was close to midmorning. Crows cried out, arcing over the house and sailing into the woods. It would be a nice day for a walk and then maybe a visit to Arborview. Ellen hadn't been out there for a few days, and she missed it. She longed for the sense of being alone and yet not alone, as her silent prayers filled the little space. The old biblical rhythms had returned to her. *Show me the way. Guide my coming and my going, deliver me to the safe place.* This was what she wanted, in the end, safety.

She folded Zach's old shirts in a pile and lifted the jacket. She gave it a good shake and, out of habit, went through the pockets. How many twenty-dollar bills had she found stuffed in pockets? Too many to remember.

In the right interior breast pocket, her fingers closed around a piece of paper. She pulled it out. A creamy piece of folded stationery, heavy, embossed, the kind which would have a watermark. Expensive paper.

She unfolded the sheet. Swirling, graceful—she knew the handwriting immediately—in sapphire blue ink:

I can't make it tonight. So sorry, my love. It's awful to have to wait until next week. I have your handkerchief tucked in my purse. I take it everywhere. Lifting it to my face and breathing you in sustains me. Even when I'm not with you, I feel you at my side. A.

Ellen stared at the page. It was Alice's handwriting, no doubt.

Alice.

Her love?

Zach was her love?

A grinding whir filled Ellen's ears. She lowered herself to the bed.

Was this a forgotten joke? A charade they had all played during a boozy dinner party? Alice didn't love Zach. She didn't even like him—at least not anymore.

There was no date, but the note was old—the paper soft and feathery at the edges, the creases of the folds deep and permanent.

Two years old? Three?

What had been going on three years ago? What were Alice and she talking about? Ellen touched her temple. A warm rush moved up her neck, a bright flash of light. She closed her eyes, shook her head. It was coming at her from all sides now. Unavoidable, bearing down on her.

Alice and Zach.

Had she ever noticed anything? A lingering look, a secretive smile?

No, never.

Then this was a joke, a misunderstanding.

Ellen's breath grew shallow, rapid. She stared at the note. *I feel you at my side.* She closed her eyes again.

Maybe the handwriting was Lydia's. Maybe Alice and Lydia shared this little quirk.

But it was signed with an A.

There had to be an explanation. She would call Alice, and Alice would explain. Alice would roll her eyes, and they'd laugh afterward.

Ellen's heart was pounding. She could feel it thudding in her throat. The thing was pressing in now, from the sides, from above and below. There was no escape, nowhere to hide. The truth is like that. Alice would not roll her eyes. They would not laugh afterward. They may never laugh together again.

Ellen's hand trembled as she reached for the phone on the nightstand and dialed.

One ring, two…

"Hello?"

Alice's voice. It was Saturday, and she was home, having a regular morning with Earle, probably drinking coffee and reading the paper.

"Hi." Ellen didn't trust her own voice.

"Ellie? I was just thinking about you."

"Oh?"

"Yes, want to grab lunch today?" Alice's voice dropped to a whisper. "We need to talk."

"I think we need to talk right now."

A pause. "Is there anything wrong?"

"I was cleaning out a jacket Zach forgot, and I found something, Alice, a note tucked in the pocket."

Ellen swallowed. Her mouth was sand dry. " 'I feel you at my side.' That's what it says. It's a note to Zach from a woman who loves him."

Ellen stopped because she could not catch her breath.

Silence from Alice's end, and then a shuddery exhale.

"It's from you, isn't it," Ellen said. "It's signed with an A. And it's your handwriting."

Shuffling sounds, as if Alice was moving to another room. "Please, listen…"

"I know your handwriting. After all these years, I know it."

"Ellen, please. Let me explain."

"You're not denying it?" Ellen heard the pleading in her own voice. It couldn't be true! Please, no. "Did you have an affair with Zach?"

Silence. Then Alice's voice, meek and soft. "Yes."

It felt like a bag of heavy, wet sand had dropped on Ellen's head. A minute passed, maybe two, with only the sound of breathing and a sniffle on Alice's end.

"We never wanted you to find out." Alice's voice cracked. "We tried to protect you. We tried so hard."

They tried to *protect* her?

"Zach protected you from so much. And I…did everything I could to…and then after to make it up to you, Ellie, to erase it all." More sniffling. "And now it's like it never happened. I don't know Zach anymore. I'm as appalled as you are by what he's done. I'm on your side, Ellie."

Ellen grabbed the edge of the nightstand to steady herself. If she had been standing, her knees would have buckled. "When?" Her voice was barely audible.

"Almost three years ago. It's all over and done with. It's ancient history." Alice sounded crazy, like she was going to break into laughter.

Ellen's lips were numb. "You were my best friend. But all this time…"

"No, listen! Not all this time. Only a little while. And it was a mistake, an awful mistake. I'm so sorry. I was going through a confused time. It was stupid. I never meant to… After Zach, I swore never again. I told myself if I could do this to you, there was something really wrong with me. I promised God as long as you didn't find out, I would never cheat again."

Ellen hung up. She sat for a moment, afraid the phone would ring, afraid Alice would call back, and she would have to hear more.

But the phone didn't ring.

Ellen stood and made her way to the stairs. She gripped the banister, placing one foot carefully in front of the other as she descended. Her legs were light, moving as if they were detached from the rest of her.

In the kitchen she filled a glass with cold water and carried it into the sunroom, where the chilled air hung still. She perched on the edge of the wicker couch, gripping the glass with both hands.

Beyond the windows, birds flitted along the hedgerow bordering the patio. They sought refuge there in winter, burying themselves deep among the branches. Peering into the hedge once, Ellen had been surprised to see a pair of glittering beady eyes staring back at her. She remembered the moment as clear as day, but she could not remember a time when Alice had seemed too interested in Zach. She had missed it entirely. What else had she missed?

And outside now, the day unfolded like any other, only her yard, the landscape itself, was altered somehow, alien. Ellen stood and walked to the window. They had completely bamboozled her. Completely.

She squinted through the sunlight to where Arborview sat perched in the corner of the yard, its wood streaked with black mildew stains. That's what too much shade and too little sun gets you. Decay. How had she not noticed this eyesore?

Who else knew about Alice and Zach?

Ellen backed away from the window. She turned and walked to the kitchen. She leaned against the counter. One thing at a time. First, she would catch her breath here. Then she would go lie down. Just a few minutes on the couch. If she held still long enough, maybe she could stop what was coming. She went to the living room, picked up the plush blanket folded over the back of a chair, and laid down on the couch, as the waves of panic and disbelief pulled her under.

Chapter Thirty-One

Rosa hated going to the mall, but Amazon was too risky. Mama was home during the day, and she could intercept the package. So Rosa caught the five-forty bus from the hospice to the mall and passed between the towering, sparkling evergreens flanking the main entrance. Thursday night, and the place was packed with Christmas shoppers.

Rosa stood to the side on the escalator, as a group of teenage boys galloped past, heading up. The bookstore was on the upper level. She glanced down at the Santa display in the center concourse. A big dude in a Santa suit sat on a throne-type chair before a line of little kids who were twisting and bouncing, holding their parents' hands. Mama had never taken Javi and her to sit on Santa's lap. Rosa could imagine now what Mama probably must have thought: *Sitting on a strange man's lap, whispering in his ear? Weird, if you ask me.* Sometimes Mama was right on.

Rosa took a left off the escalator. Yeasty, baking smells drifted from the food court. Cinnabon. She loved those things, the too-sweet icing slicking her lips, the burst of fresh cinnamon lighting her mouth. She'd get one for the bus ride home, if there was time. First, she needed a special book. Mama wasn't a big reader. She liked to watch the movies they made out of books instead. But Rosa wasn't getting her that kind of book.

She was looking for something else. She wasn't sure exactly what yet, but she would know it when she saw it.

Red, green, and gold festooned the store windows. A tall snowman, black top hat and silver scarf around his neck, waved a mechanical arm up and down from a toy store. It looked like a fun place to look around, but Rosa didn't know any little kids to shop for.

She passed Brooks Brothers, the preppy, super-expensive place. Rosa stopped before the window. A faceless female mannequin wore a creamy silk blouse and an ash-gray pencil skirt, a scarf with a motif of green vines draped around her neck. Rosa admired the elegant folds of the fabric, the shiny silk that hung like still water. When she was a famous chef, she would wear clothes like these. Not while she was cooking, of course, but the rest of the time. She had decided she was going to be more than a pastry chef. She was going to own her business. She'd be somebody in charge, like Mrs. Cahill, like Sarah would one day be, in her law office.

Sarah had seemed peaceful today. She had nodded while Rosa rattled on about the Napoleon and cheered when Rosa mentioned her summer job at Mrs. Cahill's new shop. Sarah was feeling better. They weren't poisoning her with the chemotherapy anymore, she had explained. That was the stuff killing her. She had always believed that her body, left to its own devices, knew how to heal.

The bookstore wasn't busy. A few browsers scanned the shelves, while a ringing, piped-in "Silver Bells" played in the background. Amazon must have stolen all the place's customers. Rosa scooted down an aisle, heading for the Cooking section. She knew the section by heart. The how-to recipe books were up front; the special diets in the middle; and the business-type career ones in the rear. She skimmed the titles. *What the Chef Doesn't Want You to Know. Cooking For a Living? Behind Closed Kitchen Doors: Dirty Secrets from the Restaurant Business.* No, no, and no. All too negative. Rosa needed a bit of dignity and optimism. *Becoming a Chef.* She stopped short. Simple and direct, she liked it. Nothing for Mama to pounce on and immediately proclaim a bunch of bull.

Rosa pulled the book from the shelf. Solid, but not so long it would turn off Mama. The author was Andrew Dornenburg. Rosa had never heard of him. She flipped open the cover to the table of contents. Lots of chapters. Her eyes skipped down the list. *Early Influences: Discovering a Passion for Food; Cooking Schools: Learning in the Classroom.* Even better: *Getting in: Starting at the Bottom;* and *The Business of Cooking: Operating and Running a Restaurant.* Just the kind of stuff she wanted Mama to see. Mama would of course claim to know it all already, but Rosa knew she didn't.

Rosa tucked the book under her arm and headed for the cash register. She wasn't expecting any miracles from this book. Mama was Mama. But maybe some reasonable true calm thing would emerge from the pages and lodge in Mama's mind. Rosa glanced at her phone, still plenty of time to grab a Cinnabon before she caught the bus.

The mall was filling up as she made her way back to the escalator. The evening shoppers came out in full force this time of night. She weaved among them. Then up ahead, she spotted Javi coming out of Secrets of the Boudoir, a lingerie shop. A big shopping bag with pink tissue paper poking out the top dangled from his hand.

"Javi!" Rosa caught up with him in three steps. "Hey, I didn't know you were coming here tonight."

He stopped. Was his face reddening?

"Secrets of the Boudoir, huh?" *Skank Central*, Mama called it. *What's the big secret when these girls are letting it hang out all over the place?* Rosa thought a lot of the stuff was pretty, though.

"Yeah, I, uh, got something."

"For Mama?"

"No! What is wrong with you?"

Rosa laughed. "I know it's for Tilda. Wanna grab a Cinnabon?"

"Sure."

They rode the escalator down, Javi holding his bag on the side away from Rosa. "What did you buy?" he asked, nodding at the bag she carried.

"A book for Mama, for Christmas." Rosa lifted the bag. "It's called *Becoming a Chef*. I'm hoping it'll, you know, help her see things differently, at least a little."

"You better do a lot of hoping."

Rosa shrugged. "It can't hurt, and I'm doing this, no matter what she says." Sarah's victorious smile flashed through her mind.

They stepped off the escalator, and the other shoppers split around them. Javi turned to his sister with a rare softness in his eyes. "My money's on you, you know." He shook his head in the know-it-all way which always irritated Rosa. But then he put his arm around her shoulders. "You got guts, little sister. I'll give you that. I'll spring for the Cinnabon."

Chapter Thirty-Two

Ellen wasn't sure how long she'd been lying on the couch when the doorbell rang. She gasped.

Alice had come. To confront her and drag things out, to cry and wheedle and plead. Oh, please no.

The bell rang again, and then knocking on the door. Alice would go away. She would give up and go away.

But a man's voice called out: "Ellen, your car's in the driveway. I know you're in there. It's Earle. Please let me in?"

Ellen sat up. "Earle?" His voice was like a lifeline reaching out to her. She got up and opened the front door.

Earle's hair stood out in tufts. Behind his spectacles, his bloodshot eyes were wary. He had no coat, and his blue denim shirt was buttoned wrong, the untucked shirttails hanging unevenly. Floppy brown loafers, no socks, covered his feet.

Ellen recoiled. "Did she send you?"

"No. She's beside herself." Earle shook his head. "I was there, in the kitchen. I heard everything." His breath formed smoky puffs in the cold air.

Ellen opened the door wider. "Come in."

He followed her into the living room and stood before the fireplace.

"I'm going to be honest, even though you'll end up hating me," he said.

Ellen returned to the couch.

"I've known for a while—about Zach and Alice." Earle looked away. "I kept my mouth closed because they begged me to." He stared at the floor. "You know how persistent, how maddeningly persuasive, Alice can be. But it's not an excuse. I have no excuse." He pulled off his glasses. "I should have told you."

So Alice hadn't outmaneuvered him this time. "How'd you find out?" Ellen asked.

"I walked in on them, in our house, pawing each other like teenagers, in the kitchen."

In their house, in the kitchen where Ellen had shared countless cups of coffee with Alice. Zach had been sneaking over there. And now this new one, Ned, was doing the same thing. "She never learns." Ellen's limbs were weak. "How did I not know?"

"I should have told you. I'm sorry."

"When? How long ago did this happen?"

Earle shoved his hands in his pants pockets.

"Earle?"

"It started about two years ago."

The blood drained from Ellen's head. *It started?* She leaned back into the couch. Everyone knew. They had all known for a long time. "When did it end?"

"Lydia ended it."

"Lydia?"

"Old Zach was a busy man."

Alice's hatred of Lydia had always seemed a little too pointed, a little too personal.

"But Zach got an earful, believe me." Earle's face reddened with the memory. "I told him what a scumbag he is, what a sleaze, screwing my wife and sitting at my dinner table with me. Not to mention what he was doing to you."

Yes, near the end Zach had begun making excuses to avoid getting together with Alice and Earle, claiming they had become too boring.

"They hid it so well," Ellen said. "They were so good at it. But how could I have not noticed anything?"

"Think back, two years ago, the kids were getting ready to graduate from high school, right?" Earle said. "Big transitions, lots of worries and drama…"

Ellen nodded. "Taber threw up the morning of the SAT, and Alice was hysterical because Caroline wanted to pierce her nose, take off, and travel the country. Remember that?"

"We were trying to raise our kids and be attentive and put them first and go to work every day, and pay the bills, and all the rest of it, and…"

Ellen felt the wave of frustrated regret coming off Earle. She looked at the smiling photos of Taber and Jimmy on the end table. All of these things had been happening at the same time. That was the problem—too much going on, too much noise and clutter and urgency, to understand any of it.

Earle drew a breath. "Can I tell you something? Now that it's all over?"

Ellen nodded. She couldn't speak.

"I never liked Zach. He's the kind of scheming little climber you meet every day—Mr. Big Deal with his pressed suits and pretty ties. I always thought he was too crass, too pedestrian, for a woman like you. I'm not surprised you got divorced, Ellen. Not at all. I'm surprised you stood it as long as you did."

The clock in the hall gave its soft chime. It was noon. The morning when she had learned the truth had passed. Tonight, the day she learned it would be over. Alice had become someone else. "She's getting sloppy. It's like she wants to be caught," Ellen said.

"I have a suspicion there might be a new one now," Earle said.

Ellen's heart pounded. Tell him. Show her no mercy. *There is a new one now, Earle. And there were others before Zach. Things are actually a lot worse than you imagine.*

She closed her eyes. She couldn't handle another blow right now. She couldn't sustain one, and she couldn't deliver one. Maybe when she was stronger, she would talk this through with Earle. Things were moving too fast right now. Another wave, and she would drown.

"You're probably wondering why I don't divorce her," Earle said. "I actually left her when I found out about Zach."

Ellen swallowed.

"I walked out and drove up to Vermont. My car headed north, out of habit. We've vacationed there so many times, and I love Vermont." Earle paused. "This is where it gets pathetic. I drove to the same inn where we'd stayed the year before. I was on autopilot."

"Oh, Earle…"

"So there I am, getting away from Alice, right? And her ghost is lurking around every corner, lying in the bed next to me, sitting in the dining room, giving me the Alice smile. You know the one—a little sad, a little sweet, a hint of the devil in her eye."

"Yeah, I know it." A surge of hot anger and then the first stab of loss. Ellen's throat constricted. "She's out of control. She's lost her moral compass, if she ever really had one."

"The problem is, I'm still in love with her."

"Oh, please." Ellen shook her head. "What does that matter?"

"That's what I'm trying to figure out."

"Well, you may not like the answer when it finally smacks you over the head."

He still *loved* her. Alice would devour him in the end, because that's what she did. Lying and scheming, then sweet words and smiles, were her weapons. And Earle, with his shiny spectacles and his birds, would end up wounded and flailing. What was amazing was how Alice had tricked them both, and for so long. She had been just kind enough, just careful enough. How trusting they'd been. Maybe love truly was blind.

Ellen stood. "I'm sorry. I need to rest."

Earle turned to her. "Of course."

"You're too good for her, Earle. One day you'll realize that." They walked to the foyer. "And I'm not going to reach out to her. Please don't ask me to," Ellen said.

Earle stepped forward and wrapped her in a quick hug, whispering "I'm sorry," in her ear. "It's so wrong this is happening to someone as wonderful as you."

Ellen shuddered. "It doesn't feel real. I can't get my mind around it."

"Give it time. And for what it's worth, I know how you feel."

Ellen opened the door.

Earle stepped out onto the stoop, as a gust of cold air rushed into the house. "Let me know if I can do anything?" he said. "And I won't blame you, Ellen, if you never talk to her again."

****

She made it out to Arborview in the late afternoon. It was cold and barren up in the branches, but she craved the stillness. She dropped onto the beanbag.

When the time was right, she would tell Zach. He would get another "earful." He had it coming. And Alice? Her Halloween party pantry face—wild hair, smeared lipstick—kept rising in Ellen's mind. Alice would construct a fatuous, self-serving explanation, a fishy "context" that minimized her culpability, her *choice* in sleeping with Zach. Anything, so she wouldn't have to account for what she had done. The ultimate spin doctor. Ellen should have realized that one day Alice's weapons would be turned on her. What did Alice say? *The leopard doesn't change its spots.*

Ellen wrapped her arms around her knees and shivered. The light was dying. Night would soon cover everything. The shortest day of the year had passed. She should go in and call William. She needed his voice.

They had weighed the consequences, these people she had loved, and they had proceeded. They had risked what was expendable. She had been expendable. That was the thing that surprised her most. How little she had mattered in the end. She could not understand them. Their hearts did not bend, and if they broke, she did not know.

She stood and walked to the window opening. Blackness hung beyond the trees, impenetrable. If God was out there, now was a good time for Him to show up.

In the woods, silence.

Chapter Thirty-Three

"I deserve an Academy Award," she told William when the holidays were at last mercifully over and they were together on the couch in his living room.

Ellen held a glass of wine. Her legs fell across William's lap. A single candle burned on the coffee table. The dark hum of the suburban night murmured beyond the windows. "I never let on, not to the kids, not to Zach when our paths crossed, not to anyone," she said.

"I'd say you deserve a Purple Heart." He lifted one of her tired, socked feet in his capable hands and began massaging it. "A friend's betrayal is the worst betrayal of all, isn't it?"

How did he know? There was still so much they had to learn about each other. "You speak as if from experience." Ellen sighed.

He smiled, the soft resigned expression that had caught her attention in the beginning, making him seem wise and compassionate, the possessor of some kind of absolution. Like the breeze washing through Arborview, brushing aside her failures and anxieties. *These things happen. You are not alone.*

"No word from Alice yet?" he asked.

"Nope."

He lifted her other foot. "It's probably for the best right now."

"If she knocked on my door, I don't know if I'd slam the door in her face or fall, sobbing, into her arms. She was my dearest friend."

He kneaded her toes.

"The hardest part is reconciling the two Alices. You know what I mean? There's Alice, my friend—loving, compassionate, fun, all this good stuff; and then there's this shadow Alice, hiding, scheming, tricking me for years, justifying it in her own mind. Both existing at the same time, in the same person. How is it possible?"

He shook his head. "You're a good soul, Ellen. You're not devious like most people."

"But I'm not a simpleton, you know," she said.

"No, of course not. I just mean there are people who have a real talent for compartmentalizing the stuff they don't want to look at. They're good at lying to others. They're good at lying to themselves. But you're honest, with yourself and with other people. Pretty rare, in my experience."

Ellen softened. She had no right to take out any anger on him.

He scooted down the couch and took her hand. "You're an amazingly strong and generous woman. How did you manage not to hit Zach with this? I never could have held back."

"If I'd gotten started, I knew I wouldn't have been able to stop, and Jimmy and Taber were always around. Of course, Taber knew something was up anyway. She never misses a beat." Ellen wrapped her fingers through his. "When you spend your life putting other people first, it kind of becomes your default setting. I don't know if I recommend it."

"I'll take your word for it."

She wrapped her arms around him, breathing him in. "Let's spend the weekend at my house? I'll take you up to Arborview." She gave an uncertain laugh.

The candle flickered. He closed his eyes, as if conjuring the unseen.

Chapter Thirty-Four

A new year, and Javier was gone. He hadn't wanted to wait around for the River Bend commencement ceremony in spring. "I'll have another one coming in a couple years," he'd said. "The one that really matters."

Rosa had not expected to feel his absence so keenly. His bedroom door stood open at the top of the stairs. She passed it every morning, half-expecting him to be there, hunched over the desk in the corner or sprawled on the bed, whispering to Tilda on his phone.

He was in Niagara now, Tilda with him, despite Mama's protests. "Don't you blow this and come crawling back, Mr. Big-Head," Mama had said, kissing Javier's cheek and blinking back tears when they dropped off Javi and Tilda at the bus station.

The cold grip of winter had truly set in, when the days were shortest, and the nights stretched into streaky, uncertain dawns. Rosa wouldn't hear from her colleges for a couple of months. All she could do now was dig in and hold on.

Her courses at River Bend were all academic drudgery this term. Core courses—the stuff she had to pass in order to move on. More history—dead people and old wars. Who cared? Composition, blah, blah, blah. Calculus she could barely wrap her mind around. One day maybe it would mean something more. But not now, when she had bigger battles to fight.

On top of the hospice, she was washing dishes at Sotto Voce two nights a week—arranged by Mama—and getting paid under the table. "The government sticks its hand deep enough into my pocket for both of us," Mama had said.

One night at a traffic light, Mama turned to her and said, "So you'll hear soon, right? From the cooking college?"

Rosa's heart quickened. "In the spring, March at the earliest."

The light dangling over the intersection glowed green, and Mama drove on. "I said all I have to say. It's your life."

"Uh-huh."

Mama shot her a sideways glance. "I'm not gonna ask nothing about it no more. I'm done."

"Okay."

"You don't want to hear my opinion. But you're asking me to buy into this."

"I'm not asking you to buy into anything." Rosa had decided to "turn the other cheek," as she'd heard the reverend say, as best she could, and let Mama's cracks roll off her back. It was hard to do, but easier than arguing.

Rosa looked out the window. Her nest egg was growing. The hospice salary was piling up, and they had been offering her extra shifts lately. In the spring she'd be working at Mrs. Cahill's new shop. She'd be able to get through Seasons Culinary College, at least for the first year, if only they would accept her.

The hospice had also agreed to let Rosa make the Napoleon with Sarah. The administrative guy said this in a voice which let you know he thought it was never going to happen. The reverend had raised an eyebrow, too, but Rosa didn't care. Sarah was looking better every day. They would make a special afternoon of it. Rosa wanted to tell Sarah about Mama. Sarah would know what to do, what to say. She didn't take crap from anybody.

Mama turned up the heat in the car. "It's freezing in here. I don't know how many more years I'm gonna get out of this old junker."

Rosa fiddled with the vents. A weak flow of warm air drifted through them.

Two towns away, the homes grew larger, and the bright store windows were filled with shiny cookware and delicate china, tailored clothes, and handcrafted furniture. They turned down the broad, genteel Main Street where Sotto Voce was tucked away.

"It's pretty here," Rosa said. "Reminds me of the town where my pastry teacher's shop will be."

"She still going to let you work there?"

"It's a definite." Rosa waited a beat. "I can't wait."

"Let's hope she makes it worth your time."

"Oh, she will. Mrs. Cahill is on the up-and-up."

Mama humphed.

They reached the corner where a Home and Hearth store stood at the intersection, its windows full of cozy décor and etched with stenciled snowflakes.

Mama hit her horn and raised her middle finger at the building. "Looks like we didn't need you after all," she called, although the window was rolled up.

A few pedestrians stopped on the sidewalk and looked around in confusion, one old man in a fuzzy-hooded parka staring into the intersection with an expression of startled disgust on his face.

"To you too, buddy." Mama bugged her eyes at him.

Rosa laughed out loud.

"Ah, one day Javi gonna buy us a house in a town nicer than this place." Mama hit the gas, and they blasted through the intersection.

"Or maybe I'll buy us a big house one day." Rosa waited for her mother's sharp retort, or at least a dismissive grunt.

"Fine by me," her mother said.

Chapter Thirty-Five

On a frigid Tuesday afternoon, Ellen found a letter in her mailbox. She carried the smooth envelope inside to the kitchen table, opened it, and pulled out a creamy card. An ink drawing of a peacock etched in flowing black lines filled the front, its tail festooned with glittering rows of glued-on plastic jewels.

Inside, a single sentence: *I still love you, my friend. A.*

Ellen closed the card. She reached for her phone, lying on the table. But she couldn't dial. A raw wound occupied the space where Alice had lived. It was a deep, gaping pit, swarming with ghosts hissing accusations, overflowing with layers of lies and half-truths, and a loss so deep, it frightened her. She had learned to keep away from the edge. What did Alice even mean by "love"? Ellen didn't know anymore.

In the afternoon, she climbed up into Arborview, where she felt strong, and called Zach. "I know about Alice." Ellen stared out the window opening into the trees.

"What are you talking about?"

"I think your last breath is going to be a lie," she said. She could feel his mind scrambling, as the final taut band of trust between them snapped. "Alice was my best friend."

Ellen had called him at his office. She imagined the

staid, respectable security of the space, his orderly desk and glowing computer screen, the files on the shelves, the reliability of this separate life he had built for himself. She knew it was where he would be most unsettled, most ambushed, by this intrusion. And why not? His phone calls had been ambushing her fragile peace long enough.

His voice was thick when he finally responded. "I can't excuse it."

"No, you can't." Ellen was surprised at her own composure. No waffling on this point. She hadn't shoved him into *Alice's* arms—of all people. There was no way he could turn this one on her.

Zach cleared his throat. "Listen, we weren't in our right minds."

Ellen's blood stirred. "No? What mind were you in, then? The two middle-aged cliches having a last fling mind?"

He cleared his throat again, a sign his anger was mounting.

"Tell me, how do you justify it, Zach?" Ellen asked. "Throwing people away like this? Blowing up what took so long to build?"

"Yeah, well, some things really need to be blown up."

His jaw was, no doubt, clenching right now, the way it did when he believed he had dropped the final word, the blow that would silence her. There had been a time—not long ago—when Ellen would have rethought her stance, when she would have backed up and started over. No more. Now she saw how pathetic he was, like a struggling insect beneath a microscope's piercing lens, with all its ugly hidden functions laid bare. A spin doctor like Alice. They had that much in common.

"You go right on blowing up things," Ellen said. "Never mind who's in the way. You'll step over the bodies, if you have to. We both know you can do it."

She could hear him breathing. He was quiet for once, a tense silence, percolating with a rage she could almost feel.

"Unless it's an emergency," she said, "involving our kids, don't call me again."

She hung up the phone. She was breathing hard, but a giddiness filled her. It wasn't like he didn't have it coming. *You reap what you sow*. They got that part right, the old nuns. *Vengeance is mine, saith the Lord.* Fine, but she could have the pleasure of a few well-chosen words.

Chapter Thirty-Six

The reverend was leaving. He'd taken a job as an assistant pastor at a church in the valley northwest of Hartford.

"A small town," he told Mr. Janssen. "I can have a real impact. Congregation around two hundred and fifty, big enough but you still get to know everyone." He chuckled. "Everyone who comes to services regularly, anyway."

They were sitting together in the chapel, about halfway up on the right. Rosa made her way down the aisle. Their heads turned at the sound.

"Sorry. I forgot my book." She pointed to a seat on the left.

"No worries." The reverend smiled.

"You're leaving? Sorry, I overheard you."

"I'm going back to church, answering my calling." The reverend winked.

It always embarrassed Rosa when he winked. *Nobody* winked anymore. "That's great." She ducked into the row of seats opposite them and grabbed *With Bold Knife and Fork*. "We'll miss you. Won't we, Mr. Janssen?"

"More than he realizes." Mr. Janssen looked antsy. He bounced one knee up and down.

"That's one lucky church, getting you," Rosa said.

"Why, Rosa, what a nice thing to say." The

reverend beamed. "If I'd known you were such a fan, I'd have used you as a character reference."

Mr. Janssen placed his hand on his jittering knee, as if to calm it.

"When's your last day?" Rosa asked. "I need to say goodbye."

"Let's call it 'see-you-later,' " the reverend said. "You never know when someone's going to pop up in your life again. But my last day here at the hospice is in two weeks."

"Oh, good. Sarah and I will save you a piece of our Napoleon!"

"I'll look forward to it."

"I've got to run," Rosa said.

"Good night." They said it one after another, the reverend first and then Mr. Janssen, who glanced up, as if he'd suddenly remembered she was standing there. Rosa hustled up the aisle and through the propped-open door. She hated disturbing people. But who'd have thought the two of them would be in the chapel this late in the afternoon?

In the hall, she put her backpack on a table and unzipped it. She tucked the book inside, zipped up the pack, and hoisted it onto her shoulder.

"Ellen Cahill." Mr. Janssen's voice coming from the chapel. Rosa stopped. What about Mrs. Cahill? She crept to the side of the door and pressed her back against the wall.

"I've got to tell you, Will, she sounds pretty terrific, especially given all the crap she's been through." The reverend, saying this in a way that told Rosa he knew a lot more about what was going on than she did. Being nice didn't mean he was dumb. The reverend was a pretty smart guy, from what Rosa had seen. Dorks sometimes were.

"She is," Mr. Janssen said, in a flat voice.

A moment of silence. Mr. Janssen sighing. Rosa could make a break for it now, but she was stuck, her back flat against the wall, afraid to hear what would come next and afraid to miss it.

"Since you're leaving, I guess I should spill it all now, huh?" Mr. Janssen tried to sound like he was joking, but he failed.

"Totally up to you. I'm here, if you feel the need."

The reverend probably delivered this line to lots of people. He was the kind of guy you could tell your problems to.

"I'm beginning to wonder where this is headed," Mr. Janssen said. "Don't get me wrong. Ellen is great. Such control and maturity. She really puts me to shame."

"Ah, come on. She's choosing to spend time with you, so you can't be all that bad. What do you mean 'where it's headed?' Where do *you* want it to go?"

There was nothing wrong with Mrs. Cahill. Rosa could vouch for that. Mr. Janssen was lucky to be with her.

"I'm wondering what it is Ellen envisions," he said. "What's on her mind?" Mr. Janssen's voice rose with what sounded like a hint of panic. "Long days at her shop, wine on the patio with me in the evenings, her kids spiraling in ever closer until we're all overlapping. And then what?"

"You tell me. What do you want?"

"I don't know."

The reverend sighed. "Then maybe Ellen is the

catalyst you need. You're fifty-two years old. Maybe it's time to decide."

Coughing. Rosa couldn't tell which one of them.

"Why am I still living here?" Mr. Janssen said. "The campus was so cold today. Walking back to my car, the wind cut through me. My knees ache before snowstorms. My night vision isn't what it used to be. Put a little ice on the road, and I'm an accident waiting to happen. Maybe I need a fresh start, someplace new."

"You can't run away from yourself, or from the things you've done." The reverend's voice, strong and direct now.

But it was as if Mr. Janssen hadn't heard him. "Ellen will never leave, not with the shop opening. She's dug in for good, in this frozen, unforgiving place where I've floundered for so long."

"Then why go on floundering if this woman could offer you the key to something more?" An edge of frustration creeping into the reverend's voice.

Rosa shifted her weight from leg to leg. What if a nurse came down the hall and saw her standing here?

"Do you know why I chose to volunteer at a hospice?" Mr. Janssen asked. "It's a form of penance."

"Penance for what?"

Rosa had to strain to hear what came next. Mr. Janssen's voice dropped so low. "A woman I loved, the one I told you about who passed in a hospice? I wasn't there when she died."

"Yes, I know. You told me. Is that what this is about?" The reverend was finally losing his cool. Good.

"She wanted me there, but I stopped coming to see her a few weeks before she died. I stopped showing up. I couldn't do it anymore. People told me afterward she kept asking for me. But I couldn't. I didn't want to."

"Nobody *wants* to."

"You don't understand. I *couldn't*."

Silence. And then the reverend, softly now, said, "I see."

Rosa couldn't tell Mrs. Cahill any of this. It was just too weird. She shouldn't even be hearing it.

The reverend cleared his throat. "Maybe what you need is to start looking at this differently."

Even in the hall, Rosa could feel the heavy, leaden air between them. She sensed the reverend grappling for the right words. "There are people you can talk to," he said. "You should go see someone with real experience and expertise in these issues."

Shrinks? Mama called them all nutjobs.

Again, Mr. Janssen seemed not to have heard the reverend. "Maybe I decided long ago, even if I didn't realize it, that life is so merciless, so crushing, all you can do is meet it with equal hardness, or with…with slippery detachment."

"Which you appear to have mastered."

"Call it a lack of faith."

"It doesn't matter what I call it," the reverend said. "What matters is what you call it, and what you do about it."

Rosa had heard enough. She held her breath and moved silently down the hall. What was it Javi liked to say? Keep your nose clean. She never should have listened, in the first place. She vowed not to breathe a word to Mrs. Cahill.

She reached the door at the end of the hall and pulled it open. It creaked, but she was safely out of range. Even if the reverend and Mr. Janssen heard it, they wouldn't think it was her. It could be anyone. Doctors and nurses and families, so many people, walked these halls at all hours, watching and waiting and praying, trying so hard to understand, to do the right thing.

Chapter Thirty-Seven

February was relentless. Plowed snow accumulated in lumpy, conquered mounds alongside roads. Sheets of brittle ice-covered streams ran through the woods. The songbirds in Ellen's yard pecked at frozen ground.

But Ellen had never minded February. It was a period of retreat, a month of chunky sweaters and down comforters piled on the beds, punctuated in the middle by red roses and the molten-lava chocolate cake she always baked for Valentine's Day.

Without her class to teach, and with Taber and Jimmy tucked away on their respective campuses, she was too busy with Just Desserts to worry about the weather anyway. She ordered flooring materials and furniture and oversaw their installation. She found fabric strips of sunburst yellow to drape along the window rods. She spent two days walking through a warehouse maze of industrial ovens with hefty price tags before ordering two models, used but still in good shape. She had to cut a few corners.

"It's getting real now," she told William, as they shared the molten-lava cake in his condo. "This place better turn a profit pretty quick, or I'm going to be in serious dire straits. I'm gambling so much on this shop."

William nodded. "I remember feeling the same way about my ill-fated wine bar. But you're in much better shape than I was. You've got your feet on the ground."

Ellen liked that he saw how competent she was. There was so much about her Zach had not seen. "How's the cake?" she asked.

He kissed his fingertips. "Delectable."

She laughed. "Happy Valentine's Day." The dozen red roses he'd given her stood in a vase on the table between them.

"Have you, ah, heard anything from Alice?" he asked.

"Seriously?"

He scraped his plate with his fork. "I've been hoping."

She tried to catch his eye. "Hoping for what?"

"Hoping things could be set right."

"You've been hoping for a miracle."

He shrugged.

Ellen squinted at him. "And how would we go about setting things *right*?"

"Okay, maybe I'm naïve. But what did you call them? Middle-aged clichés. Ouch."

"The truth hurts." What was he implying? That *she* had been cruel? She stood and collected the dirty plates.

"Ellen, what are you doing?"

"I'll clean up."

"You don't have to clean up."

"I should get going soon."

"Please sit down."

She stopped with the dishes, but she wouldn't sit. "Look, self-doubt and obsessing over my own minor transgressions has never gotten me anywhere. All my life, other people would run me over, and I would twist and turn, worrying my *reaction* had been too harsh. No more."

Ellen saw a tremor in the corner of his eye. But he needed to hear this. Her days of victimhood, of blind trust blinking stupidly beneath the banner of love, were over.

"I'm sorry," he said. "You're right."

She put the dishes down on the table. "I don't want to be right."

"No?"

All this posturing and negotiating, the hiding and the rooting out, the discovery of the way things stand and the bridges that must be built. Was no one immune? Ellen sat. "What I want to be is safe."

William studied her face, a wistful tug pulling at his lips. "That is the great yearning, isn't it? For people like us."

Ellen thought of Arborview, of the sense of safety, of reassurance, in the air. It did not follow her back down the tree, though, not with any reliability. Her shoulders softened. "The problem is," she said, reaching for William's hand, "I don't know that such a thing really exists."

Chapter Thirty-Eight

Rosa had a bad cold. First, in the chest with fits of coughing that left a metallic taste in her mouth, then in her head, where it lodged behind her nose and eyes, a dull, dripping pressure sending her to the living room couch for days to watch television. She missed a week of classes at River Bend, and a week of work.

"You can't go to the hospice," Mama said, chuckling. "You don't want to make nobody there sick."

Mama had a tasteless sense of humor sometimes. Javi, over the phone, loved the little joke. "Gallows humor," he called it, and then he said, "Don't let the old lady get to you."

"Easy for you to say," Rosa squeaked through her stuffed nose. She had turned off the TV for the afternoon because she couldn't stand the teary eyes and perfect hair of the reality show actresses anymore. "How's Niagara?"

"Cold, busy. It's harder than I thought it would be, the classes."

"Getting your karma leveled a little now, huh?" Rosa sneezed.

"River Bend is looking better all the time." Javi's voiced sounded detached, distant.

"Is somebody else there?" Rosa said.

"Tilda just walked in." His voice dropped to a

whisper. "She's been homesick and moaning all the time. Maybe Mama was right about her coming with me, after all."

"Yeah, well bite your tongue for me, okay? Don't go telling Mama she's right. She'll never shut up about it and how am I going to…"

"I got to go."

"Javi?"

Dead line. Tilda must have demanded his immediate attention. Rosa had thought he was stupid to bring Tilda, too. What were the odds their relationship would last? Not good, according to Mama: "If he don't cat around now, he gonna do it when he's older." Maybe Rosa would meet her husband at Seasons Culinary College. Wouldn't Mama be thrilled? Two chefs in the family.

By the weekend, Rosa was well enough to return to work. It was the day of the Napoleon. She lugged a grocery bag, heavy with plastic containers full of ingredients, to the bus stop. She'd packed a few things in ice, in case the bus was late.

Rosa headed down the sidewalk to wait on the corner. The block was quiet for a Saturday afternoon. The cold kept people indoors, but Rosa didn't mind it so much. The air felt clean when it was cold, purified. Sarah was a skier. She went to mountains in Vermont, and in Aspen, too, where her parents had a house. A "ski house," Sarah had called it. Rosa wondered if Sarah had a boyfriend. If she took him skiing in Aspen. Maybe she'd ask. They were good enough friends now.

Sarah didn't know they were making the Napoleon today. Rosa wanted to surprise her. And if Sarah wasn't up for it, that was okay, too. There was space in the little refrigerator in the kitchen to store the ingredients for another day. Rosa would label the bag.

The hospice was pretty empty when Rosa arrived. A few nurses walked up and down the hall, smiling at her as she passed, and she saw a doctor, or someone in a white coat, heading into the medical conference room—which Rosa vacuumed and dusted—but there were a lot of empty beds, room doors open wide. The place filled and emptied like this, in waves. Rosa would probably have some down time today. Sarah and she could maybe start the Napoleon a little before her shift ended.

She hung her coat, hat, and gloves on a hook in the laundry room before heading into the kitchen. Icy fluorescent light shone over the food prep table, while the recessed lights over the sink glowed a warm yellow. Mr. Janssen's office was empty. He never worked weekends, and the reverend was long gone. Rosa missed him—his awful Spanish and little jokes, how he always had something nice to say, and, most of all, the way he looked at her like he was so impressed, so happy, proud even, just to know her.

As Rosa tucked her ingredients bag into a corner of the fridge, her phone rang. She took it from her back pocket and checked the number. Javi. He knew better than to call her at work, but he did anyway.

"Hola," she said softly.

"What do you want from me?"

"Javi?"

"Uh, hello?"

She laughed. "What, did you butt dial me? It's Rosa."

"Rosa? Oh, man. I'm sorry. I thought I called

Mama back. She hung up on me. I made the mistake of telling her how tough my classes are, you know, stupidly thinking she was going to reassure me, and…"

Rosa scooted into the little pantry off the kitchen, where boxes of napkins, paper towels, and cleaning supplies were kept. Javi was wound up and needed to vent, apparently. Lucky for him this place was so quiet today. She put the phone back to her ear.

"…she went nuts and chewed my ear off." Javi's voice, like machine-gun fire. "On and on, warning me I better not screw this up, and the shame it would bring on all of us, and the five thousand dollars she'd have wasted."

"Javi, can you…"

"I'd have strangled her if I could have reached through the phone." He was nearly growling. "She never can understand how…"

But something he said swam up to Rosa, through his wave of words. "Javi…" The room seemed to be tilting. Rosa closed her eyes.

"And then she had the nerve to say to me…"

"Wait," Rosa said. "Wait. What five thousand dollars?"

He shut up. Total silence. Then Javi said, "Yeah, it was Mama at her worst, her absolute worst. You've seen how she gets. You know what I'm talking about."

"What five thousand dollars?" Rosa leaned back against the wall, because even before it hit, she could feel it coming. A trapdoor opened beneath her feet. An inkling deep within she wanted to run from rose to the surface, with sinister power, and whispered in her ear. *You already know what they've done.* They had all been living this lie, this charade, calling it anything but what it really was, for a long time.

"Mama gave you five thousand dollars for school?" Rosa managed to get the words out.

"Uh…yeah. But that ain't much. It was a little bit she scraped together and set aside."

Set aside? "You told me she wasn't giving you any money."

"I never told you that."

"You let me believe it!" Rosa forced her voice down. "You know I thought we were both getting the same deal."

"Oh, come on, don't you start on me today, too."

"We talked about money for school all the time, Javi, and you never said nothing."

"I thought it didn't matter."

"Bull." Rosa's voice was shaking. "Then why did you hide it? Why the lie of…of omission? It's still a lie."

"It's five thousand dollars, not a fortune."

"It might as well be five million to us. And you know it." Rosa hung up.

Her heart was thumping. A wave of nausea roiled her stomach. Mama had "set aside" money. Secretly set aside. Rosa had always known Mama loved Javi more. Javi was her favorite. That was just Mama. But this was too far, an abandonment that reached into the future, investing in Javi's security and success, in Javi's safety, but not in Rosa's.

She moved back into the kitchen, her legs unsteady. She pulled a chair out from the table. She had to sit for a minute.

What was it Mama liked to say? *Money is the bottom line.* She said it with a tight-jawed certainty, a bitter period at the end of her thoughts. And Javi alone was deserving of her money, and it wasn't just because Rosa wanted to cook. The boy's future mattered more simply because he was a boy. The old ways were burned into Mama's soul. Life had taught her nothing.

How Sarah would howl when Rosa told her. She would give that slow shake of her head, the one which meant "they haven't got a clue." She'd call them out, straight-up. There was no getting anything by Sarah. She was doing so much better, the hospice was thinking of sending her home, at least for a visit. Sarah had already begun packing.

Rosa reached for a napkin from the table, wiped her nose, and then stood up. She still had a job to do. And a Napoleon to make today. For once, she was going to push all thoughts of school and money, Javi and Mama, out of her mind. She could do it today. She had to.

She checked the work schedule at the bulletin board on the wall, where her supervisor left a written log of rooms to be cleaned at the start of every shift.

Rosa scanned the list. Not many, just as she thought. Three rooms needed to be cleaned top-to-bottom, 215, 110, and 107. Ninety minutes of work in the rooms, tops. Then she had to run the laundry and remake the beds, another two hours, mop the hallways. Yep, she'd be finished early. She'd start on the second floor and work her way down.

She got fresh cleaning gloves and a pail. There'd be supplies in the closet on the second floor. The chapel was up there, too. Maybe she'd stop by. It was down the hall from Sarah's room.

Sarah's room. Room 215.

Chapter Thirty-Nine

Ellen turned her attention to the menu. She would have all the expected treats and delicacies: cream puffs and eclairs, brownies and blondies, fruit tarts and macaroons, scones, biscotti, ladyfingers, shortbread, and magic bars. There would be cakes made-to-order and seasonal pies, and a "Cookie of the Day."

But she wanted more. A signature offering, a creation that would set Just Desserts apart. This specialty would rotate with the seasons. Four chances every year to leave her mark on the world, to deliver something bold and sweet and redeeming. Pastry is a defiant act in an ugly world. Maybe she would print this on the napkins.

The shop's slogan, created by the advertising agency she'd hired, was already painted in swirling red letters across the glass door: *Just Desserts: Get What's Coming to You.*

The ad agency team—three kids who didn't look much older than Jimmy and Taber, dressed in skinny black jeans and micro mini-skirts—had listened intently, scribbling notes, as she described her vision for the shop.

"It's too dark, Mom," Taber warned on the phone. "Nobody wants judgment with their morning coffee."

"Dark?" Ellen said. "Or edgy?"

"I like edgy. I'm just not sure pastry is the place for

246

it."

Ellen sighed. "What do you suggest?"

"How about something lighter, more—I don't know—hopeful. Isn't that what you're shooting for?"

Ellen hesitated. "Sort of, but it's more than that. It's…"

"We Rise." Taber paused. " 'Rise' makes you think of baking, right? Yeast makes things rise, and puff pastry rises. And there's a certain, I don't know, transcendent quality in what you're reaching for here."

"Transcendent." The same thing William had said. The word felt right in Ellen's mouth. She thought instantly of Arborview. Wasn't this what she had been doing in the old tree house? Stepping into silence and connecting—she didn't know how—with something that lifted her above the fray, so she could think, so she could begin to *see*? "How'd you get so smart, so young?" she asked.

"I'm only doing my job, Mom."

Ellen planned to open in late May, early June at the latest. She would have to call the ad agency back. They'd charge her more to change the shop's name. They'd have to print new materials. They'd have to repaint the door. But We Rise was the perfect name.

She was lining the shop's walk-in kitchen pantry shelves the next afternoon when she heard the door chimes ring. She'd forgotten to lock, which she'd promised William she would do when she was alone here. She wasn't expecting any deliveries today. She put aside the organic bamboo shelf liners the salesgirl at a ritzy kitchen shop had talked her into, reached for her cell phone in her apron pocket, and headed out to the counter.

"Hello," she called, pushing open the swinging kitchen door.

Alice stood in front of the display case.

Ellen stopped. "Oh," she said.

Alice winced. "Should I have called first?" Her voice was small, uncertain.

Ellen stood rooted for an instant. Then she forced her way to the counter and placed her hands on top. Alice looked strange. Were those sweatpants? They were—gray sweats with a red hoodie sweatshirt and white tennis shoes. Ellen couldn't believe her eyes. And Alice's hair—pulled back in a stubby ponytail with silvery streaks at her temples. Ellen would have passed her by on the street.

"Are you all right?" Alice asked. She shook her head. "Of course you're not. Why would I ask such a thing? What a question coming from me, of all people. Anyway. Earle is gone."

Ellen trembled. Earle was dead?

"He's left me."

Ellen exhaled.

Alice sighed. "Are you going to talk to me at all?"

"I'm sorry," Ellen said. "About Earle, I guess."

"You guess?" Alice—with ratty clothes and greasy hair and a husband on the lam—still raising an eyebrow of expectation, believing she was due special consideration, or some magical exemption, from consequences.

Ellen folded her arms across her chest. "Earle finally saw through your crap and walked out. I say hooray for him."

Alice raised her palms in surrender. Her fingernails were stubby and ugly and worn, like Ellen's. "I didn't come here to fight with you," she said.

Ellen steadied her breathing. "Why did you come?"

"To see how you are."

Warning lights flashed in Ellen's mind. Then a gentle nudge: *Do the right thing. She has come to you. Say the right thing.* But what was the right thing?

"Can I at least sit down?" Alice walked to a table and dropped into a chair. "I sit across the street in the library sometimes and watch your shop." She pointed out the storefront window to the building across the green. "I love what you've done with the interior. You must be proud."

Ellen moved around the counter and walked to the table. She pulled out a chair and sat. "I haven't opened yet. Let's hope I can be proud in six months' time."

"Oh, Ellie, it will be a smash. You'll be marvelous."

Ellie. The word stung. No one but Alice had ever called Ellen that.

Alice looked down at the tabletop. "I want to sit a minute with you. I know I won't be here again. There is no way back to the way we were before, is there?"

There it was. No way back. Something dropped inside Ellen. A tendril of panic wound around her heart. Even after everything, part of her still wanted Alice.

Ellen shook her head. "No one ever goes back, only forward. It's taken me almost fifty years to understand this. But there is always a way forward, if you're willing to try. If you're brave enough."

Alice gave a weary smile. "I am where I am."

"Oh, please, no more dismissive clichés, okay? What's next? 'It is what it is'—right? Things can be what you *make* them, too. You can choose."

Alice looked startled. Then she shrugged. "I've made a mess of my life, and I've come up empty-handed."

She'd come up empty-handed. It was so typical of Alice to paint herself as the victim. Always. Why was it Ellen had never realized this about her? How can you be friends with a person for twenty years and not see a thing like this?

"You know what you haven't mentioned?" Ellen asked. "Anyone else's life. What about what's happened to Earle's life? To your daughter's life? To *my* life?"

"A person can only say, 'Sorry,' so many times. I'm through with sorry." Alice raised her eyes. "And you didn't get divorced because of me."

Ah, a spark of the old Alice: deflecting all blame, minimizing when the truth loomed too near, changing the frame. The old spin doctor was still in there.

"No, I didn't. But that isn't the point, though, is it?" Ellen said. "The point isn't how, or why, my *marriage* ended. The point is how our friendship ended."

Alice looked back at the tabletop. "Look, I hate the way things ended. I wanted to tell you." She sighed. "Maybe life just hunts us all down, in the end."

"No, life does not hunt us down. Bad choices hunt us down. Lies and denials and cruelty eventually turn on you, if you give them enough time."

"Is that so?" Alice sniffed, not a teary sniff but a defiant little whiff. "I see you've become quite the philosopher, Ellie."

Alice smiled, a cold, inflectionless flash. And Ellen sensed it—a submerged strain of rigidity that Alice was battling to hide, a reluctance to *give in*. Underneath it all, Alice was angry. In her mind, *she* had been wronged. Could the clothes, the hair, be a ploy, a strategy to gain sympathy? Would she drive straight home after this and color her hair and schedule a manicure? Had she sunk that low?

A weightlessness came over Ellen, as if she had stepped into an alternate reality. "I should be getting back to work."

Alice made a show of looking at her watch. "Oh, it's getting late, isn't it?"

They walked to the door. Alice pulled a pair of gloves from her purse—a black, fur-trimmed pair Ellen knew. The sight of them made her stomach hurt. She swallowed. "Thanks for stopping by. I know it can't have been easy."

"But nothing's easy anymore, Ellie. Is it?"

Ellen looked out at the street. A car with Alice's license plate, a sapphire Mercedes Benz SUV, sat parked at the curb. Alice loved sapphire. Zach and Ellen had looked at those cars once. The prices were ridiculous. Even Zach, who loved all things status-symbol, had balked. "You got a new car," Ellen said.

"I traded up. I had to." Alice pulled on her gloves. "My attorney told me to clean out as much cash from our joint accounts as I could, before Earle files. There's no sense in letting him walk away with so much money. He'll have a much tougher time getting a car away from me."

Ellen opened her mouth to speak but couldn't get any words out. There was no point. Alice would never see herself. Ellen opened the door, and the chime jingled. A jolt of cold winter air washed over them.

"You take care of yourself, Ellie," Alice said. Their eyes met, and Alice rested a hand on Ellen's shoulder.

Ellen swallowed hard. "You, too."

Alice smiled and turned away.

Ellen closed the door and watched until the brilliant blue of Alice's car disappeared down Main Street. Then she locked the door.

****

"It's a start," William said, after she'd driven to his place and relayed the scene with Alice.

A start to what, she wanted to ask.

But she didn't press him. It had been an off-night. The encounter with Alice had drained her, and William was edgy during dinner, distracted. Maybe they both needed a good night's sleep.

Later, he seemed to drop into a deep sleep instantly, lying beside her in the dark. She listened to his breathing. The morning sun would set him straight. It had always helped her.

She woke in the night to find his side of the bed empty. She listened for the sound of him in the bathroom.

She sat up, shivering, and reached for the pink flannel robe he had bought her, a "houseguest gift," he'd called it. The gesture and the way he had placed it in her hands had sent a rush of warm gratitude through her.

His condominium was small, and from the top of the narrow staircase, she could see light coming from downstairs.

She found him in the kitchen, sitting at the table beneath the window, a glass of red wine before him.

"Hi," she said.

He startled, raising his head. "Oh, did I wake you? I'm sorry."

He was wrapped in a long, white bathrobe, the thick cotton kind that reminded her of good hotels. From the doorway, she could see the rough stubble on his cheeks and the ashy shadows beneath his eyes.

"No, don't worry." She went to him. "What are you doing?"

"I couldn't sleep." He tapped the wine glass. "This helps."

She didn't push. She could tell he didn't want her to. "The sun won't be up for a few hours. Come back to bed. It's so cold down here."

He took her hand. "I'll turn up the thermostat. I'm sorry. I must be getting addled in my old age."

She kissed his cheek, feeling the raspy stubble against her lips. She led him into the hall and toward the stairs.

Chapter Forty

Rosa spun around to the filing cabinet near the door. She grabbed the clipboard off the top and ran her finger down the list of room assignments. Room 215. No name, the little blank box where the patient's name should be written, empty.

She swallowed hard. Sarah had been discharged? While Rosa was out sick, she'd gone home.

She pictured Sarah the last time she'd seen her, sitting in the chair in her room, fully dressed, reading a book. Her suitcases half-packed to go.

She was home! A thrill ran up Rosa's spine. But would they still be friends? How would they keep in touch? Maybe Rosa could get Sarah's cell phone or her address from the hospice. Or maybe they would send Sarah hers.

Rosa took her pail and gloves and headed out into the hall. She'd start on the second floor, with Sarah's room, to get it out of the way. It would be weird to see the room empty. She'd clean it and then put it out of her mind.

Faint music drifted down the second-floor corridor, coming from the nursing station. Sarah's door was open. Marissa, one of the aides who worked the night shift, came down the hall. Marissa was nice, always smiling. Her brown hair fell in a straight bob to her chin, and she wore a silver cross necklace Rosa thought was pretty. Sometimes, coming out of the room of a patient who had just died or was nearing the end, Marissa would have this glow on her face, like she'd witnessed a special, rare thing.

"Hi," Marissa said. She wore silver cross earrings today, as well. "Are you feeling better? I heard you were out sick."

"I had a bad cold," Rosa said. Her own voice sounded strange, faint. She found it difficult to form words. She cleared her throat.

Marissa smiled. "But you're back on your feet. Young people recover fast."

Rosa nodded toward Sarah's door. Why was her heart thudding, reaching up into her throat?

Marissa followed her gaze. Then her smile melted. "It was beautiful the way she went. I was lucky enough to be here, to witness it."

Rosa bit her lower lip, which had gone dry.

"The departure everyone hopes for." Marissa gave her a worried look. "Rosa, are you okay?"

"Sarah went home."

Marissa nodded. "Yes. That's a lovely way of putting it."

What was this woman talking about? "Sarah's parents brought her home," Rosa said.

Marissa's eyes widened.

"We were going to bake a Napoleon today. We've been planning it."

Marissa put her hand on Rosa's shoulder. "Oh, honey. You didn't know. Oh, I'm so sorry. This has to be such a shock…"

Rosa stepped back, shrugging off Marissa's hand.

"Sarah passed away, Rosa. Two days ago. I'm so

sorry. I know she was your friend."

Rosa stared into Marissa's face. "We're making a cake."

"Sarah was very ill. You knew, right?"

"She's been so much better lately."

"It happens this way sometimes, a rally and then a sudden turn for the worse. But she's at peace now. You can trust in that."

Rosa grew light-headed. A gray haze pushed in all around her. Marissa's face was a mask of soft concern, but Rosa wanted to slap her.

Marissa said, "It was her time to go."

Rosa stepped back. "Are you crazy? Nobody's supposed to die this young."

"Let's get a cup of tea." Marissa reached out to take Rosa's hand. Wow, this woman was weird. Why had Rosa never noticed how weird she was?

Rosa shook her head.

"Sarah's at peace now."

Rosa spun around and started down the hall. "She's not at peace. She's dead."

Marissa didn't pursue her, and Rosa was soon at the end of the corridor. She dropped her bucket in front of the supply closet and slammed through the door leading to the stairwell. Her feet flew down the stairs, and she burst into the foyer.

The sun spilled through the stained-glass star window in watery splashes of blue and gold and amber, glowing across the tile floor, running in shards down the far wall, shifting and winking, almost like they were breathing. Rosa stood in the center, her breath the only sound, a shower of light all around. She swore she felt Sarah, a jolt of her, moving among the colors. She closed her eyes, and Sarah's face emerged, so clearly, the mint green eyes, the mischievous dimple. *Don't let anybody tell you who you are.*

"Sarah?" Rosa whispered. The word drifted upward. Rosa felt the hum of the air, laced with unseen energy, the way you can sense the presence of a person in a dark room before you turn on the light.

Rosa opened her eyes. The high-pitched ceiling loomed above her, overwhelming. She made her way to the door and down the short hall to the chapel. It was empty. She dropped into a seat, feeling her legs give way, and shuddered an exhale.

Sarah was dead. Hadn't Rosa known from the moment she saw the cleaning chart? Sarah wasn't recovering at home. She would never go home, or back to Yale, or become a lawyer. There would be no Napoleon. It was all a sick, teasing joke. If a girl like Sarah could die, for no reason, for no purpose at all, nothing was safe. This sounded like something Javi would say. *Don't place any bets, florecita.*

Javi. The money. Mama.

Sarah.

Rosa trembled, cornered. She regained her feet and headed down the aisle and out into the hall, then through the spotlight of the foyer, and back to the first floor, to the safety of the kitchen. Only the kitchen felt weirdly violated, as if a stranger had broken in and rearranged everything.

Rosa took out her phone and sent her supervisor a text, steadying her finger to zero in on the keys:

—I'm sick again. I'm heading home. So sorry. Not many rooms to clean. Can someone cover for me?—

She pulled on her coat.

Outside, the cold air stung as she hurried down the street. She would get on the next bus going anywhere, as long as it was away from here. Oblivious traffic passed, drivers focused on the road or nodding to unheard music. Rosa's hands had stopped shaking. The cold grounded her. Her breath rose in puffs. Was Sarah already buried, or cremated—burned up, so there was nothing left of her? No miracle had come. Rosa wanted to sit down on the curb, curl into a ball, and let the cold cover her. She heard Mama's voice, smug in its defeatism: *You work in a hospice. What was you expecting?*

Chapter Forty-One

Ellen leafed through the catalogue, studying the photographs of the delicately curved wrought-iron patio chairs and matching tables. She wanted to expand onto the sidewalk with an al fresco space. "Very Parisian," she told Taber on the phone. "Picture it: café tables and chairs under a striped awning, hanging plants."

Taber had gasped. "Seasonal flowers, swap them out four times a year. I'll work up a color scheme."

William had been less certain: "You haven't even opened, and you're expanding?"

But Ellen loved the idea, and the town zoning board agreed. Outdoors seating would expand the options and bring in more people. It was a simple matter of maximizing her profit by offering patrons more choices. William must have understood this.

Ellen closed the catalogue. She liked being alone in her shop at night, the lights low, the hiss of a passing car's tires outside, and this great dream blooming within her.

She gazed out the window. She had been in Arborview that afternoon, despite the cold, hunkered down on the beanbag, in a heavy coat and winter hat. She hadn't stayed long, fifteen minutes, maybe twenty, long enough to enter a moment of distilling silence. Alice's face had come to her, Alice's voice, her throaty laughter. A dull pang had pierced Ellen. There were truths Alice would never look at. She had reached the end of her tether and would go no further.

Lately, it seemed to Ellen that all people had tethers—some longer, others shorter—tying them to the past and whatever pain they had endured. Some strained at the end of the tether until it snapped, and they stepped, freed, into a new space of understanding and possibility. Others, like Alice, remained rooted, going in circles, wondering who to blame next.

****

When bus Number Eleven, not her usual bus, lumbered up, Rosa climbed aboard, flashing her pass at the driver. She didn't ask where it was going, didn't bother reading the glowing ticker-tape across the front announcing the stops. She slid into an empty seat in the back, meeting no one's eyes. A numbness stole over her, and she let her mind drift where it would.

On the highway, the bus passed the exit to her neighborhood. Mama would have left the porch light on for her. Farther along the highway, she passed the exit for the ritzy town where Sotto Voce stood. Mama must be there now, getting ready for her shift. Rosa glanced at the time on her phone. The dinner menu started in an hour. The sous chefs were chopping away. The saucier, dipping and tasting. The chefs were seasoning their pans. Gleaming white dinner plates stood stacked and waiting, as the anticipation built. But did Mama see any of this? What did she know about creation? About this world of possibilities? Mama gave up all her dreams long ago.

Sarah had kept making plans, lying in a hospice bed. Her death bed. Rosa stared through the streaky bus window. "I'm sorry, Sarah." Her whispered words fogged the glass.

The bus exited the highway. Rosa read the street signs. They were rolling into Mrs. Cahill's town. There was a bus stop in the center, near Mrs. Cahill's shop. A wave of panic. What if…no, Mrs. Cahill was not on this bus. She had a car, and anyway it was Saturday night. She was probably out at dinner.

The lights of the village green bounced off the bus windshield. Rosa slid down in her seat. There was the shop, right there, a blue and yellow awning hung over the front, and a sign above the door: *We Rise*. The bus drove past, and Rosa saw Mrs. Cahill staring out of the shop window, a warm light glowing behind her.

Rosa jumped to her feet as the bus slowed at the corner. She grabbed her bag and hurried down the aisle. The bus groaned to stop. Rosa nodded at the driver. A gust of frigid wind greeted her as she stepped down onto the sidewalk, as the bus pulled away, grinding and hissing.

The green was empty, too cold for anyone to be out walking. Rosa headed down the sidewalk. She stopped under the shop's striped awning. Mrs. Cahill had left the window. Rosa could see tables inside, chairs. She knocked, softly at first, then harder until Mrs. Cahill appeared in the doorway. Her face brightened, her mouth dropped open as she pressed buttons in the alarm pad near the door.

"Rosa." She smiled. "What a surprise."

"Hi. Is it okay I'm here? I was just, um, in the neighborhood."

"Yes, of course." Mrs. Cahill waved her inside. "Come in, come in."

Rosa sniffed, and something in the sound must

have tipped off Mrs. Cahill, because she said, "Rosa, is anything wrong?"

Rosa gave a smile so phony, it hurt her face. "Nah."

Mrs. Cahill pulled out a chair at one of the tables. "Let's sit down."

Rosa sat. "Your shop is really nice."

"Did something happen?"

"I…well…yes." Rosa swallowed hard. "Sarah died."

"Sarah?"

"A patient at the hospice, a friend of mine. The one I told you about? We were going to make a Napoleon today."

"Oh, yes. Oh, Rosa."

Then something snapped deep inside. Rosa bent over in her chair as the tears came. Mrs. Cahill's arms were around her, squeezing her hard. "Honey. Your friend. I'm so sorry," she whispered.

Rosa let herself be held. It was odd, having this intimate moment with a teacher. But it didn't feel so strange. Mrs. Cahill was more than a teacher. She was a friend now, too.

"This wasn't supposed to happen. Sarah was special." Rosa took a breath, sitting up. "She had everything in front of her, everything to live for. And she was smart as a whip."

Mrs. Cahill nodded and took her hand. "I know. I know."

"I thought maybe we'd stay friends, when she went back to Yale, and I went to Seasons Culinary College. She was so…so confident, you know? She made things seem possible." Rosa sniffed. "You probably think I'm ridiculous. Thinking this person in a hospice was going to get out and go back to college. I've been kidding myself, right?"

Mrs. Cahill nodded. "We all kid ourselves occasionally. When something is too awful to face, or to admit, we hide out for a while." She stood and ducked behind the counter. She came back with a box of tissues and slid them toward Rosa. "It's only natural to want to avoid pain. I've been guilty, too."

"Nothing makes this right." Rosa took a tissue and wiped her nose.

"Seasons Culinary College is possible," Mrs. Cahill said. "Sarah was right about that, you know. Maybe this was her gift to you."

This sounded true, and it was nice. But Rosa's smart, secret friend was still gone. No more talks and high-fives and shared recipes. The Napoleon would never be made. "Sarah thought cooking school sounded great. She thought I could do it."

"Doesn't surprise me." Mrs. Cahill scooted her chair closer.

"I thought maybe there would be a miracle," Rosa said. "Sarah and I talked about it. She believed it, too."

"I'm sorry you didn't get a miracle. They do happen."

"Do they?"

"Yes, the problem is we don't get to pick which ones. Listen, nothing I can say will make Sarah's death any easier." Mrs. Cahill leaned toward her. "But you were a good friend at a time when she needed friends the most."

"I caught the bus, but I didn't know it was coming here," Rosa said. "I just wanted to get away." She heard how foolish she sounded, hopping on a bus blindly, stupidly. "I'm sorry for coming here and making this your problem. You're busy. I should be…"

Mrs. Cahill wrapped Rosa in another warm hug. "You're not going anywhere. I could use some company tonight. Would you like a cup of tea?"

Rosa didn't drink tea, but she said, "Yes, thanks." Mrs. Cahill's arms felt so good around her.

"I've got a kettle ready to go. Hang on a minute, hold your thought."

Mrs. Cahill disappeared into the kitchen. Rosa heard clanking, and a cabinet door swinging open. Why was Mrs. Cahill alone tonight? It was the weekend. Why wasn't she with Mr. Janssen?

Rosa glanced around. The pastry display case glass was so clear, the white enamel inside so clean. The white countertops gleamed, too. Rosa loved the wooden tables with their matching seats and the overstuffed yellow couches in the corners. The warm glow she had seen from the street came from dangling silver pendant lights over the display case.

Mrs. Cahill returned, carrying a tray with two cups of tea and a plate of biscotti. "I just made them. Cherry almond."

Rosa smiled. "My favorite biscotti flavor."

"Nothing fancy, but a sure thing." Mrs. Cahill sat down opposite Rosa. "I've been baking here a little every day to break in the kitchen. It's like a new playing field, you know? I've got to get used to it before opening day."

Rosa thought how lucky Mrs. Cahill was to be cooking in a new kitchen, in her own shop, starting a great new thing, with all of the bad times behind her.

"I can't wait for you to join me this summer," Mrs. Cahill said. "Before you go off to school."

School seemed so distant now. Rosa stared into the golden amber of her tea. "I found out something else today. Mama is giving Javi five thousand dollars for college. They've been keeping it a secret. She won't give me a dime."

Mrs. Cahill blinked. "Did this happen today? You found out about Sarah and the money, too, today?"

"This afternoon, at work. I went back to the hospice, after being out sick for a week, and it all happened. Javi let the money news slip on the phone. He tried to cover it up. He tried to make it seem like nothing, like no big deal."

Mrs. Cahill nodded. "That's what people do when they're caught."

"Javi acted like I had no reason to be upset. He said it had nothing to do with me." Rosa's voice cracked.

"That's just ridiculous." A shudder of disgust crossed Mrs. Cahill's face. "It has everything to do with you and says a lot about your family." She was silent a moment, looking like she was struggling with what came next. "I'll be honest, I don't know what to tell you about this one. Families"—she rolled her eyes—"can be so stupidly vicious. Maybe with time, your mom will see things differently, and Javi will, too, and he'll come clean."

Rosa snorted. "Mama doesn't *see* anything. She doesn't believe in anything. She doesn't hope. She acts like there's nothing we can really do to change things. It's keep your head down and scrape by, especially if you're a girl."

Mrs. Cahill winced. "You'll never be like that."

How did she know that this was what scared Rosa most? Rosa hadn't found the words for it herself until now. "I won't?"

Mrs. Cahill reached to place her hand on Rosa's. "Life has overwhelmed your mother, and she's not strong like you, Rosa. I hope it's okay for me to say this."

"Yeah, it's okay. But Mama does love me, you know."

"Of course she does, in the only way she knows how. This money business is terrible. It's unjust and cruel, but don't let it derail you. Just keep going. This is your life, not your mother's and not Javi's."

If only Mrs. Cahill had been her mother, how different things would have been.

Mrs. Cahill sat back in her chair. "Does William— Mr. Janssen—know about Sarah?"

Rosa hesitated. "I don't know. Are you dating him?" The words, tumbling out of her mouth, surprised Rosa. "Sorry, it's none of my business."

Mrs. Cahill raised her palms. "No biggie. Yes, we're friends. I guess you could say we're dating."

"Oh, how nice." Rosa didn't want to go any further. Mrs. Cahill mustn't have either. Rosa sipped her tea. "I should probably get going soon."

Mrs. Cahill glanced at her watch. "Can I give you a ride after I lock up?"

"Only if it's no trouble."

Mrs. Cahill smiled. "Of course it's no trouble. You take your time. Eat something. And we'll go whenever you're ready."

Rosa lifted a piece of the biscotti, realizing how long it had been since she'd last eaten anything. She wished she could stay all night in this little shop, letting the world pass outside, taking with it Mama and Javi, and the shadows that must be falling across Sarah's bed at the hospice now.

But eventually she would let Mrs. Cahill take her home. All the way home, to her real house. There was no need now to pretend, to stop a few streets over, in front of a strange house where other people—even the women—dared to dream big.

Chapter Forty-Two

Two weeks later, and a Nor'easter was moving up the coast, winter's last hurrah. It spun out of the Bahamas and touched down in the Carolinas before tracking north. It was expected to hit New England in mid-afternoon.

This would be Ellen's first major storm in the house alone, and the prospect left her feeling hollow. The blizzards of the past ran through her mind: the watchful anticipation as the sky turned a heavy, foamy gray, the last-minute trip to the grocery store to stock up on hot chocolate—for the kids after playing in the snow—and food enough to last in case they were snowed in a couple of days. Zach making sure the storm windows were sealed tight, while Jimmy and Taber prayed for school to be cancelled, and everyone prayed for the power lines to hold.

Now, Ellen drifted through the rooms in her house out of pre-storm habit. She had enough food. No hot chocolate necessary. No schools to care about. The snowplow guy's phone number was stuck up on the refrigerator. He'd dig out her driveway. She checked the storm windows and then called William. She left him a voicemail: "Hey, it's me. Want to come over and ride out the storm together? There's safety in numbers, they say. I miss you, sweetheart."

She'd called him "sweetheart" for the first time on

Valentine's Day. He hadn't objected. In fact, he had smiled, that soft smile of his she loved. She wanted him here, on her couch, in her arms, the solid warmth of him, their shared laughter, the secret, growing alliance that was theirs alone.

The snow began falling around three o'clock, sheets of tiny, determined flakes. This was the kind of snow that meant business. There were four inches on the ground in an hour.

Ellen switched on her television, the small portable one she had placed on the kitchen counter to keep her company while she cooked. The local weather forecasters could not contain their glee.

"A monumental storm."

"Treacherous conditions."

"Estimates ranging up to thirty inches in parts of the state."

One young woman, bundled in her station's red jacket and boots, stood at a highway entrance ramp, bracing herself against the wind. "It's going to be a night not fit for man nor beast," she shouted into her microphone. "Folks, please stay home, lock the doors, and throw a log on the fire."

Ellen rolled her eyes.

Another hour, and snow falling so furiously she could barely make out the road from her window. Still no call from William. He'd never make it over here now. The roads would be impassable. Had he gotten stranded? Had something happened to him?

Ellen went to her office and turned on the computer. She should look through her email one more time anyway, in case the power did go out. She didn't like squinting at the phone and fumbling around with its little keys.

An email from William sat at the top of her queue. He'd sent it only an hour ago, after her phone call. Why hadn't he called back? She clicked it open.

Dearest Ellen,

I'm a coward. Let me say this up front.

I don't know how to explain, but I will try.

I need to leave. Not just you, but everything. I've taken a leave of absence from the college, and I'm traveling to India next week.

Yes, India. I need to be culture shocked, to be wiped clean. The chaos of the streets will erase me.

I'll be volunteering with an NGO that arranges microfinance loans to small farmers. They need accounting help, so I'll be put to good use.

To say I'm sorry doesn't begin to capture the regret I feel for hurting you. I would explain my deficiencies further, if I thought I could. I am not a man with a heart big enough for you, Ellen. You have all the self-control, all the selflessness and faith I've never been able to muster. Every time I look at you, I see how far short I fall. The mountain is just too high.

Forgive me.

Good luck with your shop. I know it will be a sensation.

William

Ellen typed without thinking, the first thing that popped into her head: *What are you saying? Is this a joke?*

Her breathing grew raspy and fast. The floor seemed to be slipping away beneath her feet. She hit send.

What was she doing? Why not call him? She

reached for her phone.

"Ding."

A response. On the computer screen, her returned email glowed, unopened. It was a bounce-back.

Had he already closed his account?

Or blocked her?

Her hands shook as she reached for her phone and dialed. The call went straight to voicemail, not even ringing first. Ellen cleared her throat, her mind racing for what to say to him, when a recorded voice said, "This voice mailbox is full and cannot accept messages at this time. Goodbye."

Was she dreaming? Had she gone crazy?

—William,— she typed into a text message. *—What on earth is going on? Please call me right away.—*

Ellen hit send. The message sat in its blue bubble. But she saw that the "Delivered" note, which had appeared under all her messages above, didn't show now.

He wasn't going to let her respond. What was he doing? How could he think this?

She felt like she had been hit with a sucker punch in the face, a fast cut to the chin. She slumped in her seat and closed her eyes. *The mountain is just too high.* What did that even mean? Such pomposity. Why had she never noticed this pompous, stubborn thread in the fine, sad lines of his smile? He was obstinate, and he drew a kind of weird power from it. He would not face her. He would not be confronted. He had digitally dismissed her.

Ellen sobbed, a rough, ragged gasp. There were no words for this. Only sounds. There is hurt too big for words. She stared at the computer screen. For how long? Two minutes? Five? Ten? Trembling rose from her core. She jumped to her feet, sending her chair crashing to the floor. She seized the computer monitor and shoved it with all her might. It rocked back before landing face down on the desk. Something shattered inside. She stared at it for a long moment. Ellen—who loved sunny yellow sweaters and sent fresh-baked cookies to her children at college, who had never so much as cut off another driver in traffic—reduced now to rage and destruction, desolation turned physical. Tears stung her eyes, hot and furious.

She wheeled around and headed for the door. Why was it that everyone else made choices? They made decisions and *acted*, while she was always left to react? Why wasn't she ever in the driver's seat?

Outside, snow buried the world. She stood at the kitchen sink, looking over the backyard. William wouldn't be there when the shop opened. He wouldn't squeeze her hand or raise a glass of champagne to her— all the little scenarios she had created in her head. He wouldn't pull her close and whisper in her ear: "I knew you could do it. You are indeed a woman of substance." Those were the kinds of expressions he used: a woman of substance. More pomposity. But those words would have warmed her, and she would have believed them. Dear God, a new day would have dawned, and she would have believed.

Tears spilled down her face now.

At the edge of the yard, Arborview sat covered in snow.

What had been wrong with her? Sitting up in that thing, bolstered by breezes, held aloft by something bigger than herself, believing it was all real. Had she lost her mind?

She hated the sight of it now.

She went to the closet and ripped a coat from a hanger. She pulled it on, along with a winter ski cap. Then she bent to tug on her old winter boots. When she straightened up, she had to lean against the wall for a minute. A dizzying lightness filled her head. She closed her eyes.

Alice would have been able to sort this all out. She was good at cutting though the drama, and the lies, in other people's lives—just not her own. She would have hit William with a few choice zingers: *Geriatric Peter Pan. Aging lothario.*

But Alice was gone, and for good. No witty words from her to fix things now. Ellen had known Alice for twenty years and still had never truly understood who Alice really was—another oversight for which she had paid dearly. Why had she thought she could ever understand William? Or even Zach?

The problem was that people stand in the shadows, visible but with hidden angles and capacities you'd never suspect. What you don't know won't hurt you until you find out, and then you're on your own. Some of them call this love.

There was a fitting credo for Ellen. Someone should carve it on her headstone.

She headed out the back door into the garage, where she grabbed Zach's old axe resting in a corner. She held the axe across her body with both hands.

Outside the storm had claimed the world. Not a bird in the sky, no squirrels scurrying along branches, everything sought refuge. Ellen trudged through calf-deep snow. A sharp wind cut across the yard, sending a blanket of frozen flurries into her face. She lowered her head. Another gust pushed her back, but she braced herself and went on.

The axe was heavier than she had expected. She heaved it up, letting it rest on her left shoulder, stumbling and raising her knees higher with each step. Her fingers were already numb, little needles and pins tingling in the tips. Why hadn't she put on gloves? Idiot.

At the base of the tree, she gazed up into Arborview's opening. It was strangely serene beneath the snow-covered boughs. While the storm pounded on, this hidden spot sat unperturbed, inviting her in. The welcome caught Ellen off guard, but she spat on the ground. Her half-frozen hands shook. "So what?" she said aloud. "This is supposed to help?" she shouted. "This is supposed to explain things? A damn tree house covered with snow?"

She stepped back, hoisted the axe with both arms, and swung at the tree trunk with all her might.

The blade connected with a solid thwack. Ellen grunted and staggered backward. The axe head slipped to the ground, the long handle still in her hands. She gasped, raising it again. Swinging was harder than she'd imagined, but she twisted to the side and let it fly.

Thwack, thwack.

The axe slipped again, the blade sinking in the snow. Ellen panted, hot bursts of breath evaporating before her face. She wanted to split the tree open. She wanted to watch the dilapidated tree house crash to the ground and splinter into hundreds of useless shards of dirty wood. That's all it was: dirty, rotting wood, imbued by her imagination with power—with comfort and clarity. Nothing more.

She hoisted and swung, connecting at a clumsy angle. Chips of bark fell. She tried to lift the axe again but found she couldn't. She let it drop and sank to her knees in the snow. She leaned forward onto her hands, so she was on all fours, then she sat back, shaking.

She'd whacked four shallow slices into the trunk, and the creamy, vulnerable wood stood exposed to the glare of the day. The trunk, beneath the rough bark, was the same shade as the dresser in Taber's bedroom, a delicate golden hue that lent the room an innocent glow. It looked like it would be smooth to the touch. Ellen sniffed. Imagine—beneath the old bark, a smooth, glowing core. *For you are dust, and to dust you shall return.*

Ellen shook her head. She was back at it again. Would she ever be able to get the nuns out of her head? She had once known the whole verse by heart. She had loved the certainty, the finality of it. *Vanity of vanities; all is vanity.*

But she was finished with all of it now. In the spring, she would hire a tree removal company. They'd come with a chainsaw and bring the whole thing down. She'd see some real dust then.

She struggled to her feet, slipping in the snow. She trudged to the ladder and brushed off the rungs. Then she climbed, wedging her feet against the tree trunk, barely managing to keep the thick toe of her boots on each one. She pushed through the narrow opening, coat scraping the wood.

It was insulated inside, cut off by the storm. Skinny strips of snow had blown through cracks in the boards. Ellen stamped the snow clumps from her boots. Flakes melted on her face. She pushed the ski cap back on her head and took a deep breath.

The familiar monastic stillness filled the space. It was as if she had stepped into a hidden holy vault. *The sanctum sanctorum*, more of the old lingo. Ridiculous. Yet it steadied her mind. She sensed the breath moving through her body. Her fingers, balled into cold fists, tingled with new warmth. All her fury, her frenzy, the swinging of the axe—and still this little room sat waiting in the branches. She could take it or leave it, but it would still be here.

A bone weariness hit Ellen. She stepped to the beanbag and bent her knees into it.

It was all over now, finished. She gazed at the splotchy ceiling. Zach, Alice, and now William, too, were gone. And Ellen knew it was for good. She knew, beyond a doubt, that whatever angst had been lurking beneath William's placid surface was stronger than his ability to overcome it. She meant nothing in this equation. His battle had begun long before he met her. It would continue without her. What had he written? *The chaos of the streets will erase me.* Anyone who saw salvation in that was beyond help, and most certainly beyond her reach.

Why, then, would she want to keep reaching? Maybe because she had built her life reaching for people, believing in them, banking on their permanence. And what had happened? They had either moved on or run away, some after inserting a few select knives in her back.

She sighed, her breath smoke in the air. Hadn't she run away from herself, too, from the bright visions, the flashing intuition of what she might have become, into the arms of something easier and more tangible? Something other people would approve of? Maybe this was the knife that cut most deeply. It was also the one she could pull out.

A tear ran down Ellen's cheek. She had read that tears carry toxins out of the body. Let the toxins flow, then. There would be no fast rebound this time. No man to cushion her crash. Not even Alice to talk things over with. Only hard times coming now, alone times, the thing they all had tried to flee.

She sank deeper into the chair. There was at least some consolation in their discomfort. She pictured Zach and Lydia squabbling over a baby, Alice trying to explain to Ned why she didn't want to get married again or begging Earle to take her back, William sweating it out on the frantic streets of a teeming Indian city.

They were lost, maybe more lost than she was. They were blind and deaf to themselves, which was maybe the worst disability of all. Ellen took sad comfort in this. Another day, far from now, she might feel differently. She was old enough to acknowledge this. Mercy could mediate. Redemption arrives, sooner or later, if you let it. The old nuns would have agreed, and Ellen—even now—couldn't deny it. This inkling of something bigger was within her, whether she wanted it or not. She felt its presence, its certainty, wedged behind her heart. It was the real story. It lifted her, spoke her name. It had always been there. She had just stopped listening.

She was listening now. She closed her eyes.

It was too cold to fall asleep on the beanbag. Evening would be here soon, but Ellen remained, feeling the silence build as snow buried the landscape, hiding the familiar outlines, erasing the edges, turning everything unknowable again.

Chapter Forty-Three

Rosa knew what was in the email the minute she saw the sender's address. She carried her phone to the kitchen table and sat down. A dampness broke out on her upper lip. Mama had gone to the supermarket for the Saturday morning shopping.

Rosa clicked on the email. She read only the first few lines before dropping the phone to the table: *Dear Ms. Rosa Escamilla, We are pleased to offer you a spot in the Seasons Culinary College Class of...*

The world seemed to fall away. Rosa's breath caught. They wanted her. There was a place for her. It was real. This was the proof, and it was only the beginning. There was no turning back.

Mama would look at her differently. This permanent thing would now be wedged between them. There had been no resolution to the five thousand dollars. Mama's response: "That's between me and Javi. Got nothing to do with you." Two days of stony silence had ensued, with the two of them passing each other wordlessly in the house and Rosa holed up in her bedroom, the door closed, whenever Mama was home.

When Rosa left for Rhode Island, Mama would be alone. Alone with her bad memories and aching feet, walking the worn floors of this house and shuffling off to Sotto Voce every night. Rising alone, going to bed alone. Growing old. What would become of her?

While this was a beginning—Rosa's beginning—it was also undeniably an end. Rosa sighed and slumped down in the seat. "There's nothing I can *do* about it," she mumbled to the empty room.

The back door creaked open. Rosa heard the rustle of grocery bags, as Mama stepped into the foyer. "What's going on in there?" She had heard the mumbling. Mama had the sharpest hearing of anyone Rosa had ever known.

Stepping into the kitchen, Mama must have seen a clue on Rosa's face. Rosa had never been good at hiding what she was feeling.

Mama was at her side in a heartbeat. "What's wrong?" She dropped her purse on the table. "Is it Javi? Did you hear from Javi?"

"No, Javi's fine." Rosa sniffed.

"Then why you…what happened this time?"

Rosa handed her mother the phone, and Mama brought it to her face. You could see the change move across her features. First, a scrutinizing furrowed brow, then the widening eyes, the hint of—a smile? "So why you crying? This is what you want, right?"

"Yeah, it's what I want. But it's not what you want."

"Well, I'm not the one going."

Rosa caught her mother's eye. "But I am."

She'd said as much so many times before, but in that moment, Rosa realized it was true. Of course she was going, with or without her mother's blessing. Anything else would have been a criminal waste.

It was as if Mama had read her thoughts. "Listen, don't worry about my blessing. I don't know what it would get you anyway. It ain't worth all that much."

Mama pulled out a chair and dropped down with a heavy thump. "But the money, I been thinking." She drummed her fingertips on the tabletop. "I can't give you anything this fall. Javi cleaned me out."

Rosa opened her mouth to speak, but Mama raised a hand to silence her. "But for next winter, I can put a little away. Okay, Miss Big Mouth?"

The sudden switch threw Rosa. She didn't know what to say. She sat breathing, and then a quiet response formed. "You don't have to," she said, as surprised at her words as her mother seemed to be. "I can handle it. I'll have loans, and I'll get a job when I'm there. I know I can do this, on my own."

Mama waved her away. "Squawk, squawk, it ain't fair, it ain't right. If I don't give you something, I'll never hear the end of it."

"You've heard the end of it," Rosa said.

Her mother glared at her. "All of a sudden you don't want the money? Well, too bad. You're getting it. And don't go running to tell Javi, either. This is none of his business, just like he was none of yours. I'm doing this because I want to. It's got nothing to do with Javi."

Rosa sat silent a moment. After all the strife and hurt, Mama's money felt beside the point now. Mama was beside the point. A joyful surge lifted Rosa, a certainty she had never known. But tears shown in her eyes.

"Don't start blubbering." Mama raised a warning finger. "If I see any more tears, I'm gonna head straight out the window."

Rosa looked at her mother's chubby hands resting on the table. "All along, I wasn't sure I'd get into Seasons Culinary College," she said. "But now it's real, and everything is going to change. Who knows what will happen to us."

Mama frowned. "Nothing gonna happen to us. Somebody better knock a little sense into you."

"I don't want to leave you." The words tore at Rosa.

But Mama didn't look the least bit surprised. She looked amused, sort of, sad, maybe a little. "Leave me?" She raised one of her penciled-on eyebrows. "You think you ever gonna get away from an old bat like me?"

Rosa thought her heart would split open in her chest, but she laughed.

"Listen." Mama leaned over the table so Rosa could see the cakey makeup in the creases of her eyelids and the last bright trace of red on her lips. "I don't know what will happen." A fierce glimmer crossed Mama's face. "But I can't wait to tell all the assholes I work with that my girl gonna cook circles around them."

Chapter Forty-Four

Ellen began spending her evenings at the shop. It was easier than sitting home as darkness fell, covering the countryside. The shop opening was only a month away, so there was plenty to get done.

In April, the days were longer, with sunlight lasting into early evening. The great thaw and melt, with its mud and slush and mess, was past. Delicate new, green life quivered in fields and on treetops.

Poised at the corner of the green, the shop offered a good view of the town center, of the cars moving through the intersections, of people passing on the sidewalk, running into acquaintances, exchanging quick hugs and broad smiles. Ellen could feel but not hear their laughter. Across the grassy green, with the trickling fountain little children found irresistible, she could see the post office with its flapping American flag, and the brownstone face of the library on the opposite corner.

She had taken to sitting in the shop window in the evening, watching the sun disappear, sipping tea, and nibbling whatever remained of the day's baking experiments. She donated most of her test recipes to the ladies at the library, but she'd still put on a few pounds eating the scraps every night. Alice would have been scandalized.

Well, the long summer evenings were good for

walking. There was the garden to get in shape, raking and weeding and carrying potting soil, and maybe she'd join a new gym. A fancy one had opened in an industrial park on the edge of town—rows of workout machines and a wall of mirrors, a hot tub and sauna. It was worth investigating.

Ellen had finished her tea one night and was wiping down the kitchen, when the bells on the front door jingled. She dried her hands on her apron, smoothed her hair, and went out to the counter.

"Mrs. Cahill!"

Rosa and a woman. A friend? No, this was Rosa's mama—Ellen recognized her from the night with William at Sotto Voce. Only Mama looked a little fresher, a little softer tonight.

"Rosa," Ellen called. "Did you get my message?"

Rosa's face glowed with an eagerness inspired by something more than Ellen's recent email asking if she could begin work at the shop in two weeks. "I did and I can." Rosa rushed up to the counter, taking Mama's hand and tugging her along. "This is my mom."

Mrs. Escamilla was matronly and solid, in a long, black skirt of shimmery material and a blue tunic that covered her ample arms. Her brassy auburn hair was piled in a loose bundle on her head.

"This one," she said, jerking a thumb at Rosa, "can't say enough about you. It's 'Mrs. Cahill this,' and 'Mrs. Cahill that.' I figured it's about time we meet, no?"

Ellen laughed. "It is." She reached out and shook the woman's warm, thick hand. "Rosa was my favorite student. I'm no longer teaching at River Bend, so I can admit these things now."

Mrs. Escamilla glanced around. "You a business owner, huh? Fancy shop in this fancy town, you flyin' now."

"Hey," Rosa said. "I have some news."

"Spill it!" Ellen gripped the edge of the counter.

"I got into Seasons Culinary College!"

"Oh, Rosa!" Ellen's hands flew to her mouth.

"And I got a kick-ass scholarship and financial aid package."

Ellen hurried around the counter and wrapped Rosa in a hug. "I knew you would get in."

"And you know, Mr. Janssen really came through with the money. He didn't stop until he knew I was all set."

Ellen held her breath.

"I went to thank him, but he's gone." Rosa searched Ellen's face. "All they told me in his office is he took a leave of absence. I haven't seen him at the hospice lately either."

"He's working in India," Ellen said.

"Oh." Rosa caught Ellen's eye, and Ellen looked away.

"I'm not surprised," Rosa said.

"You're not?"

"He didn't seem…he wasn't, you know, a happy man."

Ellen swallowed. "No?" She couldn't think of anything more to say, and she felt Mrs. Escamilla watching her.

"I'd overhear him you know, talking to the reverend. I told you about the reverend, right?" Rosa asked.

Ellen nodded.

"Mr. Janssen had some kind of guilt over an old girlfriend who died in a hospice. It happened a while ago, sounded like, but he was still pretty screwed up about it, if you ask me."

"Rosa." Mrs. Escamilla shook her head. "Nobody asked you."

"From what I heard, he kind of abandoned her while she was dying. He didn't stick around. Imagine that? Maybe I shouldn't be gossiping like this, but I…I don't know, I feel like you should know."

Ellen's mouth was dust dry.

"He sounded pretty messed up, if you ask me," Rosa said.

"Quit trash-talking this poor man." Mrs. Escamilla clucked and laughed. "You don't know what you're talking about."

Ellen managed a tight smile. "Oh, I think she might be onto something."

"Well, people move all over the world these days," Mrs. Escamilla said. "Nobody stays put anymore."

"So true," Ellen said. "Listen, you two take off your coats. Would you like a cup of tea?"

Mrs. Escamilla's brow wrinkled. "I never been a tea drinker…"

"Oh? I also have…"

"But tonight, you know, I think I'd like tea. Why not try something new, right?"

"Why not?" Ellen led them to a table before the big window and then busied herself behind the counter.

It was true, she thought as she measured out the tea leaves, nobody did stay put. Jimmy and Taber were launched into the world. Zach was in Lydia's condo, starting all over and not even certain that he wanted to.

Alice? Who knew. In the arms of a new man by now maybe. And of course William. He was thousands of miles away, swept into a new existence where there would never be a place for Ellen, and where she didn't want to go. But it was his memory that still made her breath catch, that brought her up short at odd moments, so she had to stop what she was doing and stare as the last embers of disbelief died. What a comfort he had been. What a surprise to stumble upon him, this timely, too-easy salvation. Cheap grace. She now knew there is no such thing.

Ellen brought a tray of tea and cups to the table.

Mrs. Escamilla peered at her as she filled the cups. "You divorced, huh?"

"I sure am." Ellen heard the conviction in her own voice. It belonged there.

"That's tough. But let me tell you—my husband ran around on me…"

"Mama," Rosa whispered.

"His choice, right?" Mrs. Escamilla said.

"Right," Ellen said.

"Now he's dead. Been dead a long time. I'm a widow, and I have to say being a widow is easier than seeing him run off with another woman. I done both, so I know. There's nothing like being left in the lurch."

"Nothing." Ellen nodded, and the two of them locked gazes for an instant. "You're a survivor," Ellen said.

"People gonna do what they gonna do." Mrs. Escamilla shrugged. "It's something inside them. Let 'em go, that's what I learned. That's what I've figured out after all this time. Just let 'em go."

"You are so right," Ellen said. "How much better it

would be if we could see people for who they truly are, and not who we think—or heaven forbid, feel—they should be."

Ellen was stunned at herself for saying this to the two of them, as stunned as they seemed to hear it. But it was true. If people were clearly labeled, there would be no hopeful grasping, no doomed projections.

Mrs. Escamilla's eyes reflected the last weak light of evening in the windows. "You know," she said, "I think we see things the same way, Mrs. Cahill. I can tell."

Ellen sat down, and a stillness came over her. It felt as if all the things she had only glimpsed before were closing in now, swooping by in silvery flashes, insisting she look again, more closely this time. *Seek and you shall find.* She could hear the wind moving through the trees around Arborview. She could see the sunlight slipping through cracks in the wood.

"Call me Ellen," she said.

"And you call me Luisa. You know, I'm thinking of starting something new, myself. Maybe taking a bookkeeping course at the college, something that'll get me off my feet."

"We're going to get you enrolled before I leave," Rosa said.

"It sounds like both of you are blazing new paths." The thought warmed Ellen.

"I guess so." Luisa gave a tentative smile. She sipped her tea and looked out the window. "Very pretty."

"It is, isn't it?"

The three of them sat, watching the way darkness shrouded the green and soothed the roads leading out to the hills where Ellen's house waited, and where a real estate agent would soon show up to walk through the rooms and talk money. It was time to let go. Ellen had decided last week. We Rise might bring in enough money to keep the house, but Ellen already had everything she truly needed. And it wasn't confined to a plot of land, or to a tree house at the edge of the woods. *Behold, the kingdom of heaven is within you.* That quote had moved to the top of her favorites list.

"Hey, there are some new tarts in the back," she said to Rosa. "Want to grab them? Apricot and peach with an almond crust. Oh, and red velvet cupcakes with cream cheese frosting."

Rosa smiled. "Nothing ever sounded sweeter," she said, as she disappeared though the swinging door.

Epilogue

Light streams through the windows of the sunroom. The white ceiling fan turns overhead. Outside, summer is in full, riotous bloom. A wild rabbit noses its way across the lawn. Blood-red azaleas crowd around the patio. In the corner of the yard, Arborview perches, ever patient and waiting.

Ellen sits in her favorite wicker chair, feet propped on the battered ottoman. Glittery beads of condensation run down the cold glass of iced tea on the table next to her. She cannot recall a more perfect summer day and thinks perhaps there is no sense in trying. This will be her last summer in this house, so she is determined to enjoy the best of it. A smaller place, closer to town, or even closer to the city, might be better now. There is already a buyer interested. All proceeds of the sale will be Ellen's alone. Zach had sent congratulations in the last letter he would ever send her. *You've certainly earned it*, he wrote. *A cushion to see you through, while We Rise gets established.*

Rosa is handling the shop this afternoon. She has risen to the challenges of daily baking, of special orders and queues of impatient customers, so expertly. Why not give her a chance to run the show before she heads off to Seasons Culinary College? Maybe she'd come back next summer, and Ellen would give her a title: assistant manager or something like that.

Ellen sips her tea.

On the floor, at her feet, is the latest issue of the *Town Tattler* weekly newspaper, the catalogue of small-town life Ellen has been reading for years—a citizen group protesting taxes, a new principal at the middle school, tag sales and farmers markets, and reviews of local businesses.

Ellen has circled a review on page four. It lies open, face up, on the floor, sunlight bathing the words:

'We Rise' Touches the Heavens
By Mira Rangeley, food critic
Rating: Four Stars

Transcend.

That's the word that comes to mind when I try to describe the new bakery on South Main Street.

Sitting on a corner of the town green, this little shop—the brainchild of local resident Ellen Cahill—is the place for anyone seeking a dose of comfort and connection.

Step inside, and the sweet aroma of fresh baked goods washes over you. The menu's offerings? Totally delectable. Dare I say inspired?

Cahill and her crew serve up sublime creations: crisp crusts, buttery fillings, glazes as smooth as ice, chocolate tones so rich and satisfying they make you close your eyes and stop breathing for a moment, all wrapped in pastry as delicate as angel's wings. Stand before the gleaming glass display case and choose. You can't go wrong.

The shop's ethereal ambience takes it all a step further: soft lighting, the gentle waterfall of harps in the background, nooks in which to tuck one's self away. This is a place where you'll want to linger.

So stop by, pull up a chair, and lay your burdens down. We Rise makes you believe—if only for the fifteen minutes you can spare on a coffee break—that you do not struggle through the world alone, or in vain, that solace and connection, along with a big dash of sweetness, can be yours if you know where to look.

A word about the author...

Karen Guzman is a fiction writer and essayist. Her debut novel, *Homing Instincts*, was published by Fiction Attic Press. Her short fiction has appeared in numerous literary magazines, and she is a contributor to the Collegeville Institute's *Bearings Online* magazine.

Visit her at:

http://www.karenguzman.com
www.writedespite.org

Thank you for purchasing
this publication of The Wild Rose Press, Inc.

For questions or more information
contact us at
info@thewildrosepress.com.

The Wild Rose Press, Inc.
www.thewildrosepress.com

www.ingramcontent.com/pod-product-compliance
Lightning Source LLC
Chambersburg PA
CBHW070053030726
47506CB00002B/457